Praise for Sawyer Bennett and the *Cold Fury* series

"Wow! Sawyer Bennett delivers perfect chemistry that won't be denied. *Hawke* is sexy, emotional, and fantastic!"
　　　　—*New York Times* bestselling author SANDI LYNN

"Sawyer Bennett never fails to deliver heroes I fall hard for and heroines I adore."
　　　　—*New York Times* bestselling author VIOLET DUKE

"Wow. Just wow. Sawyer Bennett is my new favorite author."
　　　　—*USA Today* bestselling author JAMI DAVENPORT

"Sawyer Bennett has scored again with *Alex,* the perfect combination of sexy and emotional. I can't wait for the next Cold Fury story!"　　　　—Bestselling author JULIE CROSS

"Sawyer Bennett has outdone herself with *Garrett.* If you like secrets, romance, hot sex, and an epically fantastic ending that leaves you totally satisfied, then this is your book."
　　　　—*New York Times* bestselling author LAUREN BLAKELY

"Emotional, intense, funny, and sexy, *Zack* has it all. I didn't want this book to end."
　　　　—#1 *New York Times* bestselling author COLLEEN HOOVER

## By Sawyer Bennett

### COLD FURY HOCKEY SERIES

*Alex*

*Garrett*

*Zack*

*Ryker*

*Hawke*

*Max*

*Roman* (coming soon)

### THE SUGAR BOWL SERIES

*Sugar Daddy*

*Sugar Rush*

*Sugar Free*

### THE WICKED HORSE SERIES

*Wicked Fall*

*Wicked Lust*

*Wicked Need*

*Wicked Ride*

*Wicked Bond*

### THE OFF SERIES

*Off Sides*

*Off Limits*

*Off the Record*

*Off Course*

*Off Chance*

*Off Season*

*Off Duty*

### THE LAST CALL SERIES

*On the Rocks*

*Make It a Double*

*Sugar on the Edge*

*With a Twist*

*Shaken Not Stirred*

### THE LEGAL AFFAIRS SERIES

*Legal Affairs*

*Confessions of a Litigation God*

*Friction*

*Clash*

*Grind*

*Yield*

### STAND-ALONE TITLES

*If I Return*

*Uncivilized*

*Love: Uncivilized*

*Sex, Lies and Rock & Roll*

# MAX

# MAX

## A COLD FURY
## HOCKEY NOVEL

### SAWYER
### BENNETT

**LS**

LOVESWEPT
NEW YORK

A Loveswept Trade Paperback Original

Published in the United States by Loveswept, an imprint of Random House, a division of Penguin Random House LLC, New York.

LOVESWEPT is a registered trademark and the LOVESWEPT colophon is a trademark of Penguin Random House LLC.

This book contains an excerpt from the forthcoming book *Roman* by Sawyer Bennett. This excerpt has been set for this edition only and may not reflect the final content of the forthcoming edition.

ISBN 9780425286517
Ebook ISBN 9781101968116

Printed in the United States of America
on acid-free paper

randomhousebooks.com

123456789

*Book design by Elizabeth A. D. Eno*

This one goes out to my Bennett's Bestie Betas and dear friends Darlene, Janett, Beth, Karen, and Lisa. Thank you for energizing me and the amazing feedback that helped me make *Max,* in my humble opinion, the best Cold Fury book yet.

# AUTHOR'S NOTE

Dear Cold Fury Fans,

Once you get started on Max's book, you should quickly start to recognize that some things sound a little "familiar." That's because Max's book takes place parallel to *Hawke*. So bonus . . . you get a little more insight into Hawke and Vale's story as you read along.

Hope you enjoy!

Love,
Sawyer

PS: If you're brand new to the men of the Cold Fury and *Max* is your first book, you can check out the other men and how they fell prey to love here: sawyerbennett.com

# MAX

# CHAPTER 1

## MAX

I stick the nozzle in my gas tank, depress the handle and flip the catch down to hold it in place. Letting the petrol flow on its own, I head across the nearly empty parking lot to the gas station that is lit up like a bright beacon out here on Possum Track Road. I'm starved and I know my fridge is empty at home, so I'm going to break down and buy some junk food for my dinner. I just won't tell Vale about it as I don't feel like listening to her bitch at me.

Vale Campbell . . . pretty as hell and nice to look at but I dread having to hang out with her. That's because she's one of the assistant athletic trainers for the Cold Fury and, most importantly, working with me on my strength and conditioning. She would most certainly say Snickers, Cheez-Its, and Mountain Dew are not on my approved list and then she'd have me doing burpees, mountain climbers, and box jumps until I puked.

So I won't tell her about this little cheat and I'll gladly take whatever she hands out to me during training camp. I'm committed to starting this season as strong as I have ever been, and I'm going to get the coveted starting goalie position, which became available when Ryker Evans announced his retirement this summer. The Cold Fury has been a championship team and I smell another winning season in the making. Not about to let two major injuries in as many years get me down.

No, I'm coming back with a vengeance and a need to prove myself to my team and fans.

Watch out hockey world . . . Max Fournier is back.

Pulling the door to the convenience store open, I immediately see two guys at the cooler checking out the stock of beer. Both wearing wifebeaters stained with grease and faded ball caps. I, myself, pull my own hat down farther to hide my face to avoid getting recognized tonight. It's late, I want to get my junk food and get gone. We've an early morning practice tomorrow and I just want to get home.

I turn right down the first aisle, which merchandises the chips and other snacks, slightly aware the other two customers are heading to the counter to check out. I keep my back to them just to be safe and peruse the options.

Funyuns.

Potato chips.

Doritos.

Corn nuts.

Reaching for a bag of salt and vinegar potato chips, I hear one of the guys drawl in a typical North Carolina redneck accent, "Hey sweet thang. How 'bout a pack of Marlboro Reds and how 'bout handing me that there box of condoms. The *extra* large size."

The redneck's companion snickers, and then snorts. I turn slightly to see them both shoot conspiratorial grins at each other, and one guy nudges the other to egg him on. While the clerk turns to get the condoms, the redneck leans across the counter and stares blatantly at her ass. The other guy says loud enough that I hear, "Mmmmm . . . that is a fine ass."

Turning my body full so I face the counter, I see the woman's back stiffen and she turns her head to the left to look at a closed doorway beside the cigarette rack. I'm wondering if perhaps a manager or another employee is in there and she's hoping for some help.

But she doesn't wait and turns to face the two assholes, squaring her shoulders.

And goddamn . . . she's breathtaking. Looking past the polyester red and gold vest she wears with a name tag—clearly a uniform—her face is flawless. Creamy skin that glows, high cheekbones, a straight nose that tilts slightly at the end, and a sexy as hell mouth that I bet would be full and lush were her lips not flattened in a grimace. Her hair is not blond, but not brown. I'd describe it as caramel with honey streaks, and it's pulled back from her face in a ponytail with long bangs falling from left to right across her forehead.

While she faces the two men resolutely, I can see wariness in her eyes as she sets the cigarettes and condoms on the counter in front of them. "Will that be all?"

Her voice has a southern accent but it's subtle. She looks back and forth between the two men, refusing to lower her gaze.

Redneck number one nods to the twelve-pack of beer he had previously placed there and says, "That was the last of the Coors. You got any in your storage room?"

"Nope, that's it," she says firmly, and I can tell it's a lie.

"Are ya sure?" he asks, leaning his elbows on the counter and leering at her. "Maybe you could check . . . I could help you if you want, and we could make use of them condoms there."

I'd roll my eyes over the absurdity of his attempt to woo a girl who is, obviously, way out of his league, but I'm too tense over the prospect that this could be more than just some harmless goofing by two drunk rednecks.

"What do you say, sweet thang?" he says in what he tries to pass as a suave voice but comes off as trailer trash.

"I say there's no more beer back there," she grits out, giving a look over her shoulder to the closed door, and then back to the men.

And that *was* a worried look.

A very worried look, so I decide that this isn't going any further. Grabbing the closest bag of chips, I stalk up the aisle toward the counter as I pull my hat off with my empty hand. I tuck it in my back pocket, and when I'm just a few feet from the men, the woman's eyes flick to me, relief evident in her gaze. I smile at her reassuringly and drop my eyes down to her name tag.

Julianne.

Pretty name for a really pretty girl.

The sound of my footsteps finally penetrate and both men straighten to their full heights, which is still a few inches below mine, and turn my way. My eyes move to the first man, then slowly to the other, leveling them both with an ice-cold glare. With the power of my gaze, I dare both of them to say something else to the beauty behind the counter.

Because I suspect the only sports these guys watch are bass fishing tournaments and NASCAR, I'm not surprised neither one recognizes me as a goalie with the Carolina Cold Fury. Clearly the lovely Julianne doesn't either, but that's also fine by me.

The sound of fingers tapping on the cash register catches everyone's attention, and the two men turn back to her. "That will be nineteen dollars and eighty-six cents."

One of the guys pulls a wallet out of the back pocket of his saggy jeans and nabs a twenty, handing it to her wordlessly. Now that they know there's an audience, neither one seems to be intent on continuing the crass game they were playing. At least I think it was a game, but I'm just glad I was here in case their intent was more nefarious.

Julianne hands the guy his change and they gather their purchases and leave without a word.

As soon as the door closes, her shoulders drop and she lets out a sigh of relief. Giving me a weak smile, she looks at the bag in my hand and says, "Is that all?"

"Uh, no actually," I say as I give her a sheepish grin. "Got distracted by those assholes. I need a few more things."

"Yeah," she agrees in a tired voice, brushing her long bangs back before turning away from me to an open cardboard box she has sitting on a stool to her left. She reaches in, pulls out a carton of cigarettes, which she efficiently opens and starts stocking the rack of cigarettes behind the counter. I'm effectively dismissed and there's no doubt in my mind she doesn't know who I am.

I head back down the chips aisle, take a bag of corn nuts and continue straight back to the sodas. I grab a Mountain Dew, never once considering the diet option because that would totally destroy the point of having a junk food night, and then head straight to the candy aisle. Two Snickers in my hand and I'm set.

When I get to the counter, she must hear my approach as she turns around with the same tired smile. Walking to the register, her eyes drop to the items that I set on the counter, robotically punching in the price of each one. I watch her delicate fingers work the keys, taking in her slumped shoulders as she rings in the last item and raises those eyes back to me.

They're golden . . . well, a light brown actually but so light as to appear like a burnished gold.

A piercing shriek comes from behind the closed door, so sharp and high-pitched that it actually makes my teeth hurt. I also practically jump out of my skin, the noise was so unexpected.

The woman—Julianne, according to that name tag—does nothing more than close her eyes, lower her head, and let out a pained sigh. It's such an agonized motion that for a brief moment I want to reach out and squeeze her shoulder in sympathy, but I have no clue what I'm empathizing with because I don't know what that unholy sound was. I open my mouth to ask her if she's okay when the closed door beside the cigarette rack flies open and a tiny blur comes flying out.

No more than three feet high, followed by another blur of the same size.

Then another piercing shriek from within that room, this time louder because the door is now open, and for a terrible moment I think someone must have been murdered. I even take a step to the side, intent on rounding the counter.

Julianne moves lightning fast, reaching her hands out and snagging each tiny blur by their collars. When they're brought to a full halt, I see it's two little boys, both with light brown hair and equally light brown eyes. One holds a baby doll in his hands and the other holds what looks to be a truck made of LEGOs.

Looking at me with apology-filled eyes, she says, "I'm so sorry. This will only take a second."

With firm but gentle hands she turns the little boys toward the room and pushes them inside, disappearing behind them. Immediately, I hear a horrible crash, another shriek, and the woman I know to be named Julianne curses loudly, "Son of a bitch."

One more screech from what I'm thinking might be a psychotic pterodactyl and my feet are moving without thought. I round the edge of the counter, step behind it and head toward the door. When I step over the threshold, I take in a small room set up to be a combo office/break room. There's a small desk covered with papers along one wall, another wall with a counter, sink, and minifridge under it, and a card table with rusty legs and four folding metal chairs to its side.

It also suddenly becomes clear what manner of creature was making the noise that rivaled nails on a chalkboard.

A little girl, smaller than the boys, is tied to one of the chairs with what looks like masking tape wrapped several times around her and the chair, coming across the middle of her stomach. Her legs are free, and the crash was apparently a stack of toys she had managed to knock off the top of the table.

"Rocco . . . Levy . . . you promised you'd behave," Julianne says in a quavering voice as she kneels beside the little girl and starts pulling at the tape. The little boys stand there, heads hanging low as they watch their mom attempt to unwrap their sister.

I can't help myself. The tone of the woman's voice, the utter fatigue and frustration, and the mere fact that these little hellions taped their sister to a chair, has me moving. I drop to my knees beside the woman, my hands going to the tape to help her pull it off.

Her head snaps my way and she says, "Don't."

My eyes slide from the tape to her, and I'm almost bowled over by the sheen of thick tears, glistening but refusing to drop.

"Please . . . do you mind just waiting out there. If any customers come in . . . just tell them I'll be out in a moment," she pleads with me, a faint note of independence and need to handle this on her own shining through the defeat.

"Sure," I say immediately as I stand up, not meaning to further upset this poor lady with the beautiful tear-soaked eyes. She clearly has enough on her plate without me adding to it.

She turns back to tearing at the masking tape, being extremely gentle, I notice, with the pieces on the little girl's arms. I glance to the two little boys, and although I see their heads are bowed down in what looks like apology, they both have slight smirks on their face.

Little hellions for sure.

I back out of the break room and consider just leaving my snacks on the counter, but I dismiss it. I want to make sure everything is okay, because unless I'm mistaken, that beautiful lady is on the edge of a serious meltdown.

She doesn't keep me waiting long, only a few minutes before she's backing out of the door and pulling it shut behind her. She gives a final plea to the kids inside: "Will you please just behave for the rest of the night, and if you do, we'll go shopping for a new toy for each of you this weekend, okay?"

*Nice. Bribery usually works with kids.*

I don't hear any type of response from the inside, and with a mighty sigh, she pulls the door shut and turns to me. She jumps slightly, maybe so lost in her thoughts that she forgot I was there, but then her eyes dart down to the items on the counter.

"I am so sorry you had to witness that," she says as she rushes to the register, then rings up the rest of my purchases, which she hadn't gotten to before the hellions busted loose.

"Not a problem," I say with a chuckle. "You handled it well."

She blows out a gust of frustrated air upward from her mouth and her bangs lift slightly before falling down. "They can be trying at times."

Finally, she looks me in the eye and says, "That will be seven dollars and fifty-nine cents."

Wordlessly, I pull my wallet out, grab a ten and hand it to her. She just as wordlessly takes it, makes my change, and then quietly puts my purchases in a plastic bag. It gives me an unfettered moment to study her face more carefully, which looks not only pale from what might be exhaustion, but has a blue tinge underneath her eyes clearly denoting lack of sleep.

I'm not sure why, but this tugs on my heartstrings a bit and I open my mouth to ask if she's okay, but the glass door to the convenience store flies open and two teenagers walk in, one of them laughing loudly at something the other said.

The crinkle of plastic gets my attention and I turn back to find the woman behind the counter holding my bag of purchases across to me.

"Have a good night," she says with a tired smile, and when I take the bag from her, she immediately dismisses me and her eyes go over my shoulder to watch the teenagers as they peruse the sodas in the glass coolers at the back of the store.

"Yeah," I say slowly. "You too."

She never even gives me a second glance, and I'm not being egotistical when I say that I usually get a lot more attention from the female persuasion than what I'm receiving right now. Mostly because I'm in the media a lot with the Cold Fury, but also because I've been told on more than one occasion that I'm hot.

Whatever.

The point being, this woman doesn't give me a second glance, and I find that I . . .

Well, fuck . . . I like it a lot.

I think I might be a bit of an oddity. While a lot of the single guys on the team revel in bachelorhood and the never-ending supply of puck bunnies who gladly give it up so they have a chance to be with a hockey star, that's not my way. Never has been. I get nothing out of a shallow woman throwing herself at me, with no real care as to who I am as a person. They see a hot goalie who makes millions, and well, that's all they see.

But this woman . . . she doesn't see anything but an ordinary guy who is easily dismissed, and yeah . . . I totally dig that.

I turn from the counter and walk out the door, making a mental note to myself to stop back in the near future and see if I can talk to her some more. Unpeel a few layers. Maybe ask her on a date.

I chuckle.

Max Fournier—professional hockey player and one of the team's most eligible bachelors—wanting to flirt with a convenience store cashier who couldn't give a rat's ass about him.

Totally like it.

# CHAPTER 2

# JULES

"Levy, please just try those carrots once," I say pleadingly as I finish cutting up Annabelle's chicken. "I swear they won't kill you."

He ignores me, his palm supporting his head, elbow on the table while he moves the carrots around on his plate. I don't bother asking again because it won't do any good.

"Okay, there you go, Annabelle," I say as I straighten, and turn to Rocco. "Do you want any more milk?"

He shakes his head with a smile, and to make me proud he stabs a carrot with his fork and eats it. I beam back at him for just a split second before I turn my wrist over and look at my watch.

Crap. Tina is fifteen minutes late, and if I don't leave in the next two minutes I'm going to be late as well.

I spin toward my purse on the counter, miscalculating how close I am, and slam my hip bone into the corner.

"F-u-u—," I start to say but change directions mid-curse. "Fudge."

It's been four months since the kids have come to live with me, and I've just about broken my pattern of cursing in front of them. I reach across the counter, fish inside my purse and pull out my phone. With a few taps on the screen, I'm dialing Tina.

"Hey," she answers on the second ring. "I was just getting ready to call you; I can't make it tonight."

I close my eyes as my free hand curls into an involuntary fist, take in a breath, and when I open my eyes the tears come. Lately I'm having a harder and harder time holding them back. I blow the air out and beg with all my might, my voice suffering a slight quaver. "Please don't do this to me, Tina. I can't miss work again."

"I'm sorry, Jules," she says in a placating manner. "But Marshall's running a fever—a hundred and two—and I think I need to take him to the doctor."

I nod . . . not with acceptance but rather defeat. I blink my eyes, force back the tears. "Okay, I understand." I'd be a shit not to, and I'd do the same in a similar situation.

Marshall having a fever I totally understand. I didn't understand Tina flaking out on me two nights ago when she couldn't watch the kids because her boyfriend, Todd, wanted to take her to a concert at Red Hat Amphitheater after he'd scored tickets on a radio show. That left me with no other choice but to bring the kids to the convenience store, which I knew was a very bad idea. I ran a good fifty-fifty shot of getting busted by the manager, Chris, as he would sometimes come by to check on me. The seven P.M. to midnight shift tended to be busy for the first couple of hours and then petered out after about nine P.M. I was usually good if I could make it to that magic number, but two nights ago he surprised me with a visit around eleven. Of course, by then the kids were conked out on the hard tiled floor in the break room, which I know wasn't ideal, but I also couldn't afford to lose this job.

I most definitely could not leave them at home alone.

So I got an ass-chewing from Chris and a warning that kids were not allowed there when I was working. Something about liability issues, or that was the reason he touted, though I think it is more that he's just an asshole boss who doesn't like kids.

"Maybe Glenda can watch them tonight," Tina suggests.

"Not an option," I say firmly.

Because she is totally not an option at night. During the summer, my next door neighbor, Glenda, watched the kids during the day while I worked my primary job. Once school started—Levy and Rocco were in first and second grade respectively—she only had to watch Annabelle during the day and just for a little bit after Levy and Rocco got home from school.

It's a good deal for me. She watches the kids so I can work my seven A.M. to four P.M. shift at Sweetbrier Nursing Home, and in return I cook and clean for her and her husband, Bill. Of course, Bill has no idea about the arrangement and assumes Glenda makes his dinner each night and keeps their small apartment tidy, but Glenda hates to cook—and even worse, hates to clean. Add on the fact that I don't have money to pay her, much less afford daycare, it's a good trade until I can get things figured out.

But while Glenda is sweet and competent and takes good care of them, her husband is a certified asshole as well as an alcoholic, and he's at home in the evenings, so I don't want the kids around that.

"I'm really sorry," Tina says again. "But I'm loading up now to take Marshall to the ER."

I hold back a sigh, because Tina doesn't need guilt from me and it seems I sigh a lot lately and I need to change that. "It's okay," I tell her, but it's really not.

*I'm fucked.*

At least I can still cuss in my thoughts, although that doesn't give me much solace right now.

Annabelle lets out a cry of despair and I spin around to find Levy piling all of his carrots on her plate. She doesn't like them either so she's completely mortified to be given extra.

"Stop, Levy," I tell him, but he ignores me. Six years old, and being the middle child, it somehow seems to give him license to disregard my directions. I haven't figured a way to work around that yet, so I let it go by saying, "It's okay, Annabelle. I don't expect you to eat all of them."

Annabelle smiles at me then turns and sticks her tongue out at Levy.

I take another deep breath, let it out . . . praying for God to give me patience and an understanding boss.

Then I dial my manager, Chris.

"Chris Bellis," he answers his phone haughtily, as if he's the most important man in the world. Asshole boss.

"It's Julianne," I say hesitantly, already dreading his response. "Um . . . my babysitter fell through and I can't make it in to-night."

He doesn't say anything.

"Unless you let me bring the kids in," I add hastily. "I swear they won't cause any trouble."

*Please, God, don't let them cause trouble.*

Finally, he talks. "Unacceptable, Jules. Our policy is strict on having children here."

"Well, then . . . I'm sorry, but I can't make it. You'll have to find someone to cover for me," I say with what I hope is a firm voice, but I'm terrified I just screwed the pooch.

"Well, then I'm sorry too, Jules, but I'm going to have to let you go if you don't show tonight," he says just as firmly back to me. "That will be twice in one week you've had childcare issues and it's obviously becoming a problem."

"No," I say quickly, and then try to add on reassurances. "It's not a problem. Just bad luck. Chris, I've worked for you more than two months now and this is the first time I've asked to take off."

"And I sense this won't be the last," he says crisply. "I've had single mothers work for me before, and they're never reliable. I don't have time to cover someone who doesn't show enough responsibility—"

"Please, Chris," I beg him, tears once again pricking at my eyes. "I really need this job."

He's not moved. "If you will come by tomorrow evening, I'll have your final paycheck ready and you can turn in your store key."

I don't even consider arguing with him any further. At this moment I am beyond exhausted. Utterly defeated. I don't have it in me to even care about how that extra money each week is what enabled me to feed and clothe three hungry kids that I'd never planned on having.

My head turns on the pillow and I look at the digital clock on the bedside table. Almost eleven o'clock and I can't sleep. Annabelle doesn't have that problem, and she's pressed up against me with one arm wrapped around my neck. This has been her usual sleeping position since she came to live with me in this dinky little apartment four months ago, but I'm used to it so that's not what's keeping me up.

I can't go to sleep because I've gotten to the point where I'm used to surviving on only a few hours each night. By the time I'd get home from my shift at the gas station convenience store, I'd be lucky to get four and a half hours before I had to get up to start my workday all over again at the nursing home.

That's the story of Julianne Bradley's life.

Work, sleep. Work, sleep. Work, sleep.

Actually, that's not quite right. It's more like Work. Sleep. Take care of kids. Work. Take care of kids. Cook and clean for Glenda and kids. Work. Sleep.

Not anywhere in that daily grind is there time budgeted for me, unless you count the quick five minute shower I take each morning. It's amazing the little things that you easily cut out from your life as being unimportant when you're on a time crunch. I can be showered and dressed for work in about fifteen minutes now. That's because I quit wearing makeup and usually put my wet hair up in a ponytail or bun. That leaves me adequate time to get the kids up, dressed, and fed breakfast before Glenda arrives. She handles getting Levy and Rocco on the bus and then stays at my apartment with Annabelle. The boys come home around four, about the time I'm getting off work. I live only a few miles from Sweetbrier, so I'm usually home by 4:15 P.M. I start Levy and Rocco on their homework and help with whatever they need. I then spend about an hour in Glenda's apartment, which is right next door, and I've got a good routine going: Mondays and Thursdays, I dust, and clean the bathroom; Tuesdays and Fridays, I vacuum and mop; Wednesdays, I get to anything that can't be held off until the next scheduled day. About the only thing I don't do is their laundry, and I told Glenda *no way* was I washing Bill's underwear.

She didn't care. She was just happy not to do the nasty stuff like toilets and even happier yet to have me do the cooking.

So after cleaning Glenda's place, I'd come back home to start dinner, making enough for her family and mine, and in between help the kids out if they're still doing their homework. If I was lucky, dinner was ready before I had to leave for work at the gas station, and I'd be able to cram some food down my throat too. If not, Tina—who is also my neighbor, but one flight down—took over feeding the kids while Glenda picked up her portion home for when Bill arrived. Thinking about this just makes me all the more tired and depressed.

There is one benefit though to not having much time to myself. That means there's precious little time for me to give in to my insecurities. All of the doubts as to whether I'm good enough to take care of Melody's children, or whether I've bitten off more than I can chew but I'm just too stubborn to admit it to anyone.

Sighing into the darkness of my room, I try not to think about my life before Melody died. I'd often bitch to my friends or my boyfriend about how hard it was sometimes to be a grown-up and live on your own. I wanted to get my hair highlighted but I couldn't because I bought a new pair of shoes that I simply had to have. Or the tread on my tires was wearing thin but because I spent all my extra money on frivolous things, I couldn't get them replaced. Or in the few days before payday I was eating Ramen noodles, but the day after I'd get my check I'd blow it on a cute top from the Gap.

I mentally roll my eyes at myself as I think about my life now and realize . . . before Melody died, I was actually living an easy and fruitful life. I had it damn good before and while I would never give these kids up, I can't help but be a little wistful over how good it felt not to have this much responsibility on my shoulders.

I didn't ask for my older sister to get cancer at the age of twenty-eight. I didn't ask to take care of her. I didn't ask to watch her die. I didn't ask for my niece and two nephews to come live with me. And I certainly didn't ask for all of the stress and fatigue that comes with raising three kids devastated by the loss of their mother, working minimum wage jobs, and not a clue in the world on how to even interact with my niece and nephews in this new family dynamic thrust upon us.

Still, I wouldn't change a thing about my circumstances right now.

Well, I'd kill for another part-time job and I'll have to get cracking on that tomorrow. But there was no other option except that the kids come live with me. Melody's husband bailed on her long before she got sick, and while he floated in and out of the kids' lives periodically, he's three years behind on child support. And there truly was no other option when Melody asked me point-blank to become their mother when she passed.

I could have never said no to her.

So with the court's approval, guardianship was legally transferred to me before she died, because their father didn't contest it. Four months ago I became an instant mother to three kids who I didn't know all that well and had no clue as to what to do with them. I only knew that it was now my job to care for them, raise them, and love them in the best way I could.

It's my duty now to make sure they thrive.

With another sigh, I carefully remove Annabelle's arm from around my neck and slide from the bed. I'm feeling too guilty just lying here when there are things to be done that could give me a jump start on tomorrow.

# CHAPTER 3

# MAX

Hawke strides in through the lobby doors and as he approaches me I stand up from the plush couch I'd been waiting on.

I grin at him and say, "You're late."

He looks at his watch and then rolls his eyes at me. "By like one minute."

I don't respond but we do our bro greeting—palm smack, back of hand smack, and then a fist bump.

"Jim's not here anyway," I tell him as I sit back down on the couch. "Just called and said he's stuck in traffic. Be about fifteen minutes late."

Hawke sits on a wing-backed chair adjacent to the couch and rests an ankle over his knee. He's dressed up, same as me, except his suit is black and mine's charcoal gray.

"Did you go to the hospital this morning?" I ask him.

"Yeah," he says. "He looks good."

*He* being Dave Campbell, father of one sassy athletic trainer— that would be Vale. Dave had a seizure two days ago and is at

Duke Hospital. He's suffering from a rare brain tumor and received some type of experimental treatment at Duke, and I'm guessing this seizure was a complication. The reason our leading defenseman, Hawke Therrien, is visiting our athletic trainer's father in the hospital is because they have history.

I mean . . . Hawke and Vale have a very long history.

And from what I learned yesterday afternoon when Hawke and I went out for a few beers, not a great history. I had sensed there was something going on between the two of them in the Cold Fury workout room. Vale tensed up the minute Hawke walked in, and I could feel weird vibes from him as well. I left after my workout, only to return a few minutes later to find Hawke's hands on her shoulders with a disgruntled look on his face. He dropped her like a hot potato when I walked back in but didn't try to hide anything from me.

Hence the beers after, and he laid it all out.

Apparently, Vale and Hawke were a hot item years back, but she broke it off with him suddenly and with no explanation. He hasn't been able to figure it out but isn't sure if he should ask either. To complicate matters, they apparently fucked the other night and now things are super awkward.

I didn't have any good advice for him. My one stab at a relationship was a miserable failure, which was totally my fault. So the most I could do was listen to him lament about Vale and commiserate with him that it was a fucked-up situation.

"This place is something, huh?" Hawke says conversationally as he looks at the huge lobby filled with comfortable furniture that's quite stylish and elegant. Thick, luxurious carpet done in light purple, gray, and cream match the floral-print wallpaper that's posh rather than feminine. The receptionist sits at a cherry desk that looks Victorian and there's a grand piano in the corner that a man sits at playing a soft melody.

It's definitely not what I'd envision a nursing home to look like, and the only thing that gives it away is the various residents I see milling around. Some wander about with walkers while others are in wheelchairs that they pull along the floor by shuffling their feet on the carpet rather than having their frail arms try to push the wheels to get them to their destination.

We're at Sweetbrier Nursing Home and Rehab Facility because one of the Cold Fury assistant managers, Jim Perry, held a fundraiser for this place. His mother was a resident here and she passed away a few months ago. He was so impressed with her care, he organized a charity live auction to raise funds to help build a new wing that would house a larger therapy gym as well as increase the dining facilities. He asked a few players to participate and I readily agreed. The fundraiser was last month, long before Hawke arrived for training camp, and I handled hosting and emcee duties for the black-tie event. Hawke's here now because he made a late donation personally and volunteered to come with us to present the check for $57,000 we'd raised to the home administrator. There'd be a big write-up in the paper, of course, and management always loved when we did shit like this.

"I hope to fuck I never have to come to a place like this, though," Hawke continues on. "When I die, I want to go fast."

"Amen, brother," I agree.

While the place is clean, smells decent, and is decorated very nicely, it still holds that overwhelming vibe of futility as I watch the elderly patients struggle to get around because their bodies are failing them. It's fucking depressing actually.

The lobby area is cut through the middle by a hall that runs left and right, presumably to the two wings of the low, sprawling building done in white clapboard with green shutters. A commotion occurs at the intersection of the hallway as one elderly gentleman tries to navigate his wheelchair around the corner but runs into the wheelchair of another elderly gentleman. Seriously, it's all I can do not to laugh out loud.

"Goddamn it, Ernie," the first man yells. "You need to watch where you're going."

"No, *you* need to watch where *you're* going," the other guy yells back. "Fuckin' blind as a bat, you are."

I snicker as I watch the two men trying to disentangle their chairs that are now stuck to each other near the footrests. The receptionist looks alarmed but like she doesn't have a clue what to do. I think she might stand up and try to assist, but then one of the nurses—I'm guessing by the fact she's wearing cranberry-colored scrubs—jogs up to the men and with some murmured words and her hands to their shoulders gets them to stop yelling. She then squats down, pulls the chairs apart, and sends the men on their way in opposite directions.

When she stands up and turns toward me and Hawke, my breath freezes in my lungs as I recognize her.

The beautiful woman from the convenience store last week.

Julianne is her name.

She doesn't see me because she's walking with her head down as she makes her way through the lobby and out the doors, carrying a brown paper bag with her.

"Holy shit," I say as I stand up from the couch, my legs involuntarily walking after her.

I'm not in the least bit ashamed to say I went back to that little convenience store three more times, hoping to catch her on duty again, but she was never there. I'd honestly given up after that third time, figuring she maybe worked a different shift or even that she didn't work there anymore, and frankly, couldn't say as I blamed her. Looked like a shit job to me.

I don't know why I wanted to talk to her again. On the face of things—her working a minimum wage job and having three unruly kids—we didn't have much in common. If I had to guess, I think it was the fact that despite what was clear exhaustion and frustration on her part that night, she still had a solid backbone when it was all said and done. That impressed me.

And let's not forget . . . she's totally gorgeous.

"Where are you going?" Hawke asks, but I don't spare him a glance.

"Be back in a minute," I mumble as I traverse around the low coffee table and follow the woman out the lobby doors.

She's tall for a girl, maybe topping out at five-nine, but that's perfect for me. I'm a towering goalie at six-five. Her hair is in a ponytail again and it swings jauntily as she turns right once she clears the doors and heads to a small courtyard. And when did nursing scrubs look so damn good on a woman before? They mold her ass perfectly, and I'm not ashamed I'm noticing that either.

Not a red-blooded male around that wouldn't look.

She waves at a coworker sitting at a picnic table wearing the same colored scrubs, which I'm guessing is a uniform, but doesn't sit with her, thankfully. Instead, she chooses a concrete bench set under a large crepe myrtle and takes advantage of the shade. Even though it's the first week of October, it's still fairly warm today.

I don't even hesitate but walk right up to her. She doesn't see me though, as she's got her head bowed over the paper bag while she pulls out a sandwich wrapped in plastic and a fruit cup. I glance at my watch and see it's only five after eleven, so I'm guessing this must be her lunch hour.

"Julianne?" I ask hesitantly when I'm just a few feet away.

Her head snaps up and she looks at me with blank eyes even though she answers almost hesitantly, "Yes?"

I push my hands in my pockets and try to look casual as I

come to a stop before her. "Met you in the convenience store last week. Well, we weren't officially introduced . . ."

She still stares at me blankly, and while her golden brown eyes are as beautiful as I remember, they're still marred by the blue circles under them. It's clear she has no clue who I am. This should wound my ego, but again the opposite occurs and I like that she doesn't recognize me at all. I like being a true mystery for once and not having immediate assumptions made about me because of my fame.

I feed her a little more information to jog her memory. "Two redneck assholes giving you trouble. Then two feisty rug rats taping their sister up?"

I punctuate that last statement with a grin, and she finally recognizes me as her mouth forms into an O.

"I remember," she says softly with just a wisp of a smile, which slides off just as quickly as it formed. "That wasn't my best night."

"Well, I think you handled it with grace," I assure her.

Another slight smile that doesn't quite reach her eyes, then her gaze drops to her lap. It's a shy maneuver, as if she doesn't know how to respond, or perhaps she just wants to be left alone. Since I don't know the answer, I press on.

I take a seat next to her on the bench, and she gives a little jump then turns to me with wide, curious eyes.

"I went back there to see you," I tell her conversationally.

Her mouth drops. "Why would you do that?"

I shrug and give her the simple but overly forward truth. "Pretty girl, I didn't see a wedding ring, and I wanted to talk to you more."

Julianne's eyebrows knit inward and she appears thoroughly confused.

So I try to enlighten her, and lean in and give her a conspiratorial wink. "It's what happens when a guy is interested in a girl. He tries to make conversation."

Well, that's not exactly true. Many guys just try to get in the girl's pants, but that was not my original intention. Don't get me wrong . . . this woman is smoking hot and I'm not going to pretend that the attraction isn't a big part, but I'm also equally intrigued by her.

She still doesn't say anything and I can't figure out if she's just a horrible conversationalist or unusually shy, both of which will really suck because I like my women to have some sort of personality.

So I try one more time to get the ball rolling. Reaching my right hand across, I hold it out and say, "My name's Max Fournier."

She finally moves, as if introductions are something she can handle, and shakes my hand. "Julianne Bradley, but my friends call me Jules."

Her hand is soft and the bones feel delicate yet her shake is surprisingly strong. I like that. I also like that she has put me in a friend category and not a weird-creeper category.

Our hands break apart. I don't like that.

"Well, Jules . . . when are you working again next? I'll drop in and keep you company. Might chase off a few more rednecks for you."

Finally, I get a true smile from her and it reaches her eyes. "Well, that's sweet of you but unfortunately I got fired from that job, so you won't be able to stalk me there."

"Why did you get fired?" I ask, a little dismayed I can't see her there, since it's the perfect excuse for me to . . . well . . . stalk her, but also a little happy because I felt that job was beneath her.

"My boss found out I had the kids that night and that's against company policy," she says sadly. "And I had to miss work one day because my babysitter fell through, *again*."

I tilt my head. "I assume this is your full-time job here. Are you a nurse?"

"Yeah, this is my full-time job. I only worked at the convenience store Monday through Friday from seven to twelve in the evenings. And I'm a certified nurse's assistant."

"So you were working two jobs and raising three kids?" I ask, astounded.

"Pretty much."

*Just . . . wow.*

"Husband or boyfriend to help you out?" I can't help but ask.

She shakes her head, accompanied by another pretty smile, but this time she drops her eyes in a definite shy gesture. She takes her hand and tucks a stray lock of hair behind her ear that has escaped her ponytail. "Just me."

Jesus. No wonder she looks like a strong wind would blow her over. And I'm guessing whatever prick got her pregnant and left her with three children should have his ass kicked.

While I'm pleased to hear there's no man in the picture, I'm still left with an unsettled feeling over her plight. "No other family to help a young mother out with her kids?"

Her face gets a little guarded and I think she might tell me to mind my own business, but I'm stunned when she says, "I'm their legal guardian and it's just me. The kids came to live with me four months ago when my sister died."

Fuck.

Just . . . fuck.

And everything is suddenly clear and fitting into place. Young woman working as a nurse's assistant and probably getting by okay on her own. Sister dies and she takes on raising her niece and nephews on what is probably a terrible salary for what she does. No wonder she was working a second job.

Hell, no wonder she looks like she's about ready to collapse.

And given how unruly those little hellions appeared to be, I bet she's in over her head.

I know that this should be causing all kinds of warning bells to go off in my head, but for some reason it merely makes me want to pull her to my side, press her head on my shoulder and assure her that I'll make everything right.

Which . . . that's fucking weird. I've never been a guy who feels like he has to rescue a girl just to prove his manliness. And besides, I remember when I tried to help her pull the tape off the little girl the other night, and she gave me a firm "Don't." I remember that tilt to her chin even though she looked on the verge of crying. I could tell right then Julianne had a backbone and I've always been attracted to independent women. She may be having troubles, but she's definitely strong.

"Max." I hear Hawke calling my name and I turn my head toward the lobby doors. Jim is standing with him. "Let's go, buddy. We're ready to present the check."

"Be right there," I say as I hold up a finger.

Hawke nods and they both turn back inside.

I look back to Jules, who still has no clue who I am, or if she does, she's not impressed by it.

I like that too.

"So . . . I know this is totally forward, but any chance I could take you out sometime?" I ask with a full smile, which I know is one of my better features as I've been told my dimples are panty-droppers.

She's shaking her head no before I even get the words all the way out, and that is a definite ego-crusher.

"That's sweet," she assures me with apologetic eyes. "But it's just . . . Well, I can't. I don't have any free time, and even if I did, I can't afford a babysitter . . ."

Her words fall off and her eyebrows knit together in confusion again, as if she's just now realizing that her life is far more complicated than she ever realized.

"Part of the date would be me covering the cost of a babysitter," I urge with hopeful eyes, and fuck . . . why do I want to go out with this woman so much? Everything about her circumstances spells trouble to me and yet it's drawing me closer rather than repelling me.

But then she smiles at me.

And those whiskey eyes go warm.

And she says, "You really are very nice, but my priority is those kids right now, and until I can get a bit more stable, I'm not doing you any favors by going out with you, not with my mixed bag of troubles."

Yes, it's clear. She's simply an incredibly intriguing woman who seems to be focused, driven, dedicated, and caring. Add on the fact she's stunning, what fucking guy wouldn't be interested in that?

Despite the fact she has no time and is flat broke and looking quite broken.

"Max," I hear Hawke call out, and he's standing outside the lobby doors again, this time pointing to his watch with a look on his face that says "Get your ass in gear."

I nod at him and stand from the bench, turning to face Jules. She looks up at me, same sweet smile on her face even as she starts to unwrap her sandwich, which had been resting on her lap.

"It was nice meeting you, Jules," I tell her sincerely. Even more sincerely I say, "I hope we run into each other again some-day."

"Nice meeting you too, Max," she says softly, and is that a tiny hint of regret in her eyes?

Hmmmm. Can't really tell but it doesn't matter.

She'll be seeing me sooner rather than later.

# CHAPTER 4

# JULES

"That will be seven dollars and thirty-two cents," I tell the guy across the counter from me. I peg him as single, because no wedding ring first and foremost, but also because he's purchasing a twelve-pack of Pabst Blue Ribbon and that just screams of a lonely Friday night to me.

He hands me a ten and I make change, passing it to him with a smile.

Yes, a smile.

"Here you go, and have a great night," I tell him with a grin that's actually genuine and fueled by a little bit of peppy energy I seem to be oddly sporting only an hour before midnight.

Here I am, back at Whalen's convenience store and gas station on the outskirts of Raleigh, going on my twelfth hour of work today, not counting the time spent cleaning and cooking after I got home from Sweetbrier, and I actually feel a little giddy.

Maybe even euphoric.

And that's simply from the fact that I'm back at this crappy job I'd lost two days ago. I'm so relieved not to have to worry about finding a new job, or how I'm going to manage things financially until I do, that I'm actually fucking over-the-moon happy to be back here.

The guy nods at me, stuffs his money in his back pocket and tucks the boxed twelve-pack under his arm. I watch him walk to the double glass doors, which automatically open on the exit side just as he reaches it, and I can't help the tiny smirk that comes to my mouth when I see Max Fournier on the other side.

He holds the door open for the sad single guy getting ready to get drunk tonight on cheap beer. Single guy does sort of a double take when he sees Max but Max isn't paying attention. He's actually sauntering in as if he owns the place.

"I was wondering when you'd be in," I say with a pointed stare that I try to level as chastising but completely misses the mark.

"Well, wonder no more," he says with an answering grin that is unapologetic. "I wanted to wait until things died down here. Glad to see you're settled back in."

"Yes, well, it was sort of hard to decline Chris' offer when he called me yesterday all in a tizzy that *the* Max Fournier stopped into his store to pay him a visit and politely begged him to give me this job back." My tone is dry, slightly disapproving, but he can tell by the sparkling tease in my eyes that I'm overjoyed to be back.

Max shrugs as if he did nothing special. "I don't like to take advantage of my celebrity but this seemed like one of those times it was warranted."

Indeed.

Yesterday, Max Fournier approached me in the Sweetbrier courtyard as I was on my lunch break and I really didn't know what to do. I immediately recognized him and he was just as insanely gorgeous . . . like the type that took your breath away gorgeous. How could I forget that face from last week when he witnessed my near-meltdown after the redneck-masking-tape-kid fiasco? Despite how tired I was, despite how stressed and worn down I was, I could not disregard his ruggedly handsome face or his wavy, stylishly messy brown hair with lighter brown streaks attesting to the fact this man likes being outdoors in the summer. Those wavy locks fell boyishly over his forehead, highlighting a pair of amazing hazel eyes that were filled with kindness and sympathy as he'd watched me peel tape off Anna-belle.

Yeah . . . I remembered him, and when he approached me yesterday I ogled the hell out of him those first few moments because I was so stunned to see him, it seemed like all my wits had melted away. Of course, by the time I'd gotten them back, he was being called away and caught me completely off guard by asking me out. My heart wanted to say yes, but my head was already saying no to him. It was just terrible timing.

So I was sad when he walked away, wondering how that might have played out had I not had the responsibility of the kids, and what opportunity had just passed me by. I tried not to think too hard on that because it would only make me feel guilty.

I always felt guilty anytime I imagine the what-ifs in my life.

While I recognized Max as being the guy from the gas station, I had no clue who he actually was. I was enlightened by Chris, who had left an urgent voicemail for me while I was working. When I got off duty from Sweetbrier and was in my beat-up old Maxima heading to the apartment, I called him back.

"It's about time you called me," Chris said urgently when he picked up.

"I'll try to get by there today to pick up my check and give you the key," I responded.

"Forget that," he said impatiently. "You've got your job back. I know this is late notice for you today, so I've got tonight covered, but you can start back tomorrow night."

"Huh?" was about as intelligent a response as I could muster.

"Girl, I had no idea you had friends in such high places," he said in awe. "Here I was today, doing inventory while Jody worked the register for the lunch rush, and *Max Fucking Fournier* walks into my store."

*Max Fucking Fournier?*

*He deserves "fucking" as a middle name?*

I didn't want to appear stupid, so I just said, "Uh-huh."

"I'm a huge fan of his, of course, and I about died. Walked right up to me . . . asked me to talk in private. You know . . . sort of man-to-man?"

"Uh-huh."

"And well, he lobbied for me to give you your job back and I just couldn't say no to him, you know?"

"Uh-huh."

"So, you can come back tomorrow."

"Uh-huh."

I did have to listen to Chris ramble on and on about what a god Max Fournier is, and I heard words like *goals against average* and maybe something about a Stanley Cup, but I was so stunned that this man had the ability to command Chris that way, I was in overload. It was only after I got home that I Googled Max and realized who in the hell he is.

Max Fournier is a professional hockey player and the goalie for our own Carolina Cold Fury.

His bio is impressive.

Twenty-seven years old and born in Montreal. He's bilingual, speaking English and French-Canadian, and that explains what's not quite an accent I'm detecting but more of a soft flow of his words together that hinted he might not be American. I hadn't recognized it for what it was until I read that.

He left home at sixteen to join the Ontario Hockey League and played for the Ottawa Stallions for two years before he was drafted into the NHL at age eighteen to the Florida Spartans. He spent three years there as first a backup goalie, then a starting goalie, before being traded to the Cold Fury, where he's been for the past four years although he suffered injuries that kept him on the bench last season.

I am not completely ignorant of hockey. I've dated guys in the past that are all about the sport and so I learned some things. I've even been to a game once before. But I didn't know enough to recognize who Max Fournier was, and I sure as hell have no idea who any of the other players are.

But it all made sense to me why Chris jumped to give me my job back. The Cold Fury are the defending Stanley Cup Champions and I know Chris is a huge fan as he's always talking about them.

I watch as Max turns his back on me and walks down the aisle that displays gum and candy on one side and chips on the other, until he reaches the back cooler and pulls out a Mountain Dew. He snags a Snickers when he comes back through and drops them both on the counter.

I ring the purchases up while casually saying, "You should let me buy these for you. It's the least I can do for you getting my job back."

"Not necessary," he says, and my eyes slide from the green digital display on the register to him. He looks back at me with an expression that clearly says he was glad he could help. He hands me a five dollar bill without even looking at the total and I take that to mean this is not his first Snickers and Mountain Dew combo he's purchased.

My heart starts beating a little quicker as I make change for him, then quicker yet when I pass him the coins and our fingers brush against each other. A flood of warmth courses through me, leaving a little prickle of excitement behind, and when he smiles at me and shoves the change in his front pocket, a feeling of serenity settles over me.

That's . . . odd and not exactly altogether unpleasant.

I wait for Max to tell me goodbye and walk back out that door—back out of my life, probably for good—but he stuns the hell out of me when he walks the length of the counter and then rounds the end to come behind the register with me. He casually leans against the back counter, setting his Mountain Dew there and opening up his Snickers bar.

"What are you doing?" I ask, stunned, with equal measures of excitement he's not leaving and terror that Chris will walk in and find him here. I cannot lose this job again.

"Going to hang out with you for the rest of your shift," he says with a shrug and then takes a bite of his candy bar.

I get sidetracked a moment by the strong lines of his jaw moving as he chews, and my fingers itch to touch the stubble there, which looks the same length as when I saw him yesterday.

"You can't," I blurt out. "If Chris comes in . . . I can't lose this job again."

"He knows I'm here," Max says calmly after he swallows, and then waves the candy bar in my direction. "Want a bite?"

My eyebrows draw inward and I shake my head at his offer. "He knows you're here?"

"Yup," he says with a grin. "Told him I was going to come by tonight for a little bit and hang until you closed up, and then make sure you got to your car safely."

"And he was okay with that?"

"He was more than okay," Max says nonchalantly, takes another bite and grins at me through his chewing.

I narrow my eyes. "You bribed him, didn't you?"

"Yup," is all he says.

"With what . . . tickets to games?"

"And signed shit," he adds on.

I shake my head, my eyes lowered in amusement. I keep them lowered, afraid to look at him again as I might just grab his face and plant a huge kiss on his cheek.

I'm saved from embarrassing myself when the door opens and a young guy walks in. Tall with light blond hair, fashionable white polo, and khaki shorts with loafers. He doesn't spare us a glance and heads to the coolers.

Max sets his half-eaten candy bar down, pushes off from the counter, steps to the end and nabs a baseball hat off a rack that holds several done in local collegiate colors. He chooses a red Wolfpack one, glances at the price tag before pulling it off. I watch all of this with interest as he puts the hat on, pulls it low, and then fishes in his wallet to hand me a twenty along with the tag.

I look down at the items in my hand, then back to him, and he winks. "Don't feel like getting recognized."

I grin and turn to the register, where I ring up the hat for $14.99 and hand him his change.

Max pulls his phone out, bends his head over it, and leans back against the counter just as the young guy puts a case of beer on the counter. He doesn't even give Max a glance and it takes no more than a few minutes for me to card him, ring up his purchase, take payment, give him the difference, and he's back out the door without once looking at the man behind the counter with me.

I turn to face Max, resigned—no, okay, excited—that he's going to spend the next hour here. Positioning myself on the opposite counter, with the register behind me, I lean back and ask, "It's kind of weird . . . a professional athlete eating a candy bar and drinking a Mountain Dew."

"We all have vices, Jules," he offers before polishing off the candy bar.

"I bet you train super hard so what's a candy bar here and there, right?" I observe.

"That's kind of my theory," he says, after which he swallows the last bit and uncaps his Mountain Dew. He holds it up toward his mouth, but before taking a drink he says, "But let's just make an agreement right here and now that if you ever meet Vale Campbell, my strength trainer, you do not tell her about the candy bars and soda, okay?"

I laugh, tilting my head back and realizing it's been a long time since I've let out an actual spontaneous laugh. When I lower my face and look back at him with a fading chuckle, he's staring at me, bottle still poised in the air.

His eyes are intense . . . pinned on me. We stare at each other, and as my laugh dies, an electric current seems to sizzle in the air between us. His gaze drops to my mouth, holds there a moment and then moves back to my eyes. A slight flash of longing and then it's gone and he's giving me an easygoing smile. "Agreed?"

"Sure," I say, desperately reaching out to grab ahold of that magnetic feeling again, but it's gone. "It's our secret."

"So what do you do to entertain yourself in here at night in between customers?" he asks casually.

I sigh internally because that pulsing vibe of attraction that was just here is absolutely gone, but I'm bolstered somewhat by the fact that Max's attention on me is no less focused.

"Um . . . let's see. I'll often read *People* magazine so I can stay up-to-date on celebrity news, or I'll just surf on my phone, but I have to be careful because my data plan isn't very big and there's no WiFi here. Oh, and I like to play a game when customers come in . . . I try to figure out what their life story is just by what I observe about them."

"For example," he prods me.

"Well, that kid that was just in here . . . I think he's from a fairly well-to-do family, probably goes to private school judging by his clothes and car. On his way to a party and he stopped in here to grab beer for the night. In fact, I bet the party is in one of these huge developments with the mega mansions and he's on his way there, probably hoping to get laid by a cheerleader or something."

"But he would have bought condoms," Max points out. "Actually, I think he had a date tonight and was stood up . . . and he's depressed and came in to buy beer so he can get drunk and drown his miseries."

"You're a romantic," I say with a grin.

"I can be," he says softly, and that causes me to flush warm again.

God, I can't even remember what it means for a guy to be romantic.

The door to the store opens again. Max pulls his cap lower and we watch as a woman of about fifty walks in wearing a black tank top with white bra straps sticking out. Tight jeans, and tattoos up and down both arms. Her eyes are done with blue eye shadow and lips are bright red. She weaves a little, clearly drunk.

She orders two packs of cigarettes and without a thank-you

walks back out. We both watch as she gets on the back of a Harley driven by a big burly guy with a long gray beard.

I turn back to look at Max and he laughs. "That's way too easy. No fun in trying to figure out her story."

For the next fifty minutes I am thoroughly entertained by Max. We make up people's life stories and in between I read him snippets from *People* magazine. I find him witty with an amazing sense of humor, and I laugh more than I have in a long time. Our conversation is casual and not very deep, but it is very easy and I appreciate that more than he'll ever know. That electric pop never happens again, but I expect it's because Max is being respectful of me, and he's showing me what a nice guy he is.

And God . . . he's so nice.

At midnight I lock the doors and turn off the outside lights to indicate we're closed. Max waits patiently as I zero out the register and fill out the paperwork that goes with it, before putting the cash into the safe.

It's when he follows me out of the store, waits for me to relock the doors, and then walks me to my car that I start to feel nervous.

I open my car door and slide into the driver's seat while Max rests his hand on the top of the door and peers down at me.

"You work again on Monday, right?" he asks.

I nod, putting my key in the ignition.

"I'll come see you then," he says.

"You don't have to—"

Max cuts me off. "I've got an away game tomorrow in Boston but I'll be back Sunday. Give me your phone number."

"What? No," I blurt out, wondering why he would possibly want to come hang out in a convenience store with me or even want my number. Getting involved with me is a terrible idea, and why he can't see that is beyond me.

"Yes," is all he says as he pulls his phone out. "Give me your number."

I weigh my options, but before I can even give adequate consideration to the first one—which is to refuse him again—he narrows his eyes at me and says, "I'll just get it from Chris. You know he'll give it to me."

I try to be mad or affronted that he's being so pushy, but damn it . . . his smile and dimples are so fucking persuasive, I give him my number.

I do it with an eye roll, but I give it to him all the same.

## CHAPTER 5

# MAX

I wait until four P.M. to call Jules. I had to force myself not to call her yesterday in order to concentrate on our game in Boston. And normally I never have a hard time locking the world out and focusing on my job in the net when it's game day. In fact, I'm usually so focused on game day, I barely speak to anyone.

But yesterday morning as I was sitting on the team plane for our flight to Boston, I actually pulled my phone out. I had come perilously close to dialing her, when Hawke threw himself down in the seat next to me and without even so much as a "Good morning" proceeded to fill me in on the saga of him and Vale. This did not include exact details but he told me grimly that Vale finally revealed why she broke up with him seven years ago, and that they had worked it out. He then told me with a stupid grin on his face that makeup sex was awesome, and then, with amused chuckles, about how one of his hookups showed up at his house with Vale there.

I winced because that did not sound funny.

He jabbered at me until the plane door closed and I was forced to put my phone into airplane mode, the call to Jules averted.

Fuck, I wanted to hear her voice and see if that connection we'd made the previous night was still there, but I also didn't want to come on too strong with her. When she told me at Sweetbrier that it was not a good time in her life, I took that as a clear indication I had to proceed slowly with her. She had so much on her plate and so many worries on her mind and I did not want to add on to that. It's why I kept things light and friendly the night I hung out with her at the convenience store.

So I forced myself to give her some space and I finally got my head in the game on Saturday. It's a good thing too because we're still in preseason, and while I think I'm the favorite for the starting goalie spot, I'm not locked in either. I got the call for the start Saturday night and I played fucking fantastic, managing to go all three periods without thinking about Jules once. And that is how it should be. When I'm in a game, I should be focused on that.

But I'm not in a game today so I can put my attention elsewhere.

It's Sunday and I'm not going to let another day pass without at least letting her know I'm still interested. I busied myself today with working out, getting my house cleaned, and grocery shopping for the upcoming week. I did my laundry and watched some golf on TV. Then I got up, got in my car, and drove to Tony's Pizza.

I have no clue where Jules lives and while I'm quite confident her manager would hand me her address without a care in the world, that's definitely too stalkerlike. But I do know Tony's is near her house because it's only a few miles from Sweetbrier, and she told me Friday night that her commute was only like five minutes. So I know I'm in the general vicinity of where she lives.

As I sit in the parking lot of Tony's, I pull my phone out and dial Jules' number, my heart pounding hard as I wait for her to answer, slightly terrified she won't.

She picks up on the second ring and answers with a tentative whisper, her tone of voice wondering who is calling her since I did not give her my number and she wouldn't recognize it. "Hello?"

"Have you started on dinner yet for you and the kids?" I ask. I'm taking a guess she's with the kids because I learned Friday night that she doesn't work weekends except for watching a friend's kid who watches her crew during weeknights when she's working at the convenience store. It's been raining all day today, so I hoped they'd all be there at Jules' apartment.

"Max?" she asks hesitantly.

"Well, of course it's Max," I tease her lightly. "Or do you have so many men chasing after you that you can't keep us straight?"

She laughs softly and it flows through my veins like a sweet lazy river. I like that sound so much, I immediately yearn to hear it again.

"You just caught me off guard," she says by way of explanation.

"Didn't think I'd call, did you?" I guess.

"Nope," she admits candidly. "I'm not exactly a great catch."

"I beg to differ," I say, but I don't want to belabor that point with her because I'm not sure I have enough breath in my lungs to have my reason penetrate her doubtful head. Besides, I intend to show her through actions that I'm interested in her quite a bit, despite the messiness of her life right now. Friday night was one of the best hours I'd spent in a long, long time. Fun, humorous conversation that was virtually effortless, and let's not forget . . . she is not hard to look at.

I continue on. "So, I'm getting ready to order pizza. You cool with New York style and just pepperoni? It's my favorite but I could be persuaded to order something else."

"Huh?"

"Pizza, Jules. Pizza. I'm getting pizza for you and the kids, and going to deliver it to you. You'll be nice, invite me in to eat with you, and then I'll be on my way."

"Pizza?" she mumbles.

"I might bring cannoli too," I add on to tempt her further.

"You're crazy," she murmurs.

"Quite possibly. So what kind of pizza do you and the kids like, and what's your address?"

"My apartment is a mess," she warns me.

"Don't care."

"The kids are kind of wired today since it's been raining and they've been stuck inside," she warns further.

"We'll stuff them with pizza and then put in a movie for them to watch," I suggest. "It'll be fine."

She huffs out a breath, remains silent for a moment, then says, "Fine. We all love New York style and I'll text you my address."

"Awesome," I tell her, and then I give a double fist pump inside my car. I can't believe she gave in that easy.


This isn't going quite how I expected, but it's cool.

Totally cool that three little kids are repetitively whipping my ass at Candy Land. I draw a card, note the blue square, and advance my gingerbread pawn and fucking land on a licorice drop.

Again.

At age six and the middle child, Levy—who I quickly realized is the true troublemaker of this crew—points a finger and laughs almost maniacally at me. "You lose a turn, Max. In your face."

*Little brat.*

But I laugh back at him, watch as Annabelle—who proudly announced to me she is four and a half years old—pulls a yellow card and advances to the Candy Castle for her third win. She lets out a "yippee" as she smirks at Levy, who's only won one game, while she's won three. Rocco is the oldest at seven and you can tell he's sort of an old soul. While he's also only won one game, he praises Annabelle for her victory.

Yeah . . . not how I thought this would go.

I showed up with hot pizzas and my nerves on overdrive as I realized I was getting ready to not only spend time with Jules, which produced the good kind of nerves, but that I'd also be interacting with her niece and nephews. It suddenly hit me . . . I want Jules to like me, and if I want that, those kids better fucking like me.

I had hoped a nice bribery of gooey pizza and then the DVD copy of *The Incredibles* would be sufficient. I'd hoped after we ate, the kids would watch the movie and I'd be able to perhaps talk to Jules, or even stare at her a bit if that's all I could finagle. But she informed me after we ate that she didn't own a DVD player and even if she did, her TV didn't work because of two active boys that may have knocked the TV over during a wrestling match.

Thankfully, neither one had been hurt, but the TV didn't survive, something inside having been jarred loose, and Jules simply couldn't afford to fix it.

So I got stuck playing Candy Land with the kids while Jules finished up laundry, got their clothes ready for the next day, and packed the boys' lunches. In between the second and third game, I found her in the bathroom scrubbing out the toilet. She just looked at me sheepishly and muttered, "Sorry . . . but I'm totally taking advantage of you keeping them occupied so I can get ahead on a few things that need to be done."

Christ . . . it was a fucking punch to the gut as I realized Jules couldn't even sit down longer than the fifteen minutes it took her to eat two slices of pizza before she was pressed into answering the call of responsibility. I wanted to pull her away, rip those nasty yellow rubber gloves she was wearing off, and make her go sit down on the couch to rest. Instead I asked, "Want me to help do something?"

She grinned at me and said, "Trust me . . . this is actually a nice break from having to entertain three rambunctious kids. You playing with them is doing me a huge favor."

I nodded and started to turn away, but she called, "Max?"

I turned back.

"Thanks. I know this is an awful way to spend your time."

Another punch to the gut.

"Jules," I told her as my eyes pinned her in place, "watching you scrub that toilet and playing a horribly boring game over and over again is the highlight of my day."

And that's the truth.

Well, mostly the truth. I'd rather have been watching a movie, but whatever. I think she got my point that I would take her how I could get her. And besides, I'm still trying to figure things out. Trying to figure out what I'm trying to get out of all of this, and whether or not I can even see any feasible way of getting some time with her alone to figure those things out.

But for now . . . this works.

I'm not in a rush.

"Let's play again," Levy says aggressively as he pulls all the gingerbread men back to the start. "I want to win again."

I groan internally but try to put a pleasant smile on my face. Luckily, I'm saved when Jules walks into the tiny kitchen that opens up into the living room and says, "Okay, kids. It's time to get to bed."

This is met by grumbles all around, but fuck . . . they're kind of cute doing it. They're each ready for bed, even though it's only a little after eight P.M. as Jules had them take their respective baths immediately after dinner. Annabelle has on a pink pajama set that has a unicorn on the front. It looks old and faded but totally comfy. Levy is wearing equally faded Batman pajamas while Rocco sports Superman pj's.

Jules levels them all with a stern look and holds an arm out, indicating for each of them to precede her down the hallway. More grumbling as Levy and Rocco mutter good nights to me, but Annabelle hops off the chair and runs around the table. "Thank you for the pizza and playing with us."

She looks so much like Jules, there's no wonder I originally thought she was their mother. This means that Melody and Jules must have looked a lot alike. Tonight I've been very impressed with how well adjusted the kids seem, despite losing their mom four months ago. And Jules . . . she's a fucking dynamo, easily alternating between loving aunt and stern guardian when needed.

"You're welcome, Annabelle. Can't wait to play with you again."

She gives me a huge grin and turns around to run down the hallway. Jules shoots me a soft smile before turning to follow the kids. That smile . . . the way in which she said thank you in about a million different ways with just that one look has me rising from my chair and following them down the hall, intrigued to see how she gets the kids to sleep.

The first door on the left is where I find all of them, as Rocco and Levy climb into a double bed and Annabelle waits patiently for Jules to tuck them in. Watching her hold the covers up so they can push their little legs in, then pulling them up to their chins . . . the way she leans across the bed and kisses first Rocco on the forehead, and then pulling back to do the same to Levy, touches me deeply. She may feel in over her head, and this I know because

I've seen the look of frustration and defeat at times, she's a fucking natural at this. Whether it's raising her niece and nephews or her own children, she was destined to be a mother one day.

Jules turns out the light, picks Annabelle up, and perches her on her hip. She sees me standing in the doorway and her look is accepting of me watching the intimacy of their bedtime ritual. I even get a soft smile as I step back from the doorway to let her by before following her to the room on the opposite side of the hall.

I immediately know this is Jules' room because this is only a two-bedroom apartment and I quickly figure Annabelle sleeps in here with her. A small bedside lamp is on, casting the room in a warm glow. Her comforter is done in mint green with tiny roses embroidered around the edges. It's a little more feminine than I would have pictured a strong woman like her having, but it works, I guess. As Jules starts the process of tucking Annabelle in, which apparently includes reading her favorite book, I walk over to a dresser on the opposite wall of the small room and pick up a frame that holds a picture of two women.

I immediately know this is Jules and her sister, Melody. They're both outside and the sun is shining brightly on them. They have the same eyes, which seem to glow not only from the rays of the sun but from sort of an inner vitality that you can tell they both possess. Their arms are wrapped tightly around each other and their cheeks are pressed together as they look at the camera and appear to be laughing at whoever is taking the picture. It's both gorgeous and sad, knowing that one of those lights has been completely snuffed out and the other has been dampened.

I set the frame down, vaguely listen as Jules reads to Annabelle about a giraffe that can't dance, and my eyes slide to a painting on the wall to the side of her dresser.

It's done in gallery wrap canvas and I'm stunned by the boldness of the colors, only enhanced by the boldness of the brushstrokes. It's a night scene, the sky done in various shades of blue darkening at the horizon and getting lighter in the foreground. A lone row of autumn trees colored in oranges and reds are lit up from below by streetlamps, and a concrete walkway runs parallel. A woman walks along the path, her back to the viewer. She's wearing a trench coat and carries a bright yellow umbrella to shield her from the rain. But I don't need the umbrella to tell me it's raining in the painting. I know this because the leaves on the trees are dewy-looking and the streetlights are reflected on the concrete, which looks shiny and slick. What really strikes me about the painting though is that I immediately recognize details like that, but it's not because of fine brushstrokes. Rather, it's done in chunky swatches of color that if you were to look closely at it wouldn't make sense, but from afar I can tell without a doubt that it's a dark rainy night.

I wonder why she's got such a remarkable painting in this room and I also have to wonder how she afforded it, because it's quality work and I'd like to know more about the artist. My mother is a freak when it comes to original pieces of art, and our house back in Montreal is filled with all of her finds. She'd love something like this, I'm sure.

I turn to the bed and see Jules has finished the story and is pulling the covers up around Annabelle, so I make my way to the bedroom door. She bends down and kisses Annabelle on the forehead, same as she did for the boys, but Annabelle responds by grabbing Jules around the neck and giving her a hug that's very fierce for such a little girl.

"Good night, Mommy," Annabelle says in a sweet voice, and I don't miss the fact that Jules' body stiffens slightly.

But she holds still until Annabelle releases her, and when she pulls back she gives the little girl a warm smile. " 'Night, pumpkin. Sweet dreams."

"Okay," Annabelle says and then turns on her side, tucks her hand under her head and closes her eyes.

Jules turns to look at me as her hand goes to the lamp, and just before she turns it off, my gut clenches when I see the uncertainty rippling in her eyes.

# CHAPTER 6

# JULES

I follow Max out of my bedroom, my heart pounding so hard I feel dizzy. Annabelle just called me Mommy and I didn't have a clue what the fuck to say to it. I've been Aunt Jules to them, and all three continued to call me that when they came to live with me. I think it was a comfort to them somewhat, as it kept it clear in their minds that they had a mommy that loved them very much and there was no pressure for them to feel anything otherwise.

I'm also stunned because while the kids have been with me for a little over four months, we still don't know one another all that well. Melody lived in Oklahoma and our ability to see each other was stunted on both sides by us each not having the money to travel for visits. As such, I probably saw the kids less than a handful of times in their short lives, so when Melody died, they were coming to live with a virtual stranger.

Thus, I'm completely shocked that Annabelle would consider

me to be her mommy right now and I'm dumbfounded by what to do. On top of that, I'm just very, very tired of the pressure that comes with trying to make decisions that don't fuck their heads up more than what they already are.

And then there's Max.

Big, beautiful Max walking into my living room and I don't have any idea what to do with him. Oh, I know there are all kinds of things I want to do with him, but I'm afraid that might be the desperate part of me that wants to grab on to something just for myself, and that's completely selfish at this point in my life.

When Max hits the middle of my living room, he points to my couch and says, "Sit."

I blink at him in surprise but his face is so earnest . . . so intent on something . . . I don't even think to disobey. Besides, my back is killing me from bending over to scrub out the bathtub tonight.

I fall onto the couch heavily, huffing out a sigh of relief to be off my feet.

Max steps into the space between the living room and the cheap coffee table I got at a flea market and sits down on it, facing me. I wince when I see it almost shudder under his weight, but impressively, it holds solid.

He leans forward, puts his elbows on his knees, and says, "That bothered you. Annabelle calling you Mommy."

I hold his gaze solidly so he gets me. "It didn't bother me. But it concerns me. I have no clue if that's appropriate or not. Should I remind her I'm her aunt and not her mom, because I'm terrified that she'll forget her mom, or should I let her call me what makes her happy?"

"Not sure there is a right answer," he tells me softly, and oddly, that helps. Knowing that he sees how murky these waters are.

I give him a weak smile and nod. "I'm thinking I need to let Annabelle do what makes her feel the most comfortable, and still work hard to keep the memory of Melody alive."

"I think that's wise," he murmurs. "And you're doing a fantastic job with them, for what it's worth."

His gaze holds mine. Solid. Caring. Steady.

I can't for the life of me figure out why this enigmatic man who is famous and rich and hot would be sitting here looking at me this way. It's as perplexing as everything else in my life, and for once I just wish I could easily identify what the hell is going on so I could deal.

It will take work to figure it out. I wasn't lying to him when I told him this was a terrible time in my life. And yet, the feeling of comfort I have right now as he gives me validation feels so damn good, I honestly don't think I could push him away. He's the first real adult I've had in my life for a while, somebody whom I don't need to take care of.

Patting the cushion beside me, I say, "Okay . . . so tell me all about Max Fournier and why in the world he is sitting in my dinky little apartment trying to make me feel good about myself."

Max's eyes crinkle with amusement and he pushes his large body off the table, turns, and drops down beside me. He's so big, the cushions depress, and I can't help that my body tilts toward his, causing our shoulders to come to rest against each other. It would be so damn tempting to just lay my head there on that solid support and close my eyes to rest.

But Max's soft voice intrigues me and I get caught up by his words. "I'm a total fan of going to the theater, horror movies being my favorite. Not those blood and gore ones. They're okay, I guess, but the ones that are suspenseful and have you about climbing out of your skin. I prefer hot dogs over hamburgers, can't stand onions, and I'm not lying when I say I really do like moonlit strolls on the beach."

I burst out laughing, angle my head on the cushion to look at him. "Such a cliché."

"Not if it's true," he says in that deep voice that has a slight softness to it, the next word effortlessly starting before the previous one ends.

"You have an accent," I say in an abrupt change of subject. "I read you're French-Canadian."

*"Je suis né à Montréal. Mon père est québecois et ma mère américaine, donc je parle couramment les deux langues."*

I give a dramatic, feminine sigh. "I bet you get all the girls to drop their panties when you talk like that, right?"

He leans forward a bit, looks at the lower half of my body with an arched eyebrow and says dryly, "Apparently not."

I should be tired as hell and not up for witty banter, but damn if he doesn't energize me with his quick wit and charm. I laugh and turn my face forward again. "But seriously, what did you say?"

"I said you're not getting in my pants, no matter how much you beg," he says devilishly.

And I can't help it, I laugh again.

But then he turns serious. "I said yes, I am French-Canadian and I was born to a French-Canadian father and an American mother."

"Your accent is very hard to detect though," I point out.

He shrugs. "I probably mimic my mom's accent some, plus I've spent the last eleven years outside of French-speaking Canada. It's probably just diluted, I guess."

"And do you have siblings?" I ask, my mind of course thinking of my one and only, who I lost.

"Three," he says in a voice that tells me he loves his siblings the way I loved Melody. "I'm the oldest, then there's Lucas, who is a year younger than me at twenty-six. He's a center for the New Jersey Wildcats. Then Malik, who is twenty-four and exercised his dual citizenship by enlisting in the U.S. Marine Corps, and finally our little sister, Simone. She's twenty-one and in her senior year at Dartmouth, where our parents met. She wants to follow in my dad's footsteps and become a doctor."

"Your dad's a doctor?" I ask curiously.

"A radiologist. His name is Laurence," he confirms with a nod, and I can hear the French part of his accent loud and clear when he pronounces it "Lor-ohnce." And damn . . . that's sexy.

"My mom, Marilyn, is a public speaking coach," he adds with pride. "My family is amazing."

"I can hear the affection in your voice," I say with a smile. "That's nice."

And it is . . . so nice.

And foreign.

"Will you tell me about Melody?" he asks softly, and his voice washes over me with such care that I don't hesitate in the slightest, even though she's been difficult to think about much less talk about.

"She was three years older than me—" I start, but Max interrupts.

"How old are you?"

"Twenty-five," I tell him and then continue on with my story. "Our mom ditched us when I was thirteen and she was sixteen, and my dad was a long-distance truck driver, so he sort of just let Melody take care of me when he was on the road. Which was fine. Melody was always really mature and she did take great care of me. Did all the grocery shopping, paid bills with money Dad left us when he was gone, made sure I did my homework. You know . . . mom stuff."

"Was that here in Raleigh?" he asks.

I shake my head. "Fayetteville . . . about an hour south of here."

"Military base there, right?"

"Fort Bragg," I tell him. "In fact, that's where she met her husband, Dwayne. He was a soldier there and they got married when she was twenty. I moved in with her and Dwayne for my last year of high school, but then he got out of the Army not long after I graduated and she moved with him back to Oklahoma, where he was from."

"That must have been tough on you," he observes.

"Really hard because Melody had just found out she was pregnant with Rocco," I tell him in a sad murmur. "But she was in love and following her heart."

"What did you do?" he prompts.

"Moved back into my dad's house. Got a job and tried to figure out what I wanted to do with my life. Finally decided on becoming a nursing assistant, and I figured I could go back to school later and complete my RN degree if I wanted."

"And that's when you moved to Raleigh?"

"Yup. Finished my degree, got a job at Sweetbrier and have been there ever since."

Max sits up from his semireclined position and turns himself to face me, raising one powerful leg up onto the cushion and slinging his arm along the back of the couch. It's not touching me but it is resting right above the top of my head. I shift my body, turn to lean on my hip so I can face him.

"What happened to Melody?" he asks quietly, his eyes pinned to mine.

I drop my gaze only for a moment, really just to collect myself, and then I look back up to him. "Ovarian cancer. By the time it was diagnosed it had spread everywhere. She went downhill really fast, maybe about three months total from the time she was diagnosed. Sweetbrier let me take a leave of absence—unpaid, of course. I went out there and took care of her until she . . . well, until the end. Brought the kids back with me."

Max's face has morphed into painful empathy and he reaches his hand out, runs his fingers over the back of mine resting on my thigh. It's an intimate move, but not a sexual one. It's full of support and care. He then wraps his fingers around my hand and squeezes.

"What about her husband?" he asks.

"He flaked out pretty much after Rocco was born," I told him with only a slight hint of bitterness. Bitter that he hurt Melody so badly but very much consoled by the fact I have the kids and he doesn't. I explain further, "He cheated on her frequently, often leaving for weeks, usually to stay with another woman. He'd then float back into her life, she'd take him back because she loved him, and lo and behold, she'd get pregnant again. Then he'd flake out again. When she got diagnosed, he'd been gone again for maybe six months. Moved to Arizona last we heard, with some woman. Never sent her any money and actually owes a few years of back support to them, but I doubt I'll ever see that."

"Did he even come back when Melody was sick?"

"Nope," I tell him now with complete bitterness. "Melody was heartbroken he didn't even care enough to come say goodbye but she defended him to the end, which drove me nuts. Said that it was too hard on him to see her that way. They had a few conversations on the phone and he made it clear he couldn't handle the kids. Gladly signed off for me to get guardianship."

"What an asshole," Max mutters, his hand reflexively squeezing mine. And it feels good and secure.

"Totally an asshole," I agree. "He was horrible to Melody and

I never got why she kept taking his shit. He's only called the kids once since they've moved in here, but honestly, I'm not sure that's a bad thing. They're used to him not being in their lives and I think it only highlights his abandonment of them when he makes such infrequent calls. At first I thought it was strange they hardly ever asked for their daddy but then I realized he really wasn't that to them throughout their lives."

"Someone should kick his ass," Max says on a low growl. "Or better yet, go kick his parents' asses for raising such a piece of shit."

He won't get any argument from me there, that's the truth. I lean until the side of my head rests against the cushion and smile at him in agreement.

Max bends his head down a little closer to me, his eyes brimming with stark admiration. "So here you are . . . probably leading a decent, stress-free life, and all of a sudden . . . you lose your sister and gain three kids. You had to cram everyone into this little apartment, and you're struggling to make ends meet because it's not cheap feeding and clothing and nurturing three children. So you work your ass off, morning, noon, and night and you make things work."

"Pretty much," I say with a heavy fatigue because my life sure as shit isn't easy right now.

"You're fucking amazing," Max says quietly and my heart seems to squeeze for one intense moment, then it relaxes into utter calm and tranquillity just by having someone affirm what I've been doing.

"Thank you for saying that," I murmur, appreciative of his validation and more than happy to have him holding my hand. Just that tiny bit of affirmation does wonders to help my confidence and almost makes me believe I can actually do this.

Is it bad that there's a part of me that just wants him to lean his head a little farther toward me, and perhaps brush his lips against mine? Just a little touch?

Instead, Max releases my hand and pulls back a little, putting an easygoing smile on his face. "Okay, that's our quota of heavy shit for the night."

"Agreed," I say with a smile, even though my hand feels cold now that his is gone.

"So what's the deal with that painting hanging in your room?" he asks curiously. "It's gorgeous and I'd like to maybe get something like that for my mother. She's really into art and collects originals."

My face actually starts to burn and I can imagine how red my cheeks are. I duck my head reflexively in embarrassment, only to find Max's fingers under my chin, lifting me back up.

"What?" he asks curiously, his head tilted to the side.

I have to fight to look him in the eye when I say, "Um . . . I did that."

His hand falls away and his eyebrows shoot sky high. "You painted that?" he asks incredulously, but not in a rude way . . . more like an *I'm-in-fucking-awe* kind of way.

"It's a hobby," I mutter, feeling my cheeks burning hotter.

"*That* is not a hobby," he says inflexibly. "That is some major fucking talent. Did you take classes or something?"

I shake my head. "Nothing formal. Art in high school, and just dabbled here and there."

Max shakes his head in an amused but disbelieving way. "You are just one surprise after another."

Okay, my cheeks are now sizzling and I can't stand it anymore so I brush him off with a forced laugh. "Well, that's all my secrets. Now you know everything."

Max's lips quirk up and he shakes his head slowly again, totally not buying that for some reason. "I have a feeling you have layers upon layers, Jules. I look forward to peeling them."

And God . . . I hope he cannot see the full-body shiver he just produced with those words.

"Do you have any more paintings?" Max asks.

My eyebrows knit together. "Um . . . yeah. A few in my closet and I've got some stored at my dad's house back in Fayetteville."

"You could sell them," Max says confidently.

"No way," I disagree.

"Yes, you could," he says even more firmly. "In fact, I have a friend that works in a really upscale florist shop in Chapel Hill and I know he'd hang them there for sale."

Oh, fucking no way. The thought of someone analyzing and critiquing my work? The thought of people hating it? I could never—

"Jules," Max says in a low voice. "You could make money off that. Give up that shitty job at the gas station. Have some real money to take care of those kids."

Okay, that catches my attention.

My voice is hesitant though when I ask, "You really think so?"

"I know so," he says with so much belief in those words, it makes me want to believe it too. "If you give me what you have here, I'll take them over there. What do you have to lose?"

"Well . . . nothing, I guess," I say guardedly, my gaze falling to my lap.

"Jules," Max says, and my eyes snap back. "You're really fucking good and I'm not lying to you about that."

I can't help it. A rush of euphoria and hope rushes through me that maybe I can be more than what I am, which isn't for me but for those kids, and I smile at him. "Okay, then . . . I'll try it."

"Excellent," he says then stands from the couch but not before grabbing my hand and pulling me up with him. "Let's get those paintings then I'm going to head out so you can get a good night's sleep."

Crushing disappointment hits me—he's leaving, and I realize . . . he's got me hooked.

He's got me fucking hooked *hard* and apparently all of my spouting off about this being a bad time in my life doesn't seem to mean shit. In fact, Max has decidedly made my life, if not a little better, at least rosier.

I sneak into my room so as not to wake up Annabelle and pull the picture he admired off my wall. It's one of my favorites and I grab four more out of my closet. When I hand them to Max, who waited for me in the living room, I tell him, "I've got more at my dad's house I can probably get next weekend."

"Definitely," he says and then turns to the door. I follow behind, again wishing he weren't leaving, but on the flip side looking forward to a good night's sleep. I know I'll have a smile on my face when I close my eyes.

Max opens the door, the paintings tucked under his other arm. He turns to face me, his eyes running over my face for just a moment as if he's checking that I'll be okay without him.

I give him an encouraging smile.

He gives me one back, then leans down to me. My eyes close and I feel his lips brush against my cheek.

"Good night, Jules," he says softly before he pulls away and disappears out my door.

# CHAPTER 7

# MAX

There's a little bell above the front door of Fleurish that chimes when I walk in. I take a quick look around, feeling slightly overwhelmed by the tables scattered about topped with massive displays of fresh flowers and plants. While Fleurish is primarily a floral shop in Chapel Hill, it also sells a variety of knickknacks and art pieces created by local artisans. I knew this would be the perfect place to see if Jules' paintings were as good as I thought they were.

"Max?" I hear from behind me and spin around to see Olivia standing by a glass cooler filled with vases of fresh flower arrangements.

"Hey, Olivia," I say with a smile as I walk toward her. I hadn't seen her at all in the off-season as I'd spent some time back home in Montreal and she and Garrett did some traveling to celebrate her continuing good health. She's just about two years postcancer diagnosis and doing fantastic. At least that's the word I got from

Garrett when training camp started a few weeks ago, but she's living proof standing in front of me.

She looks fantastic.

I reach her and lean down to kiss her on the cheek. "Have a good summer?"

Olivia smiles brilliantly at me. "The best. Garrett and I went out west and spent some time in Colorado doing a lot of hiking and stuff."

"That must mean you're feeling really good," I surmise.

"I'm feeling wonderful," she says and then her eyes drop to the paintings I'm holding under my arm. "What you got there?"

"A friend of mine is an artist and I was wondering if you could sell them here?" I tell her bluntly with no lead in.

"Let me see," she commands, and I line them up against the cooler.

"Oh, Max," she breathes out in awe. "Those are stunning."

"I know," I say, bursting on the inside with pride over Jules' talent.

Olivia turns her head over her right shoulder and calls out, "Stevie. Come here a minute."

I hear the scrape of a chair against wood flooring from the back workroom and then the megawattage personality of Stevie Magliano—owner of Fleurish—comes prancing my way.

He let his trademark hairstyle go—platinum blond spikes with neon tips—and is a bit more sedate today with what looks like naturally blond hair cropped close to his head. But just because his hairstyle has gone a little more conservative doesn't mean that Stevie himself is less flamboyant. On the contrary, he has a floral pattern of pink crystals glued to his face from the outside corners of his eyes and sweeping up his temples, with hot pink nail polish to match. Skinny white jeans, a pink button-down polo shirt with black loafers, and his ensemble screams "I'm Gay and I'm Proud of It."

"Max," he says with pleasant surprise when he sees me, then sashays my way. I have to admit, the first time I'd met Stevie I was a bit taken aback, but I don't think twice now, bending down and letting him air kiss each cheek before he pulls back and looks me up and down critically. "Oh, boyfriend . . . those jeans are dreadful. What . . . did you seriously get them at like a thrift store or something?"

I look down at my Levi's 501s that yeah . . . are a bit faded and distressed because they're old as dirt, but they still fit great.

I think.

Not sure.

"Stevie," Olivia snaps impatiently, and he turns to look at her. "Check out these paintings Max brought in."

Stevie moves to stand beside Olivia, where he has one hand on his hip and pinches his chin thoughtfully with the other as he stares down at Jules' art. His gaze is narrowed at first as his eyes critically take in the pieces, and he looks from painting to painting with thoughtful measure.

Finally, he turns to me and says, "These are magnificent."

"Can you hang them up and sell them?" I ask hopefully, prepared to do some hardcore begging if he declines. "Maybe on commission?"

Stevie gives a small shake of his head. "Not on commission. I'll buy them outright and then mark them up for retail."

"Are you serious?" I ask incredulously, because that was way better than I had ever imagined. I mean, I know Jules is good but I didn't expect anyone to take that big a leap with her work.

"Dead serious," Stevie says as he looks from the paintings to me and then back to the paintings again. "I can probably fetch four hundred dollars each. And I'd love some more. Who's the artist?"

"A friend of mine . . . her name is Jules Bradley."

"Well, have her get me more," Stevie says brusquely, all flamboyance gone, replaced by pure hardcore businessman. "And I've got a few art gallery friends I want to show these to."

"That would be great," I say enthusiastically. "How much would you buy them for?"

Turning to me, he hardens his stare and says, "A hundred dollars apiece."

I snort. "Forget it. Two hundred."

"One-fifty," he counters.

"Two hundred," I maintain firmly. "Sounds like you're going to double your money on these so that's fair."

"Fine," Stevie says with an impatient wave of his hand and turns toward the backroom. "Come on back to my office and I'll write her a check."

"Wait a minute," I tell him, and he stops to look back at me. I point down to the painting that had originally caught my eye on Jules' wall. "I want that one, so mark up a bill of sale. I'll pay you four hundred for it but I want you to ship it from here straight to my mother. I'll pay the cost of that too."

Stevie blinks in surprise, because I could have clearly got the painting at cost directly from Jules. He knows it and I know it.

But I give him an appreciative smile. "For helping her out and giving her a chance."

Stevie's eyes widen in surprise for a moment, and his mouth forms into an O.

"I get it," he drawls. "You got it bad for this girl, don't you?"

"Yup," I say, not even trying to hide it. I'm not like other guys who are afraid to acknowledge feelings. I'm not one who overly shares, but I'm not going to deny it.

While I really want that painting to give to my mother because I know she'll love it, I've got no problem admitting I have it a little bad for Jules Bradley.

My trip back from Chapel Hill to Raleigh puts me at Sweetbrier at about quarter after eleven. I knew from my first time here that Jules took her lunch a little early, so I went to the lobby, told the receptionist I was waiting for Jules, and sat on one of the plush couches.

I pulled my phone out and texted her. *I'm here to eat lunch with you. Will you share your sandwich?*

She doesn't respond but five minutes later she's walking toward me with an astonished look on her face. She's carrying her brown paper bag again, which is adorable, and I eye it suspiciously. "I don't like bologna."

Jules rolls her eyes as she comes to a stop in front of me. "What are you doing here?"

"Joining you for lunch," I tell her as I stand up. "Although I was joking about sharing your sandwich with me. I'm going to go work out after this and I ate a late breakfast."

I don't tell her that included a stop through McDonald's, where I bought three sausage biscuits. I don't tell her this because I figure someday she will meet Vale and I can't be sure Jules wouldn't rat my bad eating habits out.

"I don't know whether to be pleased or mildly annoyed at you just assuming I'd want to eat lunch with you," she says with teasing eyes before turning to head toward the lobby doors.

"You're totally pleased," I tell her as I follow her out.

"Totally annoyed," she counters.

I don't say anything else, but take the opportunity to appreciate her fine ass as she walks in front of me, leading me toward the bench she was on last week. I don't know if it's my imagination or not, but it seems she's walking with more of a bounce in her step. I'm not egotistical enough to think that has anything to do with me, but I hope it has everything to do with the fact that she got some good rest last night.

I notice that today there are a few residents enjoying the courtyard, either sitting on other benches or sitting with their wheelchairs facing each other in conversation. Jules waves to a few as she passes by and then plops down on the bench.

I hope it doesn't annoy her, but I sit down close to her.

And I mean close.

As in the side of my thigh pressed against hers.

I wait to see what she'll do, which I figure could range anywhere from a slap to just a subtle movement away from me. She shocks me when she does neither, but instead sort of bumps her shoulder against me playfully while she pulls her sandwich out of the bag and says, "Seriously. What are you doing here?"

"Can't I just come see you because I want to see you?" I ask her with my head tilted her way.

She grins as she unwraps her sandwich, her focus on that rather than me, but it's me she talks to. "Well, of course you can. But you look like a man on a mission. Maybe a man that is holding in some delicious little secret."

I grin down at her, watching as those delicate fingers unwrap what appears to be a peanut butter and jelly sandwich. With her eyebrows drawn inward in concentration, she carefully pulls the sandwich apart and, while not the neatest thing in the world, manages to split it almost equally in half.

She looks up at me with a soft smile and holds one half of the sandwich to me. "It's PB and J."

I'm not hungry in the slightest because, hello—three sausage biscuits—but I can't help but want to take the overture, because

Jules is the one offering it to me. She's sharing her lunch with me, which is too paltry to begin with, and it represents in one classic, unselfish move the core of her nature.

Instead of reaching for the sandwich, I tilt my head in toward hers and tell her as honestly as I can, "I really want to kiss you right now but I don't want the first time to be here at your place of work and in front of these elderly people. I'm not sure their hearts could handle the way I want to kiss you right now."

Jules' eyes get as big as saucers and she whispers, "Oh."

She's still holding her sandwich out to me, which is utterly fucking adorable, and although I want to kiss her, I truly don't want to do it in this setting. So I touch my fingers to her wrist and push the sandwich back her way. "Not hungry, Jules."

"But you want to kiss me," she mumbles.

"Pretty much," I tell her candidly. "Do you want me to kiss you?"

"Pretty much," she agrees softly.

"Fuck," I mutter, turning my head in the opposite direction, taking in the fact there are five people in the courtyard with us, four of whom look to be about a bazillion years old. We better not risk it.

Taking a deep breath, I turn back to her. Her eyes are sparkling and her lips turned upward slightly, but when she takes in my disgruntled look, she grins at me big. Then she takes a bite of her sandwich and chews through her smile, still staring at me.

"Tonight," I promise her. "First moment you're alone at the convenience store . . . I'm kissing you."

Still bearing an amused smile, she nods, swallows, and then asks, "But seriously . . . why are you here?"

My whole body actually jerks as I remember that I did in fact have a reason for coming here and it wasn't to kiss her. Not that

I haven't been thinking about that a lot, but my purpose in coming here was for something entirely different.

I lean to the side so I can assess my back pocket and pull out the folded check I put there less than an hour ago, after Stevie handed it to me. I give it to Jules, who sets her sandwich down on her lap and hesitantly takes it from me.

"What's this?" she asks, her gaze curious but wary.

I nod toward the paper in her hand. "Open it."

She does so, eyes dropping down, and gives a slight frown as she takes it all in. Then her head is snapping up, her frown deepens and she says, "I don't understand."

"I took your paintings to my friend Stevie's flower shop. He loved them so much, he bought them outright for two hundred dollars each."

She looks back down to the check, which is for a thousand dollars, since there were five total paintings, then back up to me. "Do you know what I could do with this type of money?"

"Get your TV fixed, for one," I say with a grin, but I know that is too frivolous for Jules to even care about.

She elbows me in the ribs playfully, but then looks back down to the check. "I can buy the kids new clothes. Not thrift store shit. And good shoes, you know? Kids' shoes are so expensive. And toys . . . they don't have much. I could even afford to enroll them in some extracurricular activities."

I swallow hard, *touched* not even the word I'd use to describe my feeling right now. I believe that I could sit here for hours and stare at Jules staring at that check in wonder, and figure all was right in my world.

And when she finally looks back up at me, eyes a little moist, her voice gives her feelings away when it cracks with emotion as she says, "You don't know what this means to me."

I can't help it. It's definitely not a kiss but I cup my hand around the back of her neck and pull her into my chest for a one-armed hug. I squeeze her as she presses her face into my neck and mumble, "I think I actually do know what this means to you."

She laughs, her breath fluttering across my skin and sending a jolt of desire through me that I feel down to the soles of my feet. I've been trying really hard to not think of Jules in that way, seeing as how I'm purposely taking things slow with her, but just that tiny little bit of sweet breath and I'm hot for her.

Just fucking great.

I gently push her back, hoping some distance will help, and she beams another smile at me. It's infectious and I smile back at her, then give another nod down to the check. "Stevie wants more paintings, so there's more money to be had. Maybe you can get something steady coming in and quit at the convenience store."

I'd kill for her to quit. Not only is it physically exhausting her, but I'm worried about her safety there. Those rednecks that harassed her still plague me.

But Jules shakes her head and I'm caught off guard when she says, "Oh no. I can't. It's a nice thought but really . . . I'm happy with this."

"What the hell?" I ask incredulously. "You can make some serious money. Stevie is going to show your stuff to some gallery owners and thinks once your name gets out there, you'll be able to charge more for your stuff."

"That's nice," she says as her thumb strokes the check. "But really . . . I just can't."

"Come on, Jules," I cajole, nodding down to the check. "You got to dream big, babe."

Jules stares at the piece of paper in her hand a moment and then looks up to me. "I can't afford to dream big, Max. I have to put my energies into those things that are guarantees. Those kids are too important for me not to play it safe."

"I don't understand," I tell her, my sense of jubilation starting to wane.

She gives a soft sigh, her eyes going warm when she sees me start to deflate right in front of her. Her hand reaches out and she lays it over mine. "Painting was never anything more than a hobby for me. I never expected it to do anything other than give me pleasure that I could create something from nothing. So this check . . . your friend buying my stuff and wanting more . . . that's great, but it's just not feasible for me to do more. Supplies cost money, and I don't have it to spend. Every cent of this check here has already been spent in my mind for necessities. And even if I could afford the supplies, which I can't, I don't have the time. Those paintings took time and focus, and those are two things I do not have at all. And to get that time, I'd have to probably give up my night job, and I just can't do that when there's no guarantees that I'd ever sell another painting. While I really appreciate your enthusiasm and belief in me, it's not a risk I can take right now."

I deflate even further, because while I think this is a stellar opportunity for her, everything she just laid out for me makes absolute sense.

If I were a woman, all alone and in her circumstances . . . I doubt I'd take the risk either.

But here's the thing Jules hasn't figured out.

She's not all alone.

# CHAPTER 8

# JULES

I pull the glass door closed and lock it, giving a tiny tug when I disengage the key to make sure it's secure. Hitching my purse up on my shoulder and tucking it in close, I turn and walk across the darkened sidewalk in front of the gas station toward my car, which is parked on the side. This is my least favorite part of the job because it's dark, after midnight, and that's when bad things happen to women who are alone.

I lift my gaze and scan the area, just like I always do, and come to a complete halt of shocked surprise when I see Max leaning back against my car. He's got his legs stretched out, crossed one over the other at the ankle, and his arms folded across his big chest.

Grinning at me.

I grin back. "What are you doing here?"

This is a legitimate question as Max had called me several hours ago and said he had some things to take care of and couldn't come by to hang with me. I understood this and frankly didn't expect anything different. While he's about a hundred different kinds of amazing rolled up into one package, I don't expect him to spend every free minute with me.

Max pushes off my car and puts his hands into his pockets while he waits for me to reach him. When I do, he peers down at me and bluntly asks, "If I gave you the money that you make here at this job, would you quit?"

My head jerks back in surprise and I immediately retort, "I wouldn't take the money from you, so no, I wouldn't quit this job."

I expect him to argue but instead he asks as he nods to his car, parked on the other side of mine, "If hypothetically I had my entire backseat and trunk filled with painting supplies, would you accept them from me?"

I groan with moderate annoyance even as sweet warmth blankets me that he'd do something so thoughtful. "No, Max. I couldn't accept."

"That's what I thought," he says brusquely and reaches into his back pocket, where he pulls out a document that doesn't look more than a few pages total, folded in half lengthwise. "So I have a business proposition I want to put to you and I even had a contract drawn up."

He waves the folded document in front of my face and my eyes follow it briefly before they go back to him. "Huh?"

Max grins as his hand drops to tap the document against the palm of his other hand. "It's getting late and you need to get home, so I'll make this fast and simple."

"CliffsNotes version," I suggest.

He nods at me. "CliffsNotes version. Okay, so here's the deal . . . I'll give you a business startup loan. It will be for $3,200, which I figure is about four months of wages you'd make here at this place, right?"

I do a quick mental calculation, and that's about right, so I nod.

He continues. "In return for that loan, you quit your job here and devote that time after the kids go to sleep to painting. You won't need Tina to watch the kids in the evening and that will alleviate your obligation to watch hers on the weekend. Of course, you still have Annabelle, Levy, and Rocco to watch, but any free time I have, I'll get them out of your hair, and you can have some time to paint on the weekends too. Are you following?"

I'm numb that he's given so much thought to this and my head spins a little. But I nod.

"Good," he says and barrels forward. "If you could paint four nights a week and maybe a little on the weekends, how many paintings could you do?"

Another quick mental calculation, which is difficult because, hello—brain is numb—I tell him hesitantly, "Two . . . maybe three. But why only four nights a week?"

Max gives me a slightly chastising look and says, "Because you need a night off, Jules. You need a damn break every once in a while."

Oh, damn . . . another rolling wave of mellowed euphoria rolls through me that someone—no, in particular Max—cares enough about me to want me to have some time off from my crazy schedule.

But I can't be overly swayed by how good that feels, because what he's proposing is overwhelming and terrifying, not to mention it sounds like I'm a charity case or something.

But Max isn't finished with his proposal. "If you can sell at a minimum two paintings a week, that's four hundred dollars and double what you make at the gas station."

"But there's no guarantee I'll do that," I point out.

"There's no guarantee Chris won't fire you the next time you run into childcare problems, and you know that's going to happen, Jules."

"But I'd be giving up a secure job."

"I guarantee you will be able to find another part-time job if the painting doesn't pan out. Trust me on that."

"You said this was a loan," I interject, because I need to clarify exactly what he's saying.

"Yeah, I knew you wouldn't take it as a gift," Max says, and you can tell he put thought into all of this. "So you can pay me back an amount from each sale. Say . . . twenty-five dollars per painting you sell."

I cock an eyebrow at him. "That would take me forever to pay you back."

"I know," he says in a low voice that's devilishly teasing. "Keeps you in my life longer."

More warmth and it makes me want to step into him, burrow my face into his chest, and snuggle in for a long ride with this man. But that's a little forward, so instead I tell him the truth of my feelings. "I don't know what to say to that. I know you say it's a loan, but really, Max . . . I'm not sure that's what it is."

He turns slightly and puts the loan document on the top of my car before turning back and stepping up to me. His face is somber as he places his large hands on my shoulders. It's a gentle touch but it's also secure. I have to fight myself not to let out an involuntary purr.

"Look, Jules," Max says quietly. "I've figured out you're the type of woman that will not accept handouts, and that you're also the type that will bust your ass to reach your goals. But I don't want you to pass up this opportunity to really make something of your talent. It's too wasteful to do that. So, don't accept a handout from me, but perhaps think of it as a hand up. If you want it to be a loan, then it's a loan. You pay me back and I accept that, although I'm completely fine with you just accepting it as a gift too as you have to know it's not denting my wallet."

I snort and give an amused shake of my head. "I have a counter-proposal. I'll accept it as a loan and quit this job, but on that fifth night, how about I clean your house or maybe cook meals for you for the week, and you can take that off the loan as well. That way I can get it paid back quicker."

Something flashes in Max's eyes and I can see it's consternation I won't take a day off from working, but his tone is light and teasing when he says, "Is it bad if I say I've got images now of you in a sexy maid outfit?"

I laugh, my head falling back because it's fucking funny. When I straighten up to look at him again, I poke a finger in his chest and tell him, "I'm being serious."

"So am I," he says with a wink.

I drop my chin and bat my lashes at him. "I'll wear a sexy maid outfit if you give me time and a half."

Max's hands squeeze on my shoulder and he groans. "Jesus, Jules . . . you're killing me here."

He stares down at me expectantly, and I chew on my lower lip as I think about it for just a moment. Well, really not even a moment. It would be crazy for me to pass this up as long as he knows I'll pay him back.

"Okay," I say with a solid nod and determination in my voice. "I'll do it. It's wild and impetuous and totally out of character for me these days, but there's something about you that makes me believe anything is possible."

Max's lips curve upward and his eyes shine with relief and happiness. He leans his face down closer to mine. "There's something about *you* that makes me believe *everything* is possible."

My heart actually expands with a burst of confidence and rapture, before contracting back inward with a replete feeling of solace. In this moment, I have to believe Max was brought into my life for a reason, and in this moment, I realize I want to give him a chance as much as his crazy ideas to turn me into a real artist.

Since I'm being impetuous and taking risks, I step into him, pressing both hands to the solidness of his chest. I can feel Max take in a breath and hold it as he stares down at me.

"Now might be a good time for that first kiss," I whisper.

"To seal the deal?" he murmurs.

"No," I tell him with a smile. "I'm still going to insist we sign the loan agreement, but the kiss is because I really, really want you to kiss me. I've been thinking about it since you mentioned it yesterday at Sweetbrier."

"I've been thinking about it a little longer," he mutters.

"Well, consider me caught up, okay?"

Max's eyes practically glow, and while I've gotten used to the soft look of care he always gives me, now I see passion laced throughout and it causes tingles to race up my spine.

He slides both of his hands from my shoulders inward to my neck, and oh, wow . . . that feels really nice. They continue slowly upward until his thumbs catch me under my jaw. With only a tiny bit of pressure, he tilts my head back and my mouth parts slightly. Holding me in place, Max leans down to me and touches his lips to mine. My breath immediately rushes out in a sigh of complete abandon and my fingers curl into his shirt.

Max holds my head gently and his mouth presses against mine in a perfect fit. He kisses me slowly . . . thoroughly. There's no tongue, only the softness of his lips against mine and the possessive way in which he holds my head in place so I can't escape him.

Not that I ever would want to. The only thing I want to do is press in closer to him, but I'm held by his strong hands so that he is in control.

So that his mouth is commanding mine what to do.

The kiss is slow, luxurious, and sweet. It's like his lips belong on mine.

It feels so very right.

And I want so much more.

A yearning for something more hits me so hard, my knees almost buckle.

I want more of this beautiful, sweet, and generous man who for some strange reason sees something in me that he wants. For the longest time, I've not considered fulfilling any of my desires because I was a low priority in the grand scheme of things.

But Max has awakened something within me. He's turned a spark into a flame. He's made me believe I can be more, and he's made me want more. And I'm not just talking about sexually. He's made me want more from life.

Max has simply changed my life.

I have no control over myself. I move into him closer, slide my hands up his chest and around his neck. I press my body up against his and feel the hard muscled planes I'd suspected were under his clothes. Max groans in response and one hand goes to the back of my head, where he wraps my ponytail around his fist, while the other slides down to grip my hip. He tilts his head, kisses me deeper, and there it is . . . his tongue slides in and I moan when it touches mine.

I burrow in even closer to Max, causing my breasts to mash into his lower chest and, oh my . . . his very hard and, by the feel of it, large erection presses into my lower belly.

The minute our bodies make contact in that sensual way, Max tears his mouth from mine. He looks down at me, his eyes darkened with need and his voice rough with desire. "I need to get going. Early day tomorrow."

I nod in understanding, because I do happen to know that the first regular game of the season is tomorrow night and Max has told me game days are always hectic.

"That kiss," he says, his voice deeper than I've ever heard before and his hand tightened its hold on my ponytail.

"Yeah, that kiss," I agree dreamily.

"Just the beginning, Jules," he whispers before leaning in one more time and brushing his lips against my temple.

He then releases his hold on me, and I swear I just sway back and forth almost in a hypnotic daze.

Damn . . . that kiss was . . .

Just damn.

Max smirks at me and then turns toward his car, which from the symbol on the back I recognize as a BMW. "Let's get the supplies transferred to your car."

*Wait! What?*

"You mean you actually went out and bought supplies today?" I ask in astonishment as I come out of my fog and trot after him to his car.

"Yup," is all he provides as he pulls his key fob out, aims it at the trunk and it opens it. And it's like the angels above start singing and the glow on the supplies isn't from the little light in his trunk but from God Himself.

I come to stand beside Max, my right arm brushing against his left. I look down at what he bought . . . tubes upon tubes of paint, brushes in all shapes and sizes, and a large gallon can of turpentine. I see a color wheel and a wood palette. He clearly had someone helping him pick out all of the right supplies for me.

"I've got several gallery canvases in the backseat," he says quietly.

I don't even know what to say, so I just reach over and slip my hand into his while I stare at the abundance before me. He squeezes my fingers gently and I squeeze back.

I shake my head slowly in disbelief, still staring at the supplies, and whisper, "Why are you such a good guy, Max?"

"It's easy for the right girl," he says back.

"And how do you know I'm the right girl?" I ask as I finally turn my head and peer up at him.

His hand squeezes mine again and he smiles. "I don't know it. I just feel it."

"I know exactly what you mean," I tell him with an answering smile.

# CHAPTER 9

# MAX

"We're out of here," Hawke says as he grabs Vale's hand and pulls her up from the bed and to the hotel door. Garrett and I grin at each other. The four of us decided for a low-key night after our game in Toronto, choosing to stay at the hotel for pizza, beer, and poker over going out to celebrate our win.

I chuckle as Garrett swipes the cards they'd just laid down on the table. Vale had a full house but Hawke had four queens. The bet was that the loser would get tied up and the winner would . . . well . . . the winner I'm sure would find something to do with the tied-up loser.

My chest gives a happy squeeze for my buddy as I watch him drag Vale out the door. I'm glad his room isn't right beside mine as I do not want to hear the headboard knocking against the wall all night. It will only reinforce to me that I'm not getting any right now, a fact that has made me perpetually horny for Jules.

"Want another beer?" I ask Garrett as I pull a fresh one out of the little minifridge.

"Sure," he says, and I take another out, walk across the room and hand it to him. I take my previously vacated seat and plop down before taking a sip of my beer. I turn my wrist over on my opposite hand, see it's about 11:30 P.M. by my watch, and figure I've got a little time to kill before I call Jules. I'm sort of glad Garrett wanted to have another beer, because I wanted to ask him something.

Ideally, I'd probably talk to Hawke. Although I'm good buds with most of the guys on the team, Hawke and I just seem to click. However, he's off with Vale and has his own set of problems with her, plus Garrett's just a bit better suited for what I want to know.

"You got that look," Garrett says as he gazes at me across the table. He's leaning back, legs stretched out in front of him and his bottle of beer perched on his stomach.

"What look is that?" I ask.

"Well, let's see if I can break this down," Garrett says as he sits up on his chair a bit. "You've been officially named as the starting goalie for the Cold Fury. Had a great preseason, did even better in the home opener on Tuesday, and tonight you got a shutout. You are fire on the ice—which is a weird analogy now that I think about it—but still, you are off to a hell of a start. And yet you're a little too laid back right now. I know you, dude, and when you come off a win, you're the type that's buzzing with energy. You want to go out and party with your teammates and relive the glory of the victory. But tonight you choose to chill out after a fucking shutout, and you look happy but mellow and even a little bit perplexed."

I give him an amused smirk. Take a drink of beer.

Garrett takes a swig of his own and points the bottle at me. "So I'm kind of expecting the next words out of your mouth are going to be something like, 'Well, you see, Garrett . . . there's this girl.' Am I right?"

"Freakishly so," I mutter. "You got all that from me looking happy and mellow?"

"No, I got that because you've been checking your watch about every five minutes and you were studying Hawke and Vale tonight like you were trying to analyze something."

"Not analyzing them," I correct him. "I'm just happy for them. I hope they work through all their shit."

"Not even going to ask," Garrett says, and I wince, as I realize Garrett doesn't know the backstory about the two of them.

But he's cool and not nosy in the slightest as he grins at me and asks, "So tell me about the girl."

"I kind of want your perspective because . . . well, Olivia had some major battles while you two were starting out, and I know it was a struggle for you when we'd be on the road and away from her. I'm just curious how you coped with it, because I know with our life . . . being away half the season sucks for both sides."

"Still doesn't tell me about the girl," Garrett pushes me.

"Girls," I tell him with a direct look, emphasizing the plural nature, and watch as his eyebrows shoot up. I laugh and then clarify, "I had a pretty serious relationship when I was young and it followed over into the NHL. The distance is part of what killed it. And now I've met a woman who I think is amazing, but she's got her own set of problems she's battling, and I worry about her. This is the first away game, and honestly . . . it's driving me a little nuts."

Garrett nods and a flash of pain crosses his face, and there's no doubt he's remembering that time almost two years ago when Olivia got really sick after one of her treatments and had to be hospitalized while the team was on the West Coast playing hockey.

He went apeshit and I remember I seriously wondered whether he would come back with the team on the road until Olivia finished her treatments.

"Wish I could tell you there was an easy way to wrap your head around it, but there's really not. There's one thing that makes it easier, and that's knowing what a great support system Olivia had here with Stevie and Sutton."

I shake my head dismally. "Jules doesn't have anyone."

"Pretty name," he tells me.

"Really fucking pretty girl," I tell him back.

"Another thing that helped is that I know Olivia is strong. I mean, really, really strong. She's one of those women that will stand against a storm because that's her inherent nature. I just knew deep down she'd be all right and no amount of worrying on my part was going to make it better."

Now, this I can understand and I nod. "Jules is strong too. She doesn't like to take help and insists on doing everything herself. She's a survivor and yeah . . . she'll be fine with or without me."

"What's her deal?" Garrett asks with curiosity.

"Her sister died a little over four months ago from cancer," I tell him, and Garrett winces hard because I know that strikes close to his fears with Olivia. "Jules is raising her niece and two nephews."

"How old are they?"

"Annabelle's four, Levy's six, and Rocco is seven," I tell him.

Garrett's eyebrows shoot up and he gives a low whistle. "Damn . . . that's a handful."

"Tell me about it," I say in amazement. "She works two jobs and then cooks and cleans for another woman in exchange for watching the kids after school. She is literally busting her ass from the time she gets up until she goes to sleep well after midnight, and I'm not talking easy jobs. She works in a nursing home full-time as a nurse's assistant and then at a convenience store at night."

"Jesus fuck," Garrett mutters.

"She doesn't even have time for herself," I mutter back.

"Then how does she even have time for you?" he asks.

"Yeah, that's also a problem I haven't been able to fully figure out," I tell him before I take another swallow of my beer.

"Well, I can only tell you my experience, and that's trust in the strength of your girl and she'll be fine when you're away," Garrett says wisely. "It will get easier with time. But dude . . . she's got to cut something out of that hectic schedule or there isn't any relationship."

"That's for fucking sure," I say with a laugh.

"One other thing, Max," Garrett says, and his voice turns serious. "I think it's fucking great you're interested in someone and I can tell by the way you talk about her that she's something special. I also get you're worried about her. But don't forget your job, and the fact that your job especially out of all of us on this team requires your head to be in the game fully. Figure a way to compartmentalize because you cannot afford to have your game affected. You're coming off two injuries and you had to battle to get that number one spot back again. Whatever you do, don't lose it."

I blink in surprise at Garrett because, honestly, I had not even thought about that. I mean, my head was in the game tonight. It was in the game on Tuesday night too. I played fucking fantastic. But I also knew that Jules was in a fairly good spot. While she insisted on giving Chris two weeks' notice, she at least had a game plan that once put into effect would help make her life a little easier. I was feeling pretty damn good about her situation, and I think that translated into my game in a positive way.

But Garrett's words hit me hard, because he's pointing out that it could easily go to shit.

"Hey you." Jules answers her phone on just the second ring, but although I can hear the pleasure in her voice that I've called, I can also hear the exhaustion.

"On your way home?" I ask as I prop myself up against the headboard. Garrett left about ten minutes ago, and I'm exhausted, but no way I was going to go to sleep without talking to Jules. It's five after midnight and I imagine she's in her car and on the way home.

"Yeah," she says, and then punctuates it with a yawn. But then she immediately says, "I watched your game tonight."

"You did?" I ask in surprise.

"I did," she says with a laugh. "Turns out that little TV in the break room that Chris has includes the NHL package. I kept the door open and watched when I could. You were awesome tonight."

Her voice is soft, definitely tired, but there's such pride in it, it sort of humbles me. That she would even have the resources available within herself to show me that pride and excitement when I know she's probably beyond exhausted.

It makes me goddamn ache with the need to just touch her. Kiss her again.

I definitely want to fuck her, but that will come with time.

But we'll have to make the time.

"I want to take you out," I tell her in a low voice. "Just you and me. No kids."

"What did you have in mind?" she asks, and I definitely hear a sexy purr inside that question. She'd probably shoot me if she knew some of the things I'd been fantasizing about.

But I don't go there. Not yet. "Maybe just out to dinner or something. I'll handle the cost of a babysitter."

"Okay, then," she says, and I can't see her face but I can hear the smile in her voice. "It's a date."

"It will be," I say with a laugh. "Now, when is your last day at the convenience store?"

"Not next Friday but the one after," she says. "He asked me to stay until the end of the month and that was only a few more days so I said okay."

I grit my teeth. I'd like her out of there yesterday, but I know Jules has to do things the way it makes her feel the best about her choices.

"Then we'll go out that Saturday," I tell her firmly.

"Awesome," she says, and then immediately follows up with, "Oh, shit . . . no wait. I can't. It's Halloween and I'm going to take the kids trick-or-treating."

"Well, count me in for that," I tell her, and I try to disregard her snort.

"You seriously want to come trick-or-treating with me and the kids?" she asks skeptically.

"Is there candy involved?" I ask sarcastically, and before she can answer I add, "Because yeah . . . I'm totally in on that."

And fuck . . . her sweet laugh of delight causes my skin to tingle. It's the best fucking sound I've heard all day. Even better than when the buzzer went off at the end of the third period and I'd put a shutout in my win column.

"But Jules," I say in a low voice, and her laugh cuts off midstream. "After trick-or-treating, I'm getting a babysitter for the kids and then I get you to myself, okay?"

"Okay," she whispers in a husky voice, and I know she's imagining some of the things I am. It sends a bolt of lust straight down to my balls.

The next two weeks are going to be torture, waiting for my first real date with Jules.

# CHAPTER 10

# JULES

The woman shrieks, "Oh my God . . . Carl . . . get out here. Zack Grantham and Max Fournier are on our front porch."

Kate snickers beside me and I watch with fascinated interest as the homeowners proceed to have a meltdown that two of the Carolina Cold Fury are at their house. Kate then snorts as we watch the poor kids holding their little plastic pumpkin buckets out for candy, but they're being thoroughly ignored while the homeowners ask for pictures.

"Is it always like this?" I ask in a hushed voice as we stand at the end of the driveway while I witness yet again the oddness of celebrity.

"Not always," she says with an amused voice. "But often."

We're currently at the end of our jaunt through Zack and Kate's neighborhood. Max suggested taking the kids to trick-or-treat here with Ben, and then Kate had volunteered to host a slumber party for all of the kids after, and thus Max and I would have our date.

The thought makes my palms sweat, but in a good way.

Kate and Zack Grantham are an amazing couple. Max filled me in on a little of their background before we came over, I think because he wanted me to feel comfortable with the kids staying the night there. Kate had started out as Ben's nanny after Ben's mom had died in a tragic car accident. The simple story is they fell in love and got married just last month, and best of all, Kate adopted Ben, the finalization coming through just the week after they said their vows.

That was the basic story, but Kate filled me in more each time the guys would take the kids up to a house for treats. Kate told me with a fond smile that Zack was a real asshole to her at first, but she said that's because he was all stuck inside his head after Ben's mom died. She said he eventually came around after he lost her—although I didn't press her for those details—and she's been living the fairy tale ever since.

That made me take pause, because that's sort of how I've been feeling. That Max is like the knight in shining armor that has come to rescue me. Although I'm not letting him fully rescue me, I have totally accepted his help and I'm not sure how I feel about that. On the one hand, I feel guilty, almost as if I'm using him, because I still can't understand what he's getting out of all this. But on the other hand, there's something about Max and all he brings to my table that just seems right. It's almost a feeling of fate or destiny . . . that I was given a terrible uphill battle with Melody dying and me taking on the kids, but that Max was put in my path for some higher purpose.

There's a part of me I believe will always feel a little guilty for all he's done for me so far, because I don't know how I could ever truly repay him. I mean, I'll totally repay the loan he's given me, but how do you truly let someone know that what they've done for you is a life changer?

On top of the guilt, I'm also suffering under a bit of fear that all of this with Max may be too good to be true. Here's a man that has the potential to be all I ever would need in this life, and I'm honestly afraid to believe in something that could actually be fleeting.

With pictures out of the way, the homeowners finally hand out candy and they go a little overboard in their enthusiasm, giving each kid a handful of full-size candy bars that barely fit inside their already stuffed buckets. Each of the kids grins, says "Thank you," and the whole group comes trotting down the porch steps toward us.

And what a group they make. Ben, who's only about six months older than Annabelle, is dressed as a little vampire. He's got his hair all slicked back, pale makeup, and dark shading under his eyes. Those little plastic vampire teeth are way too cute. Annabelle wanted to go as Tinker Bell and I was able to find her the cutest green dress with a sparkly tulle skirt that came with little fairy wings that went across her back. Levy and Rocco weren't so easily settled on their costumes, but after a lot of debate, hemming and hawing, Levy settled on wanting to be a ninja and Rocco on a fireman, and I had absolutely no qualms about spending the money on those costumes from the check that Max gave me a few weeks ago when his friend bought my paintings. My only slight regret was the plastic ninja sword that Levy swings a little too wildly, in my humble opinion.

"Look what I got," Annabelle says as she reaches me, thrusting her bucket out for me to examine. "You can have some if you want."

I ruffle her hair and tell her, "Oh . . . I so want."

"I'll give you some of mine too, Aunt Jules," Rocco pipes in, his need for affirmation evident on his face.

"You are so generous, Rocco," I tell him. "Thank you."

Levy ignores all of us, pawing through his treasure trove of treats.

"Okay, looks like the kids' buckets are full," Max says as he claps his hands together, and then puts a hand to Levy and Rocco's backs to urge them forward. "How about we get them back to Zack and Kate's house and they can get started eating all of that rotten goodness."

Kate elbows me slightly in the ribs, and when I look at her, she gives me a knowing grin.

It says, "Max cannot wait to get you alone. He's so cute in his impatience."

I grin back, and when I slide my gaze over to Max as he starts pushing the boys down the street, he shoots me an intense look over his shoulder that promises our alone time is going to be very good.

We make it back to Kate and Zack's house, and Max and I hang around for about thirty minutes to make sure my crew is settled and they're not going to wig out when I leave. Turns out, Annabelle, Levy, and Rocco are quite the independent little brood as they barely glanced at me twice when I reminded them that they were staying the night and I'd see them in the morning. I had to even prod them to stand up from the table where they were digging into their candy to give me a goodbye hug.

After farewells to everyone, Max and I walked out to his car hand in hand. He had laced his fingers with mine as we headed down their driveway to where he'd parked his car on the road. It felt natural and right, as if we'd been holding hands our entire lives.

After we both get settled in and buckled, Max turns to me in his seat before he starts the car. "Jules . . . I want you to know I have no real expectations of where tonight is going to go. It's been four weeks since we first met, but tonight is really our first date."

"I have no expectations either," I tell him, and while that's true, it doesn't mean I haven't thought about how far things might go. "I'm just happy to have a kid-free night and to share it with an amazing man."

"And gorgeous too," Max says with a grin. "I'm gorgeous, right?"

"Totally," I agree with a laugh.

"All right," he says as he starts the car. "Then my suggestion is that we have a quiet night. Take-out Thai would be my choice and then we go to your apartment or my house and just hang."

"Thai sounds great and let's do your house," I tell him. "I'd like to see how the rich and famous but mostly bachelor Max Fournier lives. I'm going to stereotype here and say I'm expecting a sink full of dirty dishes in the kitchen and clothes all over the bedroom floor."

"That's awful forward, Miss Bradley," Max says with a mock huff as he pulls away from the curb. "I'd never let a lady see my bedroom on a first date."

I snort in response, but then I wonder . . . is he teasing me or being serious?

Max's fingers brush against my temple and then sift through my hair. I shift my head as it lays on his right thigh, and I think to myself, nothing awkward about this. Again, my time with him is effortless. Conversation is engaging, silences are golden. He freely touches me and it feels natural.

The end credits roll on the screen of his sweet eighty-inch 4K TV that takes up an entire wall in his living room. Dinner was causal as we ate on the deck of his beautiful home. It's what I expected and then it's not. It's large and in a well-to-do neighborhood, but it's not ostentatious. The furnishings are comfortable; the colors are warm. It's the type of house that you don't worry about tracking mud into, but that has nothing to do with the house itself. It has everything to do with Max's casual and easygoing nature.

After dinner he suggested a movie and I happily agreed. He's right . . . neither of us have any expectations, and I can't ever remember a first date being so spontaneous and fun. I can't ever remember meeting anyone like Max and having just an innate feeling of comfort around someone.

That is not to say that there isn't some sexual tension between us. No, rather, there's quite a bit. Max and I haven't had much time together the last few weeks since our first amazing kiss. I've still been working brutal hours since giving my notice at the gas station and Max is deep into regular season hockey. He's playing phenomenally and I've learned quickly that to play at that level takes extreme dedication to your job. That means daily workouts, sometimes for two to three hours. Practices and team meetings. The games themselves. And let's not forget about travel. A two-game trip out to California had him gone for a solid five days.

But that's not to say we haven't seen each other. Last weekend Max hung out with me and the kids one afternoon and we took them to a museum. And a few times Max came and kept me company at the convenience store, and yeah . . . there may have been a little making out at the end of my shift and before he put me safely in my car for my drive home. Each one of those make-out sessions got a little hotter and our hands tended to roam further and further on each other the more we tested boundaries. The last time he kissed me, which was three nights ago, his hand ended up between my legs and mine ended up on his crotch, but totally with the material of our jeans separating us. Still, it was intimate and thrilling and both of us groaned as we touched each other and kissed.

Max ended up tearing himself away from me and muttered something about "not wanting to fuck you for the first time in a parking lot." Of course, that only guaranteed I'd fantasize about him fucking me in a dark parking lot, but I knew that wouldn't be how we came together for the first time.

And there's no doubt . . . we are going to have sex. It's what both of us want. It's the next logical step to take. I am wildly attracted to him, and it doesn't have a damn thing to do with his muscled body or his near-perfect face. It has everything to do with the fact that Max Fournier is perhaps the best person I've ever known next to Melody, and I have no qualms about giving my body to him if he wants it.

The question is . . . does he want it tonight? Max has deliberately taken things slow with me, which I find refreshing and endearing. It's frustrating too, and I'm thinking I might be the one who has to let him know it's okay to move this to the next level.

I push up on the couch, dislodging Max's fingers from my hair. He watches me as I come to my knees on the cushion beside him, my palms resting on my thighs. He's so goddamn sexy, but unassuming, which makes him sexier in my mind.

"Want to watch another movie?" he asks.

I shake my head. "It's getting late."

"Want me to take you home?" he asks with a smile, his eyes warm and open, without a hint as to what he wants.

I shake my head again.

"What do you want to do?" he asks, and there . . . right there. I hear it. His voice is low and rumbling with need.

Still, I don't want to assume anything.

"Want to make out?" I ask him with a grin.

"Fuck yeah," he says with an answering grin and then his hands are on my wrists and he's pulling me on top of him.

I willingly go, walking my knees across the small expanse of cushion, and then his hands go to my hips and he helps me maneuver onto his lap in a straddle. My hands go to his shoulders and I look down at him. His hazel eyes are darkening as he looks at me intensely, and there's no mistaking the desire I see there.

I move my hands from his shoulders to his face, palms against each cheek, and I lower my mouth down to his. At the first touch of our lips, Max's fingers press into my hips and I moan as I push my hands back and slip my fingers into his hair. Our heads tilt, the kiss deepens, and when his tongue slides against mine, a bolt of lust seizes my body and an ache starts between my legs.

Max slides one hand under my shirt and smooths his large palm up my spine. I press into him, my arms now wrapping around his neck, overlapping each other, and I lower myself down onto his lap.

Oh, wow. Onto his fully hard erection.

Max groans as I tilt my hips and rub against him, the friction igniting a fire low in my belly. This spurs me on and I rotate my hips, grinding against him while his mouth assaults mine.

But then Max's hands are on my upper arms and he's pushing back on me so the kiss breaks. His eyes are wild and his nostrils are flared as he sucks in oxygen, and my own heartbeat is racing away from me. I frown and try to lean back in for a kiss, wanting to take this connection further than we ever have before.

"Jules," Max mutters as he holds me firmly in place. I focus my gaze on him and tilt my head to the side in question. "I didn't bring you to my house for this."

"I know," I tell him softly. "You'd take me home right now if I asked you."

"It's our first date," he explains. "We've got plenty of time to get there."

I try to think how I should lay this out to him. While I appreciate his almost chivalrous attitude toward me, I also want him to know that I'm fairly forward-thinking when it comes to sex. I've never believed you have to be in love to do it, but I do believe you should have a measure of care for the person.

What I feel for Max is like nothing I've ever felt before. I'm not sure there's anything I wouldn't give him.

I don't know how to adequately convey that, so I let my hands talk for me. I drop them in between us, scoot back on his lap a few inches and start to undo his belt. I've got the leather just cleared from the buckle when Max's hands come to mine. They grip my fingers and halt my actions.

I look up to him.

"You get my jeans open," he growls at me, "I'm not going to be able to stop. I'm not a saint, Jules."

I smile at him, lean in and give him a light kiss. "You *are* a saint, Max. You're an absolute saint. But right now . . . I'm completely fine with you sinning."

Max takes just a millisecond to digest my words, then his lips peel apart in a bright grin. "So you want to sin with me, huh?"

"Oh, yeah," I say with a responding grin.

I let out a surprised gasp as Max lunges off the couch, his arms coming under my ass to support me, and my arms flying to lock around his neck. He pushes past the coffee table, through the living room, and down a very short hall to what I'm guessing is the first-floor master bedroom.

I just hang on for the ride.

# CHAPTER 11

# MAX

*Slow down, slow down, slow down.*

*Slow the fuck down, Max.*

I am trying desperately not to turn all caveman on Jules as I carry her to my bedroom. I have never wanted someone as much as I want this woman, and unfortunately, that has about reduced me to someone with the mentality of a horny teenager about to bust a nut for the first time.

I wasn't lying when I told Jules I had no expectations for to-night. I honestly didn't know where we'd end up and I really didn't care. I knew we'd get here eventually.

But the minute her hands touched my belt, I suddenly did care.

A lot.

And now I feel on the verge of losing control. It's thrilling and terrifying at the same time, and I realize that Jules is the woman that could totally destroy me.

Barreling past my bedroom door, I take a slight turn to hit one of the wall switches with my elbow to the recessed lighting in the double tray ceiling. It casts a warm, ambient glow over the entire room.

I make a beeline for the bed, crawl up onto it with Jules clinging to me tightly and lay her underneath me. Taking a deep breath, I look down at her . . . needing to see in her eyes whether I still have the go ahead.

"You good?" I ask her.

"Better if you kiss me," she whispers with a smile.

"The lady wants to be kissed," I murmur as my gaze drops to her mouth.

"Among other things," she says tartly.

I raise my eyes back up to hers. "I'll give you everything."

Her response is to clamp her hands at the back of my neck and use me as leverage to pull herself up, slamming her mouth onto mine.

*Fuck, yeah.*

I push against her, press her head back onto my pillows and devour her mouth as I rest most of my body weight onto her. My hips come to rest perfectly on hers, my cock nestled right against the heat between her legs.

Jules moans and I grind into her.

She moans harder.

*Fuck . . . Stay cool, Max. Stay cool.*

But it's hard because I find myself wanting a million different things at once. I want to kiss her until the sun comes up and I want to touch every inch of her skin. I want to hand her multiple orgasms until she begs me to stop, and I want to bury myself deep into her. I want her mouth on my cock. I want mine on her pussy. I want to eat her whole and lick her clean.

Pulling my mouth from hers, I layer a trail of kisses across her jaw and down her neck. I scoot my body down hers as my mouth moves lower, over the base of her throat and finally to her breasts, where I nuzzle them through the material of her shirt. Jules' fingers go into my hair and she grips it hard.

"Easy," I tell her as my hands go to the bottom of her shirt and I push the material up and over her breasts. She's wearing a plain white cotton bra that is slightly translucent and my mouth goes dry as I take in her hard nipples pushing against the fabric. My fingers flip the front clasp and the bra pops open, baring her beautiful tits to me.

My mouth goes from dry to watering as I test the weight of them with my hands, squeezing them gently. I pinch one nipple in between my thumb and forefinger and roll it, causing Jules' hips to fly off the bed in reaction. Christ . . . no telling what she'll do when I hit her clit.

I wrap one arm around Jules' back and roll us to our sides. Her mouth seeks mine and connects, and we kiss again. A deep, lush kiss that is all consuming, stoking the fire between us hotter.

My hands roam, as do hers. Her nails scrape up my back, and my hand goes down the back of her jeans and past her panties to cup her ass. Clothing ends up coming off, magically peeled away by our hands without ever really breaking the molten kiss that continues between us.

When we're both fully naked, we press our bodies against each other, legs intertwined. Her breasts are flattened to my chest and my cock is hard on her belly, trapped in between us. Her skin feels like satin as she strokes her leg along mine.

I swear I could fucking do this for hours, even though I'm near-delirious with the need to get inside of her.

Jules pulls her mouth away from mine and her eyes are glazed as she pants out to me, "Max . . . give me more."

"Tell me what you want, baby," I urge her as my hand skims down from her ribs to her hip.

Lightning fast, she grabs my wrist as she pulls her pelvis away from me and pushes my hand in between her legs. My pulse skyrockets and my fingers easily find her pussy, which is soaked. I brush my fingers through her curls and lightly circle her clit.

"Like this?" I ask her.

Her hips tilt forward and she gives me an affirmative moan.

"Or like this?" I ask her as I twist my hand and sink a finger into her.

"Oh God," is her answer this time.

And Christ . . . her pussy clamps down hard on my finger and I go dizzy with the need to fuck her.

Leaning in, I put another kiss on her mouth before I pull my hand from between her legs. She makes a growl of protest but I soothe her by saying, "Just a minute, Jules. Let me get a condom."

I push up to my knees and lean across her with one hand on the mattress to reach into the drawer of the bedside table. My weight almost buckles under me as Jules wraps a hand around my cock.

My head drops and my eyes flutter closed as Jules' hand starts a firm stroke up and down my shaft. I can feel pre-cum leaking out, coating her hand and making my skin slick.

I take a deep breath in, open my eyes and rear upward. Jules never misses a stroke while I dig a condom out and slam the drawer closed. I fumble with the foil, finally get it open and pull the rubber out.

Jules rubs a thumb over the tip of my cock and my balls start to tingle. I reach down with my free hand, grab her wrist and gently pull her away. She makes a small sound of protest but then purrs when I reposition myself on my knees between her legs. Her eyes are darkened to a bronze color and she watches me keenly while I put the condom on.

"Jesus Christ," I mutter. "My fucking hands are shaking."

And they are . . . badly.

I want to be inside her so bad, my entire being is shaking.

But then Jules reaches out and lays her hands over mine.

My gaze slides to hers and she smiles at me softly. One soft, understanding smile with a message back to me that she understands. That she's feeling what I'm feeling and that both of us are getting ready to have our worlds rocked by the other.

A measured calm courses through me, enough to steady my hands but in no way diminishing the lust that's still sparking through my body. Instead, I become singularly focused and the condom rolls on smoothly as Jules' hands go to her breasts and she plucks at her nipples.

"God, that's sexy," I praise her, then I hunch over her and push her hand aside with a nudge of my cheek. I roll my tongue around one of her nipples, then bare my teeth before biting at it. Jules bucks and moans and when she says, "Max . . . I need you inside of me *now*," I'm spurred to action.

I push up off her again, press one palm to the mattress and with my other hand guide my cock to her entrance. I rub the tip through her wet folds and then slowly feed myself into her. I can feel in exquisite detail as her pussy stretches and molds around me, hot and wet and oh so fucking tight.

I sink slowly into her, inch by inch until I bottom out and I just go still.

I take in everything about this moment. Jules' eyes dark and blazing with desire. Her chest heaving and her pussy contracting around me. Her delicate hands on my ass, nails poised to sink into my flesh and my cock already straining for release.

I drop my face, place my forehead against hers and whisper, "Jules?"

"Yeah, baby," she says on a throaty moan of need.

I pull my head up and look at her. "Tell me what you want."

Her hands slide up my back, over my ribs, and come to rest on my chest. "What do you mean?"

"Well," I say as I bring my lips to hers and give her a short kiss. "You're all kinds of beautiful and sweet and I could fuck you slowly, drawing our first time out and we'd both come long and steady. But you're also feisty and strong and I could fuck you really hard and fast, guaranteed we'll both blow apart viciously. I'm not quite sure what to do with you, and just so you know, whatever you choose, we'll do the opposite next. But lady's choice . . . how do you want it?"

Jules chuckles low in her throat, her eyes sparkling with mischief and humor. I'm lodged balls deep in this woman and she's amused by me.

I fucking love it.

"Hmmm," she says as she thinks on her options. She spreads her fingers out over my chest before sliding them down and pinching both of my nipples. I buck against her from the sizzle of lust that sparks through me, and she says, "I think our first time, we're both going to lose control a little. So I think hard and fast is the best option."

"You sure?" I ask with a little push of my hips against her.

She nods at me before sliding her hands up and around my neck again so she can pull me down to her. Just before our lips connect she murmurs, "Give me all you got, Max. I'm going to give it right back."

"Christ," I manage to mutter before I kiss her, and then I proceed to give her all I've got.

• • •

My back arches off the bed and I slam upward into Jules, lifting her clear off the bed. She screams, her own back arches and her nails dig into my chest as my orgasm rips through me.

*Holy mother fucking Jesus.*

"So good," Jules chants as I fall back to the bed and she collapses on top of me. "So good."

My chest is heaving and her body slides against mine because we're both sweaty as fuck. I wrap my arms around her back to hold her in place. She turns her face into my neck and kisses me softly.

"So much for slow and sweet," I tell her in between sucking air back into my lungs.

She giggles. "We'll get there."

"Fifteen minutes," I tell her.

She snorts.

"Okay, half an hour," I amend.

Because fuck . . . the second time was just as all-consuming as the first and my body is wrung the fuck out. Two of the hardest orgasms I've ever had in my life.

Three total for Jules because the first time she came just with my cock pounding inside of her. The second time, I started off with my mouth between her legs, made her come, and then she climbed on top of me and rode herself to another orgasm.

She was fucking glorious. I guarantee that will be my go-to memory when I jack off on road trips now.

I roll us to the side and groan as my half-hard dick slips out of her. I press my mouth to hers lightly before I tell her, "Let me go take care of the condom."

She nods and I roll the opposite way, right off the bed, and pad into the bathroom. I dispose of the condom quickly and do a double take as I catch myself in the mirror. I've got a bruise on my chest where Jules had latched her mouth onto me the first time and nail marks down my abdomen where she clawed me as she rode my cock. If I had any reservations about fucking her hard, they're gone. As she promised, she gave hard right back to me and I loved it.

But I am looking forward to attempting a slow steady fucking. Bodies pressed tight and staring into her eyes. Just rocking slowly against her. Yeah, that will be equally as epic I'm sure.

When I get back into the bedroom, I find her burrowed under the covers, her cheek resting on the pillow and her eyes following me as I walk across the room. When I reach the edge of the bed, she pulls back the covers and I'm invited in. I slide across the mattress and she flips the sheet and comforter over me.

Laying on our sides, our faces only inches apart, we just stare at each other. And yeah . . . I could just stare at her for hours too. Those eyes that change with her mood and even the tiny smattering of freckles over her nose and cheeks, which I found out tonight she has matching ones across her shoulders. I've certainly noticed the ones on her nose before, but up close they're beautiful and add so much character to a face I've come to think of as beyond stunning.

Jules gives me a smile, her eyes lightened up and shimmering with satisfaction. "Why are you such a good guy, Max?"

I wrinkle my nose. "No guy wants to be known as 'the good guy,'" I tell her teasingly. "That sounds so boring."

She rolls her eyes at me and it's adorable. But then those eyes darken slightly, going almost café mocha, and I know this means she's serious. "Explain it to me. Why are you so gallant? Why do you put so much energy into me? Why would you spend your time on a woman that just doesn't have a lot to give back?"

My arm goes out, slides over her waist, and I press my palm to her back as I scoot my body a little closer to hers. I know it's poor form to answer a question with a question, but it's necessary here.

"Jules . . . why don't you see what I see? Why don't you understand about yourself what I understand about you?"

"Because we never see ourselves the way others do," she whispers, and she's not wrong about that.

"Then open your eyes a little wider," I admonish her gently before I lean in and give a quick brush of my mouth against hers. When I pull back, I tell her the truth of what I see. "You are one of the most caring and generous people I've ever met. Your work ethic is amazing. You've got fortitude and strength. I've never heard you have a negative thing to say about anything or anyone. You work in a really hard job caring for geriatrics, which is a shit job by most people's standards, but you do it because you have an empathy inside of you for them. You're loyal and just recently I've found out that you're willing to take risks. You love your niece and nephews beyond all measure and you willingly gave up your carefree life at a great sacrifice to your own personal happiness to take care of them. You're smart, funny, and I even adore your sarcasm at times. So I hope that makes it clear to you, I think you're pretty much a one-in-a-million type of woman, and babe . . . those are a rarity. It was imperative I snatch you up fast before someone else scooped me."

She giggles, her eyes sparkling . . . turning golden brown again. "Well, you're really very good at this whole sweeping-a-woman-off-her-feet kind of thing. You must have had a lot of practice."

"I've actually only had one serious relationship before," I tell her candidly. "And I wasn't very good at it."

"Do tell," she quips.

"I didn't put the effort in," I admit. "It was first love type of stuff. Met her when I was sixteen and then we dated long distance for a while when I went into the NHL, and then she eventually followed me to Florida when I played with the Spartans."

"What happened?"

I give her a wry smile. "Nothing happened. I just didn't put in the effort, you know? I thought it was enough to be in love, and I just figured things would work out. Apparently, she fell out of love long before I realized what was going on. She broke it off because I couldn't devote enough of my energy to her."

"But surely she knew that being with someone in the NHL . . . someone that had to travel and—"

I cut her off. "No, it wasn't about the amount of time we spent together, or lack thereof. It was about the quality of the time. She just didn't feel that she was important enough to me, and that's all on me."

She considers that for a moment, her gaze dropping down momentarily before coming back to me. "Sounds like you may have learned some lessons from that experience then."

"Yeah," I tell her softly, bring my hand from her back to cup her cheek. "I learned if someone is important enough, it's not all that hard to give them what they need. It kind of comes naturally."

Her eyes go round, and yeah . . . she gets what I'm saying.

She understands that she's important to me.

"Max?" she whispers.

"Yeah, babe?"

"I hope I can give you back what you give me," she says hesitantly. "I want to. I want to give you everything that you deserve, but sometimes I feel like the world is pressing in on me and it can be hard for me to prioritize. I really, really like you and I want you to be a priority in my life. If you ever feel like you're not, you have to let me know."

I lean in and kiss her, and when I pull back, I tell it to her straight. "You're doing just fine, Jules. And I really, really like you too."

# CHAPTER 12

# JULES

I know I should be watching the hockey game but I can't stop staring at Max in goal. I'm sure there's plenty of action at the far end, but I still watch Max.

I wonder if he'd think that was weird.

"Stop staring at Max," Kate says as she leans across the two kids that separate us, namely Annabelle and Ben. I've got Levy and Rocco to my right.

I grin back at her. "Can't help it."

"No, I suppose you can't," she quips sympathetically.

I can't even believe I'm sitting here. Max surprised us with tickets when he showed up at my apartment this morning. That included a very hot kiss because as soon as I opened the door, he pulled me out so the kids couldn't see and proceeded to kiss the daylights out of me.

It was a deep kiss filled with longing and frustration, because it's been a long, long week since we'd had sex. Granted, on Halloween night we'd had a lot of sex, but it wasn't enough to tide each of us over. And I suppose these past seven days is probably a good preview of how our relationship is going to be tested over the incredibly busy lives Max and I lead separate from each other.

After we both woke up Sunday morning, he made love to me first, then he took me to Kate and Zack's and we picked up the kids. He then treated us to breakfast before dropping us off at my apartment. The rest of his day was spent between a workout, practice, and a team meeting. I spent that evening painting.

Monday through Thursday was no better in the amount of time we had with each other. I did my normal work routine at Sweetbrier from seven A.M. to four P.M. and then spent good quality time with the kids until it was time for them to go to sleep. I then painted from about eight to midnight. Max traveled to an away game, so I didn't see him at all on Tuesday and Wednesday, but he did come over and eat dinner with me and the kids on Monday and Thursday. Friday he had an evening team meeting, so I didn't get to see him. The way I calculated it, we saw each other a grand total of four hours for the week, and out of that time we shared a few hot kisses once the kids were in bed. But then Max left me to my painting, because as he said I wasn't going to get paid unless I produced something.

This was a bitter pill to swallow. I wanted to use my talents to help support me and the kids. Max helped me with an amazing opportunity, but it did nothing to alleviate my time crunch, and thus limited my time with Max. This truly sucks because for the first time in a very long time I want something for myself, and for the first time in also a very long time I don't feel guilty for wanting it. Max has sort of made me see that it's okay to have something for myself. He helped make that true with getting me started back with my painting, something I love doing, and it's just an added bonus that I can make something from it.

"So what are you and Max going to do tonight?" Kate asks when there's a break in the action on the ice.

She taught me all about TV timeouts, and while my eyes stayed pinned to Max as he skated slow circles in front of the net to stay loose, I told her, "He said the team usually gets together over at a bar across the street from the arena after and he wanted to take me there."

Yes, Max wants to go out after the game, and while I'd personally like to spend just another quiet night with him, I got the distinct impression from Max that this was important to him.

"Houlihan's," Kate says with an understanding nod. "He wants to show you off."

Max, unbeknownst to me, earlier in the week had asked Kate if she would watch the kids again for the night. I didn't feel great about this because it seemed like a huge imposition on Kate and it made two Saturdays in a row she'd watched my three little ones.

I don't give any credit to her theory that Max wants to show me off, not because it doesn't deserve it, because it's probably true, but because I have something more pressing. Turning in my seat and finally taking my eyes off Max, I ask Kate, "Are you sure you don't mind watching the kids tonight? I'm not feeling the best about this."

Kate waves an impatient hand at me. "Please, girl . . . game nights in our household are very low-key. Zack won't want to do anything but relax in his recliner with a beer, and the kids will zonk out as soon as we get home. It's a late night for them."

This was true as evidenced by the fact that Annabelle's been rubbing her eyes for the last fifteen minutes. While Levy and Rocco are totally into the game, Annabelle's been a little bored, and if it wasn't for Ben sitting next to her, she probably would have conked out long ago. Even though Ben's the same age, he's got a vested interest in the game and has been around hockey his entire life, so he was into the game too. But he's such a sweet boy . . . he'd be cheering for his dad out on the ice one minute and then the next he'd turn in his seat and chatter away with Annabelle.

"If you and Zack ever want a date night, all you have to do is call me. I'll take Ben in a heartbeat," I offer her.

"You're sweet," she says with a smile. "I'll take you up on that. Besides, that's what we do. The Cold Fury is a family."

Those words cause me to jerk in my seat because they pack quite a punch. Am I part of the Cold Fury family? I mean . . . I'm not married to Max, and we've only known each other about five weeks now, but still . . . he seemed like it was no big deal for him to ask Kate and Zack to watch my kids. Is that because he's thinking because we're together I'm automatically brought into the fold?

"So listen," Kate says as she leans toward me a bit more. "I was in Fleurish the other day and Stevie and Olivia showed me your paintings, and, Jules, they are stunning. I mean, Max told me they were amazing but when I saw them . . . I was just blown away."

My face flushes red but I try to maintain some semblance of grace. "Well, thanks . . . that's really nice of you to say, Kate."

She nods. "And I was wondering if I could commission you to paint something for me to give to Zack for Christmas. I swear he's so hard to buy for, but I was thinking of having a portrait done of Ben, but not like just a regular portrait. I'd want it done in all those fantastic bold colors . . . make it slightly abstract."

A zap of pure happiness runs through me and I eagerly nod at Kate. I've never been asked to paint something for someone before, and it's beyond flattering. "I'd love to. But no way are you paying for it. I'd be happy to just give it to you."

Kate rolls her eyes at me and then leans over farther and pats me on the knee. "You're really cute, Jules, but seriously . . . wise the hell up. This is your business. It's how you make a living. You charge for your talent."

"But, I couldn't—"

"You can," she rolls right over me, and then in a voice that does not mess around, she says, "If it bothers you that much, cut me a five percent deal or something, but I'm paying you or I'm not going to let you do it."

My jaw drops slightly from her fierce attitude, but then I snap it shut. Cheeks red, I give her a nod. "Okay, if you're sure."

"I'm sure I'm sure," she says with a grin. "Now turn back around and watch your man's ass while he's in goal."

My head snaps toward the ice and I immediately lock eyes on Max, the puck having been dropped and action commenced. And damn . . . even in those big, bulky goalie pads, he still looks phenomenal.

It really didn't hit me until I walked into this arena tonight with the kids.

My boyfriend plays professional hockey.

My boyfriend is Max Fournier . . . the starting goalie for the Carolina Cold Fury.

Not once in the past five weeks have I really had that sink in, and it's probably because Max and I haven't really spent much time together, but our developing relationship was never about something like that. It was about a man seeing a woman who he wanted to help and lift up, and a woman taking a chance on a man who believed in her.

But here . . . listening to the fans chant his name or scream at the top of their lungs when he makes a great save . . . it's a heady feeling knowing that he's mine.

• • •

After the game, Kate brings me and the kids to the family gather-ing room that's just down from the locker room. We wait with a host of other wives and kids, waiting for the guys to have a quick team meeting and get showered. Kate introduces me to Olivia Case, who works at Fleurish. She's waiting for her boyfriend, Gar-rett Samuelson, and she spends five minutes gushing about my art. It embarrasses me, but I end up kind of falling a little for Olivia. She's got such a sunny personality and a hippie vibe, it's hard not to be drawn to her. In the few evenings Max had eaten dinner at my place this week, he filled me in on his other team-mates and their significant others. I knew about Olivia's cancer and that she's in remission right now.

I also get to meet Sutton, who's married to the team captain, Alex Crossman, and also happens to be Olivia's cousin. She's just as awesome and it truly feels like I'm being welcomed into the fold. By the time Max walks into the room, looking amazing in a dark gray suit with a pink dress shirt, hair still wet from his shower, I'd made tentative plans to get together with the three women standing around me. When I would do that was beyond me as I had almost no free time, and what little I did have, I wanted Max to have it all. But we exchanged phone numbers and we'd figure something out, I'm sure.

Max spends a few more minutes introducing me to some other people and then I give hugs and kisses to Annabelle, Levy, and Rocco with promises I'll see them first thing in the morning. It's not lost on me when Annabelle holds on a little longer than normal, and just before she lets go, she whispers, "Love you, Mommy."

My voice quavers as I whisper back, "Love you too, Anna-belle."

Max watches quietly, and when I stand up, his hand goes to my lower back, where his thumb rubs against me in acknowledg-ment of that emotional moment.

Then he takes me out through the back exit that leads to the players' parking lot. He opens the passenger door and I climb in. After Max gets into the driver's seat I give out a little cry of surprise when he grabs me behind the neck, pulls me halfway across into his seat and kisses me hard.

As he pulls away, he puts his forehead against mine and murmurs, "I missed you and I cannot wait to get my mouth on you tonight when we get back to my place."

"We could bypass Houlihan's and head right to your place," I suggest with a grin, although I really kind of want to go to Houlihan's. I'm curious as to what Max is like when he's out in public and has to play the role of star goalie.

"We could do that," he agrees. "But I really want you to meet Hawke and Vale and they agreed to meet us there for a few beers. But we won't stay long."

"Deal," I agree readily, because honestly, I don't care what we do as long as I can be in his presence.

So Max starts his car, puts it in gear, and drives the less than one mile to Houlihan's so I can meet more of his friends.

# CHAPTER 13

# MAX

I walk into Houlihan's holding tight onto Jules' hand. I've been here hundreds of times, many of them after a game such as tonight. It's where the Cold Fury hangs out and it's always packed shoulder to shoulder on game night, mostly with fans who hope to get a picture or an autograph. That's usually what these visits are about. Hanging out and giving back to the fans.

But tonight is different for me because I want Jules to see this part of my life, and I want this part of my life to see Jules. I want my teammates to meet her and see how fabulous she is, and I want them to know that she's important.

Which isn't to say I haven't brought women I've dated here before, because I have. While it's true I've only had one serious relationship in my past, it doesn't mean I haven't had relationships. I'm the type of guy who likes dating one woman. I like the intimacy of having that person's full attention, and I like the security that comes with it. So yes, I've dated before, and some of them have lasted months. Some of them I've brought here.

None of them hold a candle to Jules, including Christine, who was the first woman I loved. And I did love her, but it just wasn't the type that could be sustained.

Yes, I like commitment and monogamy. Maybe I'm a romantic at heart, and that's probably due solely to my parents, who have a solid, passionate, and deep connection that they've had for almost thirty years. So it's only natural I want that too.

That is also not to say I haven't had one night stands. Not to say I haven't gotten blind, stinkin' drunk and fucked women that I couldn't even remember their names. I did go through a bit of a wild period after Christine broke things off with me and I spread myself around with meaningless sex.

So you see . . . I've had it both ways, and the way I feel right now with Jules by my side . . . it's a fucking no-brainer. I do believe she's what I've been searching for.

I do believe she's what I'm ready for now.

Leading Jules through the crowd, I nod at a few familiar faces I see. The hardcore fans that are always there to either celebrate with us or mourn a loss. They're also the ones that tend to be unobtrusive, and over the years I've gotten to know some of them pretty well. I take Jules toward the back of the restaurant and away from the bar area where most of the team is congregated around a bunch of tables. While the kitchen is still open, hardly anyone here this late orders sit-down dinners, and the management doesn't mind us invading this part of the restaurant.

The Cold Fury group is diverse, with a mix of players, team management, training staff, and significant others. The players are diverse as well, some married, others in committed relationships, and still others yet that are complete men-whores. And with the men-whores come the throng of women who are trying to get noticed by them, some accepting that it's just frivolous sex if they hook up but many hoping for something more lasting.

Cassie Gates is one such woman, and I see her standing next to her sister, Allie, who's married to one of our defensemen, Kyle Steppernech. Great player, greater douche. Allie is a bitch. Cassie has her claws poised to sink into any available player. At one point she had her sights set on Alex Crossman, our team captain, and he took advantage of that for sure. But after he met Sutton, it was all over with Cassie. That didn't mean she went away though, and for a brief moment she turned her attention to me. I shut that shit down fast and made her perfectly aware I wasn't interested. Looks like tonight though her current target is poor Mikkel Erat, who is also a defenseman.

Cassie's wearing a tight Cold Fury T-shirt that's straining to hold her breasts in, her cleavage so deep her navel's practically on display. She's got both arms wound tight around Mikkel, almost as if she's afraid she'll get left behind. She doesn't need to worry though. Mikkel can barely keep his eyes off her tits. He's not going anywhere tonight, and I sort of feel bad for the dude. His English is horrible and his accent thick, so I'm pretty sure he's not had the pleasure of having a deep conversation with her, so he probably doesn't get he's being manipulated.

"Well, that's an interesting outfit she has on," Jules mutters dryly as she leans into me. I look down at her and see her eyes are pinned on Cassie.

"She's a puck bunny," I tell her with an amused smirk.

"A what?" she asks, her eyebrows furrowing as she takes Cassie in, perhaps trying to see if she's got secret bunny ears or a tail.

I laugh and pull her in tighter. "It's just a term for those women that want to hook up with a hockey player."

"Oh," she says thoughtfully, then gives me a grin. "Well, I

totally want to hook up with you so I guess that makes me a puck bunny like her."

Shaking my head, my lips curved up, I tell her, "You are nothing like her. You are so not a puck bunny."

As Jules laughs at me, I lead her over to a table where I see Hawke, Vale, Garrett, and Olivia. They've all got beers in their hands and just as I reach them a waitress materializes and takes our order. I ask for a Molson and Jules goes standard American with a Bud Light.

"That's just nasty," I tease over her choice of beers.

She sniffs, gives me a slight elbow to my ribs and retorts, "We can't all be as refined as you, Mr. Fournier."

I throw my head back and laugh, because fuck, she's cute. She ignores me and turns to Garrett, who has his arm around Olivia. Jules puts her hand out. "And you must be Garrett?"

"Good guess," he says with a smile and shakes her hand.

"Well, I met Olivia in the family room so I figured that's who you were . . . you know . . . with your arm all wrapped around her."

Garrett laughs and Jules turns to Hawke and Vale. She has no clue who they are, but it doesn't prevent her from sticking her hand out. "I'm Jules."

"Hawke," he says as he shakes her hand, then nods to Vale. "And this is Vale."

Jules shoots me a taunting look before she faces Vale—I'm assuming for my Bud Light smackdown—shakes her hand and says, "I just want you to know . . . several times a week Max eats Snickers and drinks Mountain Dew."

Vale's eyes snap to mine and her lips flatten. "Is that so?"

I smirk and wrap my arms around Jules from behind, right over her chest so she's trapped, and pull her up against me. I lean down and put my lips to her ear and whisper, "You're going to pay for that tonight."

She shivers in my hold and I loosen my grip just enough to put a little space between us as I'm dangerously close to getting hard, and well . . . that would just be fucking embarrassing. Still, I give her a last parting shot when I say, "That might involve tying you up and spanking you."

She shivers again, and I chuckle as I kiss her neck, and then I do release her because I will get a hard-on if I don't.

The waitress arrives with our beers and I give her a twenty, tell her to keep the change. I hand Jules her—gag—Bud Light and take my Molson, holding it up as I say, "Cheers."

She taps her bottle against mine with a grin. "Cheers."

"So, Jules," Garrett says conversationally, and she turns to face him. "Just curious what you see in this big dork."

I roll my eyes but then turn to Jules curiously, because I'm wondering what she'd tell my friends about me when put on the spot. While I notice her cheeks turn a little pink, she looks at Garrett and simply says, "He's my hero."

Typical funny man that he is, Garrett makes a gagging motion, but grins at her with bright eyes. Olivia and Vale give dreamy sighs and Hawke just looks appraisingly at me, almost as if he's trying to find the superhero cape I'm hiding.

My chest fills with pride hearing Jules say that, and I drop my hand to her lower back and just press it there to let her know that touched me.

Garrett immediately goes in for the kill. He leans in conspiratorially to Jules and says, "Did Max tell you about that time he got drunk in Los Angeles after a game and locked himself out of his room wearing nothing but his underwear?"

Jules' eyes get big and she cranes her neck to look at me, an eyebrow cocked. She then turns back to Garrett. "No, he didn't tell me that. But I think you should."

Everyone laughs, including me, because fuck it's hilarious and so uncharacteristic of me. I decide to go ahead and take the wind out of Garrett's sails as I tell Jules, "Let's just say I may have drunk some bourbon that night and it didn't agree with me."

"How did you get back in your room?" she asks curiously.

"Walked down to the lobby," I say.

"Stumbled," Garrett adds on.

"Stumbled down to the lobby," I agree with him. "And just walked up to the front desk and asked for a replacement key. Of course, I had no ID on me and the clerk didn't recognize me so they refused. They finally had to get the manager to let me in, and I just hung out in the lobby in my underwear until he came and rescued me."

"Oh, good God, Max," Jules says in mock dismay. "You're an embarrassment to humanity."

"Right?" Garrett adds for emphasis.

"Well," Hawke says dramatically, with an evil grin aimed at me, and I cringe because I know what that fucker's getting ready to tell Jules. "Not nearly as embarrassing as Max getting nominated as one of America's hottest sports bachelors by *Sports World* magazine."

I groan and close my eyes, but I can feel Jules' gaze on me. I open them up and see her staring at me in astonishment.

"Really?" she asks.

"I was going to tell you tonight," I mutter with embarrassment. "My agent sent me a text just before the game. I have to do a photo shoot next week or something."

"The winner will be announced next month and that hottie will grace the cover of the magazine," Hawke adds with an even broader but no less evil grin.

"How will the winner be chosen?" Jules asks me.

I groan again, because I am not enthused about this. No way I could decline though, because as my agent explained, press coverage in any form is crucial to keep me relevant to the sporting world. Even if it is for a special issue that will draw in female fans so they can ogle.

Hawke answers with a lecherous smile aimed at me. "The readers will vote online, and I can tell you . . . I'm totally voting for Max. He's so dreamy."

"Fuck off," I mutter as I pop him in the chest with my fist. Not hard enough to really hurt but enough to get his attention. "You're totally ruining my hero image with Jules."

"Nothing could ruin that, babe," she says as she leans in, peers up at me and wraps an arm around my waist.

And well, that warrants a kiss. So I give it to her, completely uncaring that four sets of eyes are pinned on us. I give her my mouth and she gives me hers back. I vaguely hear Olivia and Vale sigh again, but surprisingly, no gagging noises from Garrett. When I pull back, I shoot him a look and he just winks at me and I know despite his teasing—because that's the way Garrett is—the fucker is happy for me.

A quick glance over at Hawke and I see the same on his face.

"So what did you think about your first Cold Fury get-together?" I ask Jules as we drive to my house. We discussed briefly going to her apartment but immediately discarded it, because her bed is too small and her neighbors too loud.

"It was great," she says, and I can hear the smile in her voice. "Most everyone was so nice, and I really like Olivia and Vale."

"Most everyone?" I ask, my hackles rising that someone would dare to not be nice to my Jules. We weren't pinned to each other's sides all evening so I must have missed something.

She gives a husky laugh. "Just once in the bathroom . . . that woman Cassie was in there with her sister, Allie. At least I think that's what Olivia said their names are."

"She say something to you?" I practically growl.

"Not to me," Jules says. "But she was doing her makeup and talking to her sister, and talking about boning that player she was with . . . What was his name, Mikkel?"

"Yup," I acknowledge.

"Well, it was just crass," Jules says with a slight hint of disgust. "And she said that he was just a stupid Swede and wouldn't know what hit him by the time she was done with him."

"She's a bitch," I tell Jules point-blank as I turn into my neighborhood. "And her sister is too. There's a few associated with the team that are like that, but you just have to ignore them. They love the attention, even if it's negative."

"I never did understand women like that." Jules laughs. "It's an embarrassment to our gender."

"See," I tease her with a quick glance her way. The interior is dark and I can just make out the glow of her in the dashboard lights. Just exquisite. "I told you that you were one in a million, and that's why I snapped you up."

"Garrett's right . . . you *are* a dork," she tells me, again teasingly, but her voice is a little husky. She then turns in her seat, leans across the console and puts her hand on my thigh. The muscles immediately jump in acknowledgment of her touch.

"That right?" I murmur as her hand drifts up my leg.

"Mmmm-hmmm," she purrs, and then she's palming my dick, which starts to get hard. I barely realize I have another left turn to make and I curse when she grips me through the material of my pants.

"Baby," I mutter, my hands holding the wheel tightly. "Want me to wreck?"

"Nope," she answers as her fingers grasp my zipper and give it a little tug. "Better concentrate."

"Christ," I mutter as my cock goes fully hard and the zipper slides down.

One in a fucking million.

# CHAPTER 14

# JULES

Pure lust-induced adrenaline courses through me as Max responds to my bold move.

Totally bold.

Totally unlike me.

I've never been an aggressor or an initiator, but there's something about Max that is always beckoning to me to step past the edges of my comfort zone. Tonight was just one round of extreme awesomeness in my life, and it's left me feeling jubilant and playful.

Definitely hungry for Max.

The hockey game tonight was awesome and was hard fought. At the end of regulation play, the Cold Fury and the Vancouver Flash were tied 2–2. I had no clue what that meant but Kate filled me in that the teams would play a five minute overtime period with only three players on each team out on the ice, in addition to the goalie. That five minutes about had my heart stopping several times as Max battled for his team.

When that ended with the game still tied, Kate then filled me in on the shootout, and I have never screamed louder in my life each time a Flash player streaked down the ice toward Max. But he was brilliant and perfect and amazing and yes, he pulled the victory out for his team by stopping all the shots while the Flash goalie let one slide by.

Our time at Houlihan's was just as awesome. The vibe was electric, watching players and fans celebrate the win, and I really had no clue how serious this community took the sport and their team. I watched with pride and wonder as Max posed with fans for pictures and signed autographs. I stood next to him most of the time, his arm wrapped protectively around my back. He was openly attentive to me, which was not something I expected or needed, but something I appreciated, since I was the new girl on the block. And when Max was called away to pose for pictures or even talk with some of his teammates, Olivia and Vale kept me amused with stories about this crazy group of guys.

Even the horrid experience of listening to that girl Cassie in the bathroom wasn't enough to even remotely dampen my fun, because it made me realize how lucky I was to have someone like Max and to be a part of his world.

Yes, a night of complete awesomeness, but I have a feeling all of that will pale in comparison to where we're headed right now. It's been a long week since we've been together, and sex with Max was beyond anything I could have ever imagined. I've never been with someone that was so singularly compatible to me in almost all ways, but most assuredly in the bedroom. For as sweet as Max is in his normal life, he's a bit of a freak in the bed, and while this was not something I was used to as my own sex life had been quite boring, I found myself loving every bit of it.

I responded to every bit of it because I was yearning to be as close to Max as I could, and that meant opening myself up fully to him. The minute I decided to let myself go and trust in what he was doing to me, I had the most explosive orgasms I've ever had in my life. They were brutal and terrifying in the way that made me realize I could become addicted to his brand of love-making, but they were beautiful and fulfilling too.

I ached to have that again, and that feeling coupled with the magnificent time I had tonight watching Max in his world has me feeling frisky.

So I figure I'll start tonight's adventure with a little bit of a bold move on my part.

I manage to easily slide his zipper down and that's only because it's pulled tight over his straining erection. The belt though is impossible to work with one hand, so I quickly sit up and undo my seatbelt.

"Jules," Max warns, but then his mouth snaps shut when both hands get to work on his belt buckle.

I get it open along with the button just as he makes the last turn onto the street his house sits on. Max's breath hisses through his teeth and he manages to lift his hips a bit so I can pull his pants open and free his cock.

And I take in a tremulous breath as I see it through the dim light of the dashboard.

It's fucking beautiful. Everything a cock should be. Long, thick, and beautifully veined.

The things he did to me with that cock.

My mouth waters and I feel Max's car start to slow, figure we're on the verge of pulling into his driveway, so I don't waste any time. I scramble to my knees, stretch across the console and drop my head. The minute the head of his dick hits my tongue, Max curses, thrusts his hips up, and he hits the brakes too hard, causing my body to start to roll toward the dashboard.

His arm is lightning quick as it wraps around my waist, and without even missing a beat, I sink lower onto him, taking him as far back in my mouth as I can get him.

"Fuck, Jules," he groans as I pull up to the tip, lick around the head and then suck him back in. His hand goes to the back of my head and he palms it gently although his hips rotate in a silent plea for me to keep going.

His lust becomes my lust and his need becomes mine. I want to suck every inch of him down and I want him to give me every drop he has. I start to bob on his cock, the sounds of his panting and groaning urging me faster. I wrap my hand around the bottom of his shaft and I squeeze and twist on my upward pulls.

Max's fingers tighten in my hair and he mutters, "Jules . . . slow down."

Um . . . no.

I go faster.

Max tugs on my hair. "Jules . . . hold up."

I suck harder.

"Fuck, Jules," Max growls as he grips a handful of hair and pulls up my head, placing his other hand on my cheek. He tugs gently and I finally unlatch my mouth to look up at him.

I blink, momentarily surprised that I can see his face clearly from some type of illumination outside of the car. I turn my head, look around and get my bearings, realizing we're in his garage.

I have no clue how or when we got here, I was so lost in what I was doing to Max.

Turning back to look at him, I grin as I manage to stroke upward on his cock with my hand. "When did we get home?"

He doesn't answer me but groans again over the sensation and then his hands are on my face and he's kissing me savagely. I fall into him, one hand still wrapped around his shaft, the other curling into his shirt. He possesses my mouth, causing me to moan in surrender to him.

When he pulls away, he rubs his nose along mine and murmurs, "Loved that mouth on me, babe, but I want inside of you too badly."

My eyelids flutter closed over the gentleness of his voice mixed with yearning.

He wants me.

He wants inside of me.

"Let's go in," I whisper.

Max pulls his face back from mine, and despite the tenderness of his words, his eyes are raging with need and lust. It causes a cramp to hit me dead between the legs, and I swallow hard over the lump of emotion brewing down deep as I can see just how much Max wants me written all over his face.

We stare at each other a fraction of a moment, then both of us are pushing away from each other and scrambling out our respective doors. He waits for me at the front of the car, his pants half zipped up to hold them on his lean hips but the head of his cock sticking out of the top, shiny with pre-cum and my saliva. His hand reaches out to me and as soon as we lock digits he's dragging me through his garage then lets me precede him into the house, finally pushing me up the two small steps that lead into his laundry room.

With his hands on my hips, I don't need him urging me forward, and we practically take off running through his kitchen, past the wide hall that has a staircase that leads to the basement and into the formal living room, with his master bedroom just on the other side. In fact, I see the door to his bedroom within sight, but suddenly his hands are gripping my hips hard and he turns my trajectory to the left.

Right to the low-backed sofa done in cream with a geometric print of various-size rectangles in burgundy, mocha, and khaki.

I gasp when he pushes me right to the back of the sofa so the tops of my thighs hit against it, and then his hands are at the front of my jeans and he's tearing at my button and zipper. I can hear him breathing harshly behind me, the pants of air from his mouth hitting my cheek as I crane my head around to look at him.

Just as he gets my jeans open and starts to push the denim and my panties down, his eyes snap up to mine and he gives me a dark look of frustrated need, even as his lips curve upward.

"Sorry, baby . . . but said I needed inside you badly," Max says by way of explanation. "You wet for me?"

"I'm thinking that's a sure bet," I murmur with a smile.

"Better check," he says devilishly and his hand is between my legs. The minute his fingers brush against me, we can both tell that I am indeed soaked for him, and my head drops, my eyes flutter closed.

But it's only a teasing touch because he pulls away and starts to pull my jeans and panties down to my knees.

His breath fans across my thighs as he rumbles, "You are so fucking beautiful."

A ripple of pure lust fans out across the base of my spine, pulses through my belly then settles low between my legs. The tremor in Max's voice as he roughly pulls at my clothes and the reverence are enough to have me panting for him, my pussy clenching with need.

"Hurry," I whisper as I brace my hands on the back of the couch.

A rumble . . . maybe a snarl from Max as he continues to yank at my tight jeans. Definitely a snarl next and he mutters "Fuck it" before he stands back up. I hear foil ripping and turn my head to see him quickly rolling a condom on. Then his hands are pushing my shirt up my back and I feel the tip of his cock rubbing between my legs from behind.

He pushes tentatively at my entrance, and while my legs are spread somewhat only by the grace of stretchy denim, he still has to work to get inside of me.

Finally, my slick folds give way and he punches in a few inches. He hisses in pleasure and I moan over the fullness just the tip of his cock provides me.

"More," I murmur as I wiggle my hips a little.

He slides in more and I hear another rumble of satisfaction deep within his chest. I arch my back, pushing my belly button downward and raising my ass to give him a better angle.

He praises me. "That's it."

He sinks in another inch and I almost start to sigh with relief, but then he's sliding back out.

I make a sound of protest, curl my fingers into the cushion on the couch, and try to push back at him. But then he's slamming inside of me and I can't help when I cry out, "Yes. God . . . Max . . . just like that."

"You want it hard?" he growls as he pulls back, almost to the tip, and slams in.

It knocks the breath out of me so all I can do is frantically nod and rotate my hips, silently begging for more.

"Feel good?" Pull out, slam back in.

Again I nod viciously and grunt like an animal when he bottoms out.

Max's hand runs up my spine—under my shirt, over my bra strap—gently stroking my skin, even as he pulls out and drives back in with brute force, with one hand still holding tight to my hip.

It glides all the way up until his strong fingers grasp the back of my neck. I hear a low hum from deep within his throat as he pulls back once again, his cock slowly sliding out of my wet channel, pausing just a moment so he doesn't slip free.

His hand tightens on my neck. His fingers dig down into my hip.

Then he drives into me harder than ever and I cry out in pleasure because he just exploited some magical spot inside of me.

With him pinning me by my neck and hip so I can't move, Max sets a brutal pace on my body, tunneling in and out of me forcefully. I want to turn my head to look at his face. In my imagination he's flushed red and his eyes are pinned to my ass as he watches his cock pistoning into me.

But I can't because I'm held in place by strong hands, and I realize . . . I'd rather have that. I'd rather have him controlling me in this moment, letting him finally take something he wants, all with the knowledge I've driven him to this almost animal state.

"You okay?" Max rasps out as he fucks me.

No . . . as he throws himself into me.

"More than," I manage to get out in between grunts and pants.

"You feel so good," he manages to huff as he slides the hand from my hip to between my legs from the front. The pads of his fingers find my clit and he presses down on it, creating a friction against it from within as he thrusts in and out of me.

It comes out of left field, catching me by surprise. An orgasm to end all orgasms, it seems to reverberate through every square inch of my body all at once and with a force so brutal I open my mouth to scream but I can't because I'm robbed of air.

I shudder hard and my pussy contracts involuntarily around Max's cock and I know he feels it because he falters a moment before pulling out almost all the way and hammering home one last time, where he roots himself deeply into me.

My name seems to rip free of his throat, one long groan hitting each syllable. "Julianne."

He grinds against my ass as he comes, his fingers loosening and contracting around my neck seemingly in sync with the bursts of semen I know are filling the condom up.

I can hear Max suck in a deep breath and then his hands go to the back of the cushion to rest beside mine. He lowers his body until his stomach and chest are pressed to my back and he nuzzles into my neck.

"God, Jules," he whispers in a way that tells me he's robbed of breath too. "You make me crazy."

"In a good way?" I whisper back with a smile.

"In the best of ways," he says, then presses a kiss to my cheek before he straightens up.

I'm wrecked so I just stay in my position as he pulls out of me, but when he mutters a harsh, "Well, that's just fucking great," I pull myself up and turn to face him.

"What's wrong?" I ask, and then follow his gaze, which is pinned on his dick, surprisingly still thick and long.

Aside from the beauty of his cock, I gape at the condom, which has a huge hole in it starting from the top and tearing halfway down his shaft. His semen is leaking out and a large drop falls to the floor just as I feel a trickle start to run down my inner thigh.

"Oh, shit," I whisper in astonishment.

His eyes raise to mine and they're filled with disgust. "Did I just hurt you?"

I jerk with surprise, a baffled look on my face. "What? No!"

"I fucked you so hard I shredded the damn condom, Jules," he spits out as he stares down at the mangled piece of rubber, contempt for himself evident in his tone.

Oh, my God. The look on his face . . . so full of consternation and befuddlement. Me standing there gaping at him with my pants in a stranglehold around my knees and Max's joy slipping down my legs.

My hand flies to my mouth and I manage to clamp it over my lips just as the first snicker works its way out. But it's not enough to hide it and Max's head snaps up and his eyes narrow onto me. "You think it's funny?"

My eyes crinkle with amusement and I pull my hand away, giving him a chastising smile. "I think the way you look right now is fucking adorable."

Max rolls his eyes at me and mutters, "The condom broke, Jules."

"Yes, it did," I agree and then I can't help but sigh. "And that was the best fucking I've ever had in my life."

"Seriously," he asks as he eyes me with wonder. "That's all you have to say?"

"Um," I say as I bat my eyelashes at him. "I'm on the pill so chances of me getting pregnant are slim to none. And I'm clean so there's nothing for you to worry about."

"I fucked you so hard," he grits out again, seemingly unable to get past that, "that I shredded the goddamned condom. I've never lost control like that. Never had that happen to me before."

I grin at him impishly. "I take that to mean you're clean too, right?"

"Jules," he growls at me, but I see the tiniest of curves to his lips. "I'm being serious. And of course I'm clean."

I take a hesitant, waddlelike step toward him, careful not to trip and fall on my face because my legs are so constricted. "I'm being serious too, Max. That was awesome and I'd like to do it again, just like that and soon. Although, I do feel like we should write this condom company and tell them their product sucks and that it can't hold up to the big, power cock of Max Fournier. Who knows, maybe they'll reformulate the product and then offer you an endorsement deal."

"Jesus, you're fucking cute," he says as he smiles at me, then brings a hand to the back of my head to pull me in for a kiss.

I readily return it.

When he pulls away, he says, "Let's get cleaned up and head to bed."

"We going to do this again?" I ask with my head tilted.

"Damn right we are," he says quickly. "And I guess this means we can dispose of the condoms, right?"

"They're not worth a shit anyway," I say in agreement.

Max laughs and kisses me again. I wobble slightly but manage to stay upright.

"What did I do to deserve you?" he asks in wonder.

"All the right things, apparently," I tell him, but I'm smiling hard on the inside because I'm the one who's been granted a miracle when this man was brought into my life.

# CHAPTER 15

# MAX

"Okay, we have chocolate concrete with brownies," I say as I push the cup of ice cream across the tabletop to Levy. "Plain vanilla with caramel sauce for Rocco, and a banana split for Annabelle."

I parcel out the ice cream and then spoons and napkins. It's a required treat after we spent the last few hours roaming around the Durham Life and Science museum, looking at bears and wolves and lemurs, walking through the butterfly house and playing on all of the outdoor equipment.

I'm completely fucking wiped but the kids still look like they have a ton of energy.

They dig in, dipping their spoons in and then pulling out massive globs of ice cream and assorted goo that's way too big for their mouths but still somehow manages to fit in.

I smile as I watch them and then give a quick check of my watch. Jules should be getting home within the hour and I'd hoped to have the kids all fed, bathed, and ready for bed by the time she got there, but we're running late.

We're running late because we had a seriously awesome fucking day today, and well . . . who wants to stop the awesome?

I didn't think today would be as great as it turned out because if I'm being honest with myself, I'd rather be spending it with Jules and not three kids, who are very cute and a ton of fun, but they aren't who I want to be spending the majority of my day with. The weekends are special opportunities for me and Jules because her schedule is far too hectic during the week to spend much time with me, and my weekends are hit or miss depending on our travel schedule. It's sad to say that most of the time Jules and I are bonding via phone calls and FaceTime, which isn't without merit. We've had conversations that have lasted a few hours at a time, which I know if we were together we'd spend it fucking, so in a way we're getting to know each other even better.

Jules and I have shared so much over the phone, and it's safe to say she knows more about me than anyone in my life maybe except my parents and siblings. I definitely know all about her too, which includes deep talks about death, loss, and grieving. We talk about Melody a lot actually.

She's also let me know how scared she's been these past months, having lost her best friend when Melody died, and not having anyone else to depend on. I learned all about her dad, whom she loves, there's no doubt, but who you can tell is completely undependable. He's on the road so much that he only sees Jules every few months and usually only for a few days at a time.

I was gone most of this past week with a three-game road trip, and thus I'd really, really wanted to have Saturday to spend with Jules. Sunday we have a home game, so that blows most of the day, which meant Saturday was my golden opportunity.

But then Jules told me last night, before the team boarded the plane to return to Raleigh, that Olivia and Stevie had invited her for a spa day with them, and she wanted to know what I thought about it.

And I most definitely had thoughts.

My initial and most selfish thought was "no fucking way" because I wanted Saturday with her, even if that included the kids, which it would.

But my second thought, and the one that ultimately felt right, was that Jules could really use a day off. She's still working essentially two jobs, between the nursing home and painting at night, and she basically runs on fumes. A spa day of relaxation would do her a world of good, and "spa day" didn't truly mean all day. It was really only about four hours and they'd booked it for the afternoon, so I could spend time with Jules that morning.

So I told her, "Baby . . . that sounds awesome."

"Really?" she asked, and I could hear the worry in her voice. "You don't think it's frivolous? I mean . . . Stevie said he had some coupons, and I've sold more paintings than I had figured, so I have a little extra cash—"

"Jules," I admonished her. "Will you just do something for yourself, please? You deserve this."

She huffed, then was silent as she contemplated. I waited for her to think it through, and when she finally spoke, she utterly warmed my heart. "But that's four hours I'll be losing that I could spend with you."

I had to give a little cough to clear my throat, but I couldn't keep the smile out of my voice when I said, "Jules . . . go to the spa, have a great time. I'll take the kids and we'll do something fun, so you can save on the babysitter."

"You seriously want to take three rambunctious kids on for half a day?" she asked skeptically.

*No.*

"Of course I do," I assured her. "I'll come over and we'll do breakfast, then hang for a while. Then we'll do lunch. Then you'll go get buffed and polished or whatever it is you do at a spa and I'll handle the kids."

"I have no idea what you do at a spa," she said with a laugh. "I've never been."

That made me sad. Someone like Jules deserved to be pampered, and I vowed that I'd make her regular spa appointments and watch the kids for her so she could get rejuvenated.

Ultimately, she agreed to go, and I got to spend the first half of the day with her, even if part of that time was spent hanging at her apartment so she could do laundry. I only conceded to this because Jules promised she'd come to tomorrow's game with the kids, and in order to do that, she had to get some shit handled today. That included getting all the kids' clothes washed and apparently it also meant the floors had to be vacuumed and mopped.

And even though part of my day with Jules included me helping her to do these things, there still wasn't any place I'd rather be.

I watch as Annabelle attempts a massive spoonful of ice cream toward her mouth but it bobbles and starts to slip off the side. My hand shoots out just as it falls and I catch it square on my palm. She looks down at my hand and then back up to me with a grin. "Oops."

I laugh, grab a handful of napkins and wipe my hand. "How about you take some smaller bites. There's no rush to get it all down."

"Can't help it," she says as she grabs another big spoonful. "It's too good and we hardly get to eat ice cream."

I blink at her in surprise and ask, "What do you mean *hardly?*"

"We get to eat ice cream," Rocco says as he looks at me across the table. "But it's usually the cheap stuff from the grocery store. Or Popsicles."

"It's all Aunt Jules can afford," Levy adds matter-of-factly.

I look at all three kids, my gaze sweeping around the table, completely blindsided that this is a major treat for them and utterly astounded they understand the concept of Jules' struggles.

"But it's okay," Rocco adds quickly, and I'm thinking he caught something on my face that has him struggling. "Aunt Jules takes really good care of us and she'd give us more if she could."

"She will," I say, my voice hoarse with uncertainty. "Her paintings are selling really well, and it's just a matter of time. Maybe she'll even be able to quit that job at Sweetbrier."

"Nah," says Rocco as he digs his spoon back into his ice cream. "She loves that place."

"I don't understand why," Levy mutters. "She took us there one time to visit those old people and it stinks."

Rocco elbows Levy in the ribs, and Levy throws a punch to Rocco's shoulder and glares at him.

"They can't help it," Annabelle pipes up with a sweet voice, and I turn to look at her as she stares Levy down. "They're old, and when you get old there's some things you can't help. Aunt Jules says we need to be nice to them."

Levy's head hangs down in shame and I find that fascinating. Rocco calls him on the carpet and he fights back. Annabelle dresses him down and he gets repentant.

"Well, here's the thing," I tell the kids as I continue to dab at my sticky palm with the napkin. "Your Aunt Jules loves you three very much, and so she's working really hard to give you a good life. And I'm working really hard to help her out, because I care about her too."

"Do you love her?" Annabelle asks, and whoa fuck . . . just . . . what the fuck?

"Um," I stammer, then stammer again. "Um."

"Well, do you?" Rocco asks somewhat aggressively. "Because I think she loves you."

I jerk in my seat and there's no denying the feeling of euphoria that spreads through me at that proclamation. I lean toward Rocco. "You do?"

"She talks about you all the time," Rocco says with a sage nod. "And she's always so happy when you call her."

"And we've seen her kissing you," Levy adds in. "You kiss people when you love them."

"And she's really happy now," Annabelle offers in a sweet voice. "Since she met you, she smiles all the time."

Jesus fuck.

These kids.

I put my elbows on the table and steeple my hands as I look at these three little wise and perceptive rug rats. I don't know if they know what love is, but I have an inkling. I'm not sure if that's what I would call what I feel for Jules or vice versa, but I know for sure it's something damn close to that. I know I've never felt this before in my life, and I have to say . . . it's utterly fucking reassuring that Annabelle has recognized her aunt is happier since she met me.

"So here's the thing about your Aunt Jules and me," I say carefully to the kids. "We care about each other a great deal, and I'm glad I make her happier. She makes me very happy too."

"So you love her," Levy presses, and because this kid wants an answer and because I can't lie to him, I need to do a very quick evaluation of my feelings.

Jules is an amazing woman. Her attributes are many, varied and spectacular. She's devoted to the kids, a hard worker, and totally gives of herself. Not a selfish bone in her fucking body.

She makes me laugh . . . so fucking hard.

She makes me smile just by being in her presence.

She also makes me hard just by being in her presence.

I think about her all the time and I constantly yearn to be with her.

I look forward to my future and try to imagine her not in it, and I just can't do it.

Cannot even fucking envision it.

Even with all of the problems we face, and the limits on our time, and the fact that she comes with three kids, and I travel fifty percent of the time for my job, and things are so unstable for her right now . . . I cannot imagine being with anyone else but her.

I look Levy square in the eye and I tell him the truth. "Yeah, kid . . . I love her."

I know it's only been six weeks since I first met her, but I think I may have fallen a little in love with her that first night in the convenience store when I tried to help her peel the tape off Annabelle, and even though you could tell she was on the edge of defeat, she still had perseverance.

"You should tell her," Rocco says.

"Don't be afraid," Annabelle says, and I turn to face her.

"I'm not afraid," I assure her. "Just want it to be the right time, you know?"

She nods.

"So how about we keep this between ourselves, okay?" I ask the kids, turning to look at each one in succession.

I get three smiling nods in return.

"Okay, get cracking on those ice creams," I tell them. "But we're going to order pizza for dinner, and you each better eat at least one piece of pizza so your Aunt Jules doesn't know I fed you ice cream this close to dinner."

# CHAPTER 16

# JULES

I look down at the pale blue shimmery polish the technician is painting on my toenails and I'm happy with the choice. Stevie made it for me, and perhaps it's the artist in me, but I appreciate his funky style. I knew Olivia was someone who could become an amazing friend just from that one night last week we hung together, but it only took me about twenty minutes after I met Stevie Magliano to know that he could be my soul brother.

Not that I would impede on his best friend status with Olivia, although it's clear she's not proprietary. They have a special bond that can't be touched, but right off the bat Stevie made me feel utterly like his second best friend.

This may have had something to do with the fact that our spa day started off with massages together. As in all in the same room. As in Stevie had no qualms with dropping trou right in front of me before climbing on one of three tables that were arranged in a private room smelling of sandalwood and lavender with faint chiming music in the background. I hastily averted my eyes but figured . . . what the hell. He's gay and clearly not interested in me, but I vaguely wondered if Max would be mad if he knew I got naked—albeit temporarily—in front of another man.

I'm thinking not, because he knows Stevie and knows he's like one of the girls.

At any rate, twenty minutes into the massage and Stevie had managed to pull out my entire story. I told him and Olivia all about Melody and how close we were, and how horrible it was to watch her die. Stevie started crying, and he then went off on a tangent—a very important tangent—and told me about Olivia's cancer. I knew a little bit about it from Max, but I got the full story. Then Stevie pointed me back in the direction of what he called "the really juice stuff" and had me spilling my guts about how Max and I met, and with no shame I admitted to him and Olivia how hard I was falling for him.

After the massage, the conversation was halted somewhat as we got facials, but then resumed again once we started in on the manis and pedis. And now we're finishing up and I feel happy and refreshed.

"So, seriously," Stevie says as his nails get painted a bold neon yellow. "You and Max have got to figure a way to have some more quality time together. While I'm sure your niece and nephews are adorable beyond measure, you and Max need more alone time."

"Totally agree," I say wistfully, thinking back to the last time we were together intimately. One week ago to be exact when he fucked me so hard over the back of his couch, only to take me into his bedroom and fuck me slowly and tenderly.

I still can't decide which one I like better.

"If you need help with the kids, you only need to ask," Olivia says. "Garrett and I will watch them."

"Me too," Stevie says. "I am an absolute child whisperer and I am way more fun than Olivia and Garrett."

Olivia snorts but doesn't contradict him.

I huff out a frustrated breath. "It's not just finding time away from the kids. It's finding time period. I've got to make a certain amount of money to give them what they need and pay my bills, and that means work, work, work."

"Max told Garrett how worried he is about you," Olivia murmurs.

"He did?" I ask curiously. Because I didn't really think men talked about stuff like that.

Olivia nods. "He cares about you a great deal, Jules. Even if he hadn't told Garrett, who told me, it's plain to see."

"I care about him too," I say softly, my heart squeezing in absolute abandon when I think about Max and how much he's come to mean to me.

"You should just marry him," Stevie quips. "He's rich as all get out and you wouldn't have to work."

I snort, as does Olivia, and I don't take him seriously. I think Stevie and Olivia have figured out I'm not a gold digger since part of my story to Stevie earlier included telling them about the loan Max gave me and how I insisted on paying him back from each painting.

"I just wish I could give him more of myself," I say glumly. My true fear is that Max will get tired of waiting for me to give him more.

"Well, if your paintings keep selling the way they are, you could potentially give up your other job and that would free up time," Stevie says.

And he's not lying about that. He quickly sold the ones that Max originally brought him and I've been working my ass off over the last four weeks and my art has been selling as fast as I'm producing it. Stevie had reached out to some other trendy business shops in the area and three of them are also stocking my work.

On top of that, Stevie told me today that a friend of his that's a gallery owner wants to talk to me about putting together a collection to possibly show next spring, which means more painting.

But even if I could make enough to get by just on my artwork alone, I'm not sure I would do that. I mean, I love my job. I love working with the elderly. I think it's my calling.

So if I keep my job at Sweetbrier, and I keep painting, and the kids keep being my first priority, where exactly does that put Max?

Once again at the bottom, and that weighs heavily on me, because not only is that not fair to him, but damn it . . . it's not fair to me either. I think I deserve something too, right?

"I don't know how to make it all work," I say with a voice heavy with sadness. Or is that self-pity?

"Look," Olivia says from her pedi chair beside me, and I crane my neck to look at her. "Maybe you find the compromise in there. Your art is selling well and you're making good money now. Maybe you could go part-time at Sweetbrier to free up your schedule."

I blink at her, but then my lips curl upward. That's not a bad idea at all. I could totally cut my hours back at Sweetbrier, as long as I was secure enough in myself that I could keep selling my art. That way I could continue to do a job I love, continue my art, and then have more time for Max and the kids.

A sudden wave of jubilation sweeps through me and I grin big at Olivia. "You know . . . that could work. I mean . . . I'd have to run numbers on what I could make with the paintings, but that could work."

Of course, I'd want to talk to Max about it and see what he

thought. I trust his advice over anyone's and I know he'd never steer me wrong. Most importantly, Max knows how important it is to me to do things on my own without any handouts, so he'll help me analyze the situation.

I cannot wait to get back to the apartment and talk to him about this.

I'm practically skipping down the hall to my second-floor apartment. As I pass by Glenda and Bill's, I hear them in there yelling at each other, but even that can't dampen my mood.

Knowing that Max is just on the other side of my door, and that I'll see his face, and yes . . . I'll even kiss it and it doesn't matter if the kids see it or not.

Knowing that perhaps I've found a way to give me more time with that man.

I turn the knob and push the door open, only to find Max waiting for me just inside the doorway, and the look on his face causes every happy feeling within me to vanish and a pit to form in my stomach.

"What's wrong?" I whisper, my heart galloping frantically as I brace for bad news. I can see it written all over his face. "Where are the kids?"

"Their father is here," Max says gravely, and my knees almost buckle.

"What?" I ask in astonishment, my purse slipping from my shoulder and falling to the floor.

"He's got them down in the complex playground," he says, and I immediately spin toward the door, for some reason panicked that he's with them and not within my sight.

"Relax, Jules," Max says softly as his hands come to my shoulders and he turns me around. "I made him give me his car keys and wallet before I let him take them down there. He suggested it to the kids and they were so excited to see him, and I didn't think I had the right to say no."

I nod in understanding but my head is buzzing from trying to take it all in. And yeah . . . I could see why Max felt uncomfortable in denying Dwayne's request to take the kids out to play, but am totally impressed with his quick thinking to get his keys and wallet. Not that Dwayne would kidnap the kids. He's not stupid.

Just completely unreliable and an overall douche for abandoning them and their mother.

"What does he want?" I whisper fearfully.

"I don't know," Max says. "Caught me off guard. Was waiting outside your door when I got here. The kids immediately ran to him, but I had him come inside for a while to talk. He seems chill, and says he just wanted to spend some time with them. But I honestly don't know what his agenda is, baby."

"I need to go talk to him," I murmur, although it's the last thing I want to do.

"Want me to come with you?" Max asks, his hands skimming up to either side of my neck and his face leaning in to me.

I nod. "Would you?"

"Yeah, Jules. Of course I will."

We head back out of the apartment and down to the complex playground. I immediately see Dwayne pushing Annabelle on a swing, while Rocco and Levy play on the monkey bars.

Rocco sees me first as we walk up behind Dwayne and he jumps off the equipment, running to me with a big grin on his face. For a moment my heart sinks, thinking that happiness emanating from him has everything to do with his father being here, but then he yells, "Aunt Jules . . . we had the best time with Max today. We got to see the wolves and some bears, and then he took us for ice cream, although we promise we'll eat dinner."

Rocco slams into me, his arms coming around me and his face pressing into my stomach. My arms immediately wrap around him and I sigh with utter relief that he doesn't seem to be taken in by Dwayne. Annabelle jumps off the swing and also runs to me. She looks up at me with bright shining eyes and says, "And I know a secret that Max told me but I can't tell you."

"You do, huh?" I ask with a smile as I run my fingers through her curls.

She nods enthusiastically. Levy jumps down from the equipment and walks over to us, not as enthused, but he gives me a bright smile before turning to look at his dad with a measure of confusion.

And that's when I turn to Dwayne. I keep my tone light but I get to the point. "What are you doing here?"

Dwayne reaches a hand up, scratches at the back of his head and shrugs. "Wanted to see the kids."

"You could have called first," I tell him point-blank.

"Didn't think you'd let me come if I did that," he snaps, and I immediately turn to look at Max, as I sense this isn't going to be pretty and I don't want the kids to see it.

"Will you take the kids back up and maybe get dinner ordered?"

Max's gaze burns into me and I can see him warring with wanting to stay there to have my back and wanting to protect the kids. Finally he nods, shoots a hard glare at Dwayne that clearly conveys he doesn't like him. He then reaches into his pocket and pulls Dwayne's wallet and keys out, handing them to him. Max turns to the kids and says, "Come on, little minions. Let's go order pizza."

They all herd around Max and he swings Annabelle up and over his shoulder. She shrieks with delight and for a moment I watch them all walk away before I turn back to Dwayne.

"Seriously, why now?" I ask him. "You couldn't even bother to come to Melody's funeral. Couldn't even be there for your kids when they were grieving."

"Did you ever think it was hard on me, Julianne?" he asks, and of course he calls me by my full name because he's never really been a friend of mine in all the years I've known him. He barely tolerated me when he and Melody first got together, and after he started his cheating and abandoning ways, I made no secret that I didn't like him.

"Not as hard as it was on me, Dwayne," I hiss at him. "I'm the one that held her hand when she took her last breath, you asshole, and you know what really burns me up . . . she fucking loved you until the end."

If I thought that might touch him in some way and make him feel guilty, I would have been sadly mistaken. He doesn't seem sorry or apologetic.

"Look," he says brusquely. "I didn't come here to fight."

"And we're back to the start," I say sarcastically. "Why are you here?"

"I'm thinking about taking the kids back," he says without looking me in the eye. "You know . . . take them off your hands."

"You cannot be fucking serious," I growl at him, some mama grizzly bear rage filling me up.

"I met someone," he says, still refusing to look me in the eye. "She wants to get married but she doesn't want that damn child support payment hanging over me. And she wants kids . . . so you know . . . I figured I'd take the kids back."

I swear, for a moment I think I might stroke out as my vision goes dim, and then a red pulse of light obscures his shameful face before me. I'm so angry, I'm seeing fucking red.

I advance toward him a step and poke him in the chest, "You do not just get to decide you want your kids after years of not being there for them, just because you fucking met a woman that wants kids and you don't want to pay child support. That's not how it works."

"They're my kids," he snarls at me, pushing his body against my finger and causing me to go back a step. "And if I want to take them, I'll take them."

"You better be prepared to deal with the law then," I warn him. "Because I have legal custody and you signed off on that, or have you forgotten, Dwayne? Those kids are mine in the eyes of the law and if you take them that's kidnapping."

"Then I'll fight you for them in court," he says darkly, and my insides turn to Jell-O at the thought.

Still, I tilt my chin up and tell him, "I'll fight you every step of the way. I'll spend every dime I have fighting it."

"They're my kids," he says angrily.

"Come on, Dwayne," I say softly, hoping to appeal to his common sense. "You've been out of their life far more than you've been in it. They're excited to see you when you first get here because you do something fun with them or bring them a toy, but then that wears off. They don't know you. And more importantly, you weren't there when their mother died . . . when they needed you the most."

He doesn't say anything for a moment, but just looks at the ground.

Finally, he looks up to me and says, "That's how it's gonna be?"

I sigh. "Look, if you want some visitation, we can work things out, but you'll have to catch up on the child support. You know the court requires that, and you'll have to pay it going forward. It's not cheap raising three kids, Dwayne, and I've been busting my ass to give them a good life."

If I expected that to shame him, I'd be wrong about that too, and instead his eyes shimmer with something I can't quite put my finger on. "I see you're fairly cozy with your man."

My body stiffens but I don't say a word.

"Max Fournier," Dwayne taunts, and it's clear to me he knows who Max is. "That guy's rolling in dough. I'm quite sure you're not suffering taking care of the kids."

"I support those kids on my own," I grit out. "Max doesn't give me any money."

"Maybe," he concedes and then nods at me before turning toward his car. He calls over his shoulder, "But I wonder if he would."

Well, fuck . . . what the hell does that mean?

# CHAPTER 17

# MAX

I stand in Jules' bedroom with her and watch as she stomps back and forth across the carpet. Her hands are balled into fists and her cheeks are bright red with fury.

"That son of a bitch can't have them," she yells at me, her arms waving wildly to punctuate her resolve.

"Jules," I say in a lowered voice. "You need to calm down. The kids can hear you."

She looks chastised and takes three paces to get in my face. She whispers harshly, "He can't do it. That fucking asshole has no right. He can't just waltz back into their lives now that they're settled."

"Honey . . ." I try to placate.

She just hisses at me. "That fucker wants those kids so he doesn't have to pay child support again, and do you think he's going to spend the money on them that they deserve—hell, that they fucking need to survive—if he can't even be bothered to pay a fraction of what they cost in child support?"

Tears gather in her eyes and she starts shaking. I pull her into me, wrap my arms hard around her as I tell her, "It will be fine. I've got your back. He's not going to do anything."

She pulls her face back and looks at me, one tear slipping out, and it guts me. "I can't lose them, Max. They're all I have left of Melody. They are Melody. I can't do it."

She lets a sob out and presses her face into my chest. I hold her there for a minute, and because Jules is one of the strongest women I've ever met, she only submits to her anger and grief for a few moments before she swallows it down and pulls away from me. She rubs her finger under her eyes to wipe away the remaining tears and her voice quavers, "I'm fine."

"You are not," I mutter and I reach into her back pocket to pull out the phone I know she keeps there. I thrust it into her hands. "Call Tina. Ask if she can watch the kids for an hour. I'm going to take you out to dinner, ply you with a few glasses of wine to relax, and then I'm coming back here with you. I'll sleep on the couch."

"What?" she says, trying to push the phone back at me. "No. I don't need you to handle me, Max."

"Yes you fucking do, Jules," I growl at her, refusing to take the phone. "So let me do it. Call Tina. Now."

I think she might argue but then she just nods at me silently and calls Tina, who fortunately was home. Jules briefly told her about Dwayne's visit and that she needed about an hour to cool down. Tina gladly agreed and within five minutes she and her son Marshall arrived and I was ushering Jules out the door.

I take her just about two miles from her apartment complex to a cozy Irish pub that I had spied one evening after I left Jules' apartment and before I hit the I-440 Beltline. It's packed because it's Saturday night but we're able to get a booth in the bar after only about a ten minute wait, and I think it's possibly because I was recognized by the hostess.

Whatever. I'll gladly take that so I can get Jules settled down.

A waitress comes quickly and there's no doubt that I've been recognized because she stares at me with wide eyes, gets flustered as she takes our drink orders, and calls me "sir" about twenty times too many.

Once she leaves, I hold my hand across the table, palm up, and Jules without any further prompting puts her hand in mine.

I curl my fingers around hers and squeeze gently. "What's your biggest fear?"

"That the court will give Dwayne the kids," she answers immediately and with no thought.

"What would he have to do for that to happen?" I ask.

She shrugs. "Hire a lawyer. File something, I guess. Get it before a judge."

"And what does he do for a living?"

"He's a mechanic," she says, her eyebrows knit together. "It's what he did in the Army, but he never holds a job long. He's always off chasing the next piece of tail and he has no qualms with women supporting him."

"What a loser," I mutter then squeeze her hand again. "Listen . . . for him to fight for the kids will take money, and he clearly doesn't have it. He can't even pay child support."

"But maybe that woman he's with will front him the money," she throws out.

"Um . . . excuse me, Mr. Fournier," I hear from my right, and my head turns slowly to see a boy of about thirteen sitting there with a pad of paper. A man—I'm guessing his father—stands behind him with his hand on his shoulder. "I'm really sorry to bother you, but do you think I could get your autograph?"

Inside I'm screaming, *No. Fuck off, kid. Can't you see my woman is having a meltdown?*

But there's no way I could ever do that to a fan, much less a nervous-looking kid with stars in his eyes.

"Sure thing, buddy," I say as I release Jules' hand and reach out for the paper and pen. "What's your name?"

"Andy," he says.

I start to scribble a personalized autograph as I ask, "You play hockey?"

"Yes, sir," he says. "Goalie."

"Awesome," I say as I sign my name and hand the paper and pen back to him.

"Um . . . could I get a picture with you?" he mumbles, and while I don't feel it, I manage to give him a big smile.

"Sure," I say as I slide from the booth.

His dad whips out a camera and snaps a few pictures as I drape my arm over the kid's shoulders. I know this now has everyone in the bar area watching us, and if others hadn't recognized me before, it will spread through here like wildfire. I also know that this will start a wave of people approaching me and I'm thinking this was a bad idea.

After the kid leaves I start to slide back into the booth just as the waitress returns with our drinks. She places Jules' wine in front of her and then slides my Smithwick's onto my side of the table as she murmurs, "Um . . . your beer is from a few fans up at the bar."

I turn my head as the waitress walks off and look to the bar, trying to suppress a groan when I see three women there, all turned to look at me. They're dressed super slutty and clearly out for a wild evening. I give them a nod in acknowledgment, and because I can feel the weight of Jules' stare on me, I turn to face her.

Her face is impassive and I have no clue what she's thinking. This is really the first time we've been out in public—excluding Houlihan's, of course, but I'm not counting that as a true outing. That's different, with its long-standing fans, as a place to celebrate our wins. We go there knowing we'll be recognized and knowing it's to interact with the fans.

But tonight I do not want to be fucking recognized. I want to put Jules' mind at ease.

With a grunt, I push back out of the booth, round the table, and start to slide in next to Jules. She immediately slides over to give me room.

Turning to face her, I drape an arm over the back cushion and give the rest of the world my back so she knows all I see is her.

"Jules . . . I highly doubt some random piece of ass that Dwayne has hooked up with is going to front him money for an attorney so he can take on the expense and burden of three kids."

"They're not burdens," she mutters.

I roll my eyes. "I know that and you know that, but he doesn't know that. *He* sees them as burdens or else he'd have been there for them. He'd have paid his fucking child support. Now, do I think that man wants something? Fuck yeah, and I'm going to guess it's money."

She blinks at me. "Money?"

"Yeah," I tell her softly. "Think about it. He shows up and gets you all wigged out about taking the kids. Makes a remark at the end about me rolling in dough."

"But he didn't know that you were seeing me when he came," she points out.

"Agreed. So I'm thinking he was going to roll you for a little money but once he recognized my name when I introduced my-self, I think his plans got bigger."

"Son of a bitch," Jules hisses and her eyes fire up with fury. "That asshole."

"Agreed, baby," I tell her, dropping my arm from the cushion to come down around her shoulders. I pull her in for a quick squeeze. "But you and I both know he's going nowhere with that. So I need you to stop worrying about him and to put your worries toward the things that matter . . . namely those little minions."

That gets her and she finally gives me a smile. She takes a deep breath, lets it out and murmurs, "I'm sorry he made me so crazy. Thank you for getting me calmed down and making me see things in a different perspective."

"You're welcome," I say and then lean in to graze my lips against hers.

When I pull back, she gives me a tiny shove against my chest. "Okay, buddy . . . how about go back on your side of the table so I don't get a crick in my neck from trying to look at you sideways."

I chuckle and lean in, grab another quick kiss and then push back along the booth. When I stand up, my foot steps on something and I realize it's someone else's foot.

"Oh, shit," I say as I spin around. "I'm sorry."

Standing there are the three women who sent me a beer, which I now realize Jules never even said a word about. I wonder what she's thinking now.

"Could we get a picture with you, Max?" one of the women says breathlessly as she pushes her chest outward.

"Um . . . I'm kind of on a date," I mutter and take a step back toward the seat I'd just vacated.

"Please," one of the other women says, and I can't tell her apart from the one that just asked me for the picture. They all look the same. Long hair, tiny dresses, big boobs that look fake, and a lot of makeup. "We're such big fans and you took pictures with that little boy a minute ago."

I don't dare turn around and look at Jules, not because I'm afraid she'll be mad but mostly afraid she'll laugh at me.

"Fine," I say with a sigh, and the women all giggle while they swarm me as a waitress gladly steps up to take the phones from the women so she can get pictures for all of them. Their arms go around my waist and I'm assaulted with heavy perfume, and even though I try not to look, standing above them by almost a foot I can't help but see all three of their cleavages. I paste on a smile and keep it there while the waitress snaps photos.

Finally, she finishes and I start to pull away from the women and turn my attention back to the only woman who gets my motor running, when I feel a hand slip into my back pocket. It's quick, there and gone, and then the women are walking off with backward waves at me and continual giggling.

I reach into my back pocket as I turn to face Jules and pull out a piece of paper. It has a name—Maevery—as well as a phone number.

"Did that woman . . ." Jules says, and my gaze slides from the paper to her. "Did that woman just put her phone number in your pocket?"

"Appears so," I mumble as I hand it to her and then flop down in my original seat.

Jules' lips are pressed flat as she grabs the paper, eyeballs it for only a moment, and crumples it in her hand. "She just . . . she just propositioned you while you were on a date."

I just stare at her, waiting for her to blow.

"A date with me," she reiterates.

I nod. "Yeah . . . sorry about that."

"Does that sort of thing happen often?" she grits out, and I'm torn between loving this flash of jealousy from Jules and hating the fact she's upset when she really has had enough upset today.

I tell her the truth. "Not often, but it does happen."

She tilts her head. "And what do you do then?"

I nod down to the paper crumpled in her hand. "I do what you just did. I'm not into random hookups, Jules."

She narrows her eyes at me so I quickly amend, "I haven't been into random hookups in a very long time."

This she should know because I told her truthfully about my bit of a wild period after I broke up with Christine.

Jules gives a heavy sigh and tosses the paper aside. Her eyes are slightly sad but also resolved. "I guess this is the first time I've gotten a glimpse at the ugly side of your fame. It's a bit disconcerting."

"Like I said," I tell her as I reach my hand back across the table, palm up. She doesn't hesitate and puts her hand in mine, where it belongs. "That shit doesn't happen often. It's mostly younger kids who want the autographs and pictures."

"That was kind of cute," she says as her eyes crinkle with amusement.

"It doesn't matter though," I tell her. "I've only got one woman on my mind and that's you."

"Well, that's good," she says with a sweet smile. "Because I've only got one man on my mind and that's you."

"Which is a good transition for me to ask you for a favor," I tell her as I lean across the table. She sits up a little straighter, her look welcoming and eager to give me something.

She wants to give me something.

She wants to make me happy and she's excited to do so.

"I've got three things to ask you for, actually," I tell her.

"Okay," she says, eyes still shining. "Lay it on me."

"First, Thanksgiving is right around the corner and it's not something I traditionally celebrate because, hello . . . Canadian here. But we have a few days off and I was thinking of maybe having a dinner over at my house. Would you be willing to help me?"

"Of course," she says excitedly. "That would be awesome. But I think my dad's going to try to get in for a visit. Is that cool?"

"Totally," I say, and then as an afterthought, "Maybe I should invite my parents for a visit?"

"Oh my God," she says with a laugh. "Are we meeting each other's parents?"

"I guess we are," I tell her with a grin.

"Okay," she says with a nod. "That's one thing. What else do you want?"

"You know I'm flying back on Tuesday afternoon from our game in Pittsburgh, and *Sports World* magazine wants to do my photo shoot that evening. Do you think you could maybe give up painting one night, get a sitter and come with me? I hate that shit and would really like you to be there . . . you know . . . to make me feel not so fucking stupid."

Jules' eyes warm and her lower lip purses out in sympathy. "Of course I will. I'll hold your hand and everything."

I breathe out a sigh of relief because while I really don't need Jules there, it would make it at least bearable and I'd get some extra time with her that week.

"And the third?" she prompts.

"This coming weekend we have back-to-back games in Boston," I tell her hesitantly. "I'd really like you to come with me."

"You want me to come to Boston with you?" she asks, her brows furrowed. "With the kids?"

I give a shake of my head. "No. I want you to myself. I've already asked Kate and she said she'd be glad to have them for the weekend."

"I can't," Jules blurts out without giving my request any thought. This I understand, as she's operating from an overly protective place as well as a place of insecurity in her role as a mom and determining what is appropriate.

I have to let her work this out, but I'm going to make her work it out. "Why not? What's holding you back?"

"I just can't leave the kids for two days," she says firmly.

"Technically it will be three days," I tell her, but before I can let that deter her further, I say, "And who says you can't? Where does it say that mothers can't have time away from their kids?"

"Well," she stammers, "it's just . . . they're just getting settled in with me—"

"Five and half months," I tell her bluntly. "They're settled."

"I don't want to keep pawning the kids off on Kate," she murmurs, and I sense we're getting closer to the heart of the issue.

"Kate has watched the kids twice for you," I point out. "So you and I could go out. And if I'm not mistaken, you've taken Ben one night for a slumber party so she and Zack could have some alone time."

"Yeah, but—"

"No 'buts,' Jules," I say firmly, and I squeeze her hand a little harder. I lean across the table and lower my voice so she knows I'm serious. "You are an incredibly hardworking woman and you are devoted to those kids. You kill yourself to give them what they need. But . . . I need you too and we don't have a lot of time together as it is. I'm asking you . . . please . . . come away with me for a few days and give me some time, okay?"

Jules' face immediately crumples before me. Her brow furrows and her lips flatten for a moment in disgust.

"I am so fucking sorry," she says in a small voice. "I wasn't thinking. Fuck . . . of course we need some time to ourselves, and

God . . . I'm so sorry. You're always the one that takes the back-seat to everything."

"It's okay," I assure her quickly as I see the sheen of tears forming in her eyes.

"No," she says in a ragged breath as she jerks her hand away from mine, only to fling herself out of her side of the booth and onto mine. Her arms fly around my neck and she pushes her face against mine, cheek to cheek, as she whispers, "God, Max . . . I'm so sorry. So selfish. Yes, I will go with you. If you still want me to."

I press my palm to the back of her head, hold her there for a minute before I gently push her away. Her eyes are swimming with apology.

"I'm so damn sorry—" she starts to say but I put my mouth right on hers and make better use of it.

I kiss her hard and fiercely, leaving her breathless and without words when I pull away. I use it as an opportunity to set her straight. "I don't take a backseat to everything, Jules. You're the one that does that. This trip will be as much for you as it is for me, okay?"

She nods at me, smiling, her eyes still looking like they might be on the verge of filling with tears. I want to tell her I love her and that I will do whatever I can to make this work with us, but it's not the time. That time has to be special.

So I tell her the next best thing. "I adore you, Jules. And I know I'll adore you even more tomorrow, and even more the day after that."

And the tears fall.

"Fuck," I mutter as I pull her back to my chest.

She gives a tiny laugh and mumbles. "I adore you too, Max. More and more each day."

And that is enough for now.

# CHAPTER 18

# JULES

"So this is kind of exciting, right?" I ask Max as I stand a few feet away from the stylist chair he's sitting in. He looks extremely uncomfortable with a plastic drape secured around him while the hairstylist works some magic on him.

Not that he needs magic, because he could roll out of bed and easily win the hottest sports bachelor title, but apparently he needs some type of special makeup for the camera—which has already been done—and his hair needs some trimming, which I disagree with. If he didn't look so miserable, I'd have to laugh, but I can't do that to him.

"That's not the word I would use to describe this," Max responds flatly and I have to fight with myself not to grin at his sullenness.

I take a look around. The photo shoot is being done in a downtown Raleigh studio, with nothing but a plain white backdrop and Max. Well, there will be a few different outfits, or so we've been told by the reporter from *Sports World* magazine who is overseeing the shoot and will interview Max at some point. I'm really looking forward to the one that will just be done in training shorts with him curling some dumbbells and flexing his eight-pack, but I don't tell him that because he would not get a kick out of me getting a kick out of this. So I try to look as somber as he does while the stylist runs clippers over his neckline.

I didn't realize there would be this many people here for the photo shoot. In addition to the stylist currently working Max over, there's a makeup artist who is at the next station organizing her implements and a wardrobe specialist who is currently choosing Max's outfits from a clothing rack on wheels. There's also the photographer and his assistant who are right now working on lighting, as well as another woman, who appears to be a general gofer of sorts, but for the most part she hangs in the background and does a lot of texting on her phone while Max gets beautified.

The studio door opens and two women walk in. Both are tall and thin with long flowing hair—one brunette and the other auburn—and without them even saying a word, I know they're models. They're two damn beautiful to be anything else.

"Leigh . . . Amber . . ." the makeup artist says as she spies them. "One of you hit wardrobe, the other go to my chair and we'll get started."

The brunette veers off toward the wardrobe person, who I now see is pulling what looks to be tiny little bikinis off the rack. The blonde heads our way, giving a slight smile to me as I stare at her, then her eyes connect to Max's through the mirror he's facing while his hair gets styled.

His eyes immediately come to mine through the mirror, both eyebrows raised, and he gives me a little shrug.

I give him a little shrug back.

Guess he's going to have some models in the shoot with him.

"Okay," the hairstylist announces as she whips the plastic cape from Max. "You're all done and you can head to wardrobe."

Max shoots out of the chair as the stylist calls out, "Amber . . . I'm ready for you."

Amber takes three hangers of bikinis from the wardrobe person and spins our way, walking quickly to the stylist. She looks again at me, then Max, giving a nod with a smile, and takes the seat he just vacated. I have to wonder what in the hell the stylist and makeup artist will do to these women, because they already look perfect to me.

Max steps into me and his hand goes to my lower back. He starts to push me along with him over to the wardrobe rack. His head leans down to mine and he whispers, "I hate this shit, just so you know."

I struggle not to laugh but merely give a grave nod. "I know, honey. It will all be over soon."

His hand slides up my back, curls around my neck, and he stops me in mid-stride. Bending down, he brushes his mouth against mine lightly before saying, "Thank you again for coming with me."

I turn in to him, bring my hands to his chest and peer up into those fabulous hazel eyes. "You never have to thank me for being there for you. It really is my pleasure, babe."

He grins down at me before his hands encircle my back and he pulls me in close. He lays a quick kiss on top of my head and then releases me before heading over to the wardrobe rack.

It really is quite impressive how everyone seems to move with efficiency, almost like an assembly line of beautiful people getting polished to make them über beautiful. While the wardrobe stylist starts going over the outfits with Max—again, the training shorts being my favorite—the reporter comes up and starts the interview, asking just some basic short questions to get the process started. I take that as my cue it's time for me to get out of the way, so I head over to a long couch up against the back wall, where the woman I pegged as a gofer continues to type on her phone.

When I approach, she looks up and gives me a welcoming smile. She's young . . . maybe late teens, early twenties, and really pretty. She's got long blond hair that seems naturally wavy and she's dressed super trendy in black skinny jeans and ankle boots. She has on a white dress shirt with a tight-fitting light gray sweater over it, the bottom of the shirt sticking out. On her head sits a black fedora, and she has a plethora of Alex and Ani bangles on both wrists.

"Hey," I say as I take a seat on the opposite end from her.

Her smile gets bigger and she turns to face me, crossing one leg over the other and resting her phone facedown on her thigh. "Hey. I'm Camille. This is my dad's studio."

"Oh," I say, clearly having pegged her wrong. "So your dad . . . he's the photographer?"

She glances over at him, her lips curving upward and her eyes shimmering with adoration. "That he is. I'm just hanging out with him this evening and then we're going to catch a late dinner together."

"Cool," I say with a nod and then point a finger at myself. "I'm Julianne but I go by Jules to most everyone."

She tips her head Max's way. "I'm guessing girlfriend, right?"

I give a soft laugh even as my cheeks go pink a little, because I think that's the first time I've been referenced by someone as Max's girlfriend. It kind of feels nice.

"Oh, my gosh," she says as she taps my forearm with her hand. "You're adorable . . . how that just got you a little embarrassed."

My eyes shoot to Max, who looks extremely bored with everything, and then back to Camille. "Well, it's all still a little new and overwhelming to me."

"How long have you two been dating?" she asks, sliding a little closer to me with a look that says, *Hey, let's dish about hot guys.*

"Just a little over six weeks," I tell her. "But it seems like just yesterday we met."

"So how does one go about meeting a famous hockey star?" she asks with a grin. "Because I want to go hang out there."

I laugh and lean in a little closer to her. "We met at a convenience store where I was working."

"No fucking way," she says, her eyes going round.

I nod with a chuckle. "Yeah . . . two rednecks were harassing me and Max sort of ran them off."

"Oh my God . . . that's so romantic."

Sighing, I slide my eyes back over to him and keep them there when I tell her, "You don't even know the half of it."

"Well, we're in for a lot of photos and wardrobe changes and I'm not going anywhere. I want to hear all about it," she says with a grin.

Over the next hour, Camille and I watch from the couch as Max poses for photo after photo. The two bikini models were only used in one setup and that was where he was in his training shorts and nothing but his training shorts. I know it probably should have bothered me, watching Max flex his biceps while each skimpily clad woman flanked his sides, but I couldn't find it within me. They were extremely professional, and in between sets, Max only had eyes for me.

Camille entertained me with stories about famous people she'd met through her dad's work and I learned that she was a senior at the University of North Carolina. She was also very knowledgeable about photography, taking the time to explain some of the lighting and posing techniques.

Finally, when it was all done, Max practically bolted to the bathroom to scrub all the makeup off his face, and when he came out, he looked utterly exhausted and for the first time I felt bad for him. He'd had a really long day, flying back from Pittsburgh and straight into a photo shoot, and while I had my fun teasing him a little bit, it was time to get him home and to bed.

"I want to stay at your place tonight," Max says in the car as we head out of the downtown area.

"Baby . . . you're exhausted. You should sleep in your own bed tonight. As much as I love having you with me, your body's going to suffer for it."

And that's the truth. Max stayed at my house on Saturday night after the "Dwayne fiasco" and again on Sunday, and because Annabelle sleeps in my bed, that meant he slept on the couch.

It also meant I slept on the couch, and while couches are great for cuddling and snuggling for movies or something else that lasts no longer than two hours, they are not great for getting a good night's sleep. In order for both of us to sleep, we had to press ourselves close to each other, which is great in theory but not so great in practicality when you're constantly trying to shift to get comfortable and the temperature of your two bodies together rises to about a thousand degrees Fahrenheit.

"You're probably right," he mutters and then punctuates that with a yawn. Yeah, he's exhausted and needs a good night's sleep. "Maybe you and the kids could stay at my house sometimes," Max suggests.

My nose wrinkles slightly and I tell him straight up, "I don't know. How do we explain that to them? I mean . . . is it kosher to bring them to my boyfriend's house for an overnight? For them to see us sleeping in the same room together?"

"They saw us sleeping on the couch together," he points out, and I giggle when I think about Sunday morning when Annabelle ran out of the bedroom and jumped on top of both of us when she saw us there.

"Let me think about it," I hedge, because while I would love nothing more than to take him up on his offer, I'm just not sure morally that's the right thing to do.

My heart becomes heavy as I realize that Melody would know what to do. She was such a good mom and always seemed to know exactly what her kids could handle and what they needed to be shielded from.

"You know," Max murmurs, breaking into my thoughts. "You could move to a bigger apartment. A three-bedroom."

"Maybe," I say thoughtfully, and on its face, that would definitely give Max and me more time together as he could stay the night. But on the flip side, again . . . is that cool to do with young kids in the house? Again I hedge. "I'd have to check the cost out and see what I could afford."

"Speaking of things you can and can't afford," Max says in a slight change of subject, "I did something that might piss you off."

My head snaps to the left and I look at him across the dim console. He turns his head briefly and glances at me but it's too dark to see much. When he looks back to the road, he says, "I bought you a TV. It's being delivered tomorrow."

"What?" I blurt out.

"Your TV is broken and you need a new one, so I bought you one," he says, and I note there isn't an ounce of apology in his voice.

"Max," I exclaim. "I do not need you buying TVs for me."

"You wouldn't buy it yourself," he points out.

"Because I can't afford it," I retort.

"And I can," he says simply . . . and again, unapologetically.

"I can't accept," I say firmly, crossing my arms over my chest and glaring out the window.

"You can," he says.

"I won't," I promise him.

"Fine," he says with a shrug. "Just don't accept the delivery. They can leave it outside your door. I'm sure someone in the apartment complex could use it. Figure it will get stolen as soon as the sun goes down."

I growl low in my throat and turn in the seat to face him, my eyes narrowing, which is completely lost on him since he's paying attention to the road. "Max . . . it's too expensive. Too extravagant."

"Are you not worth it?" he asks quietly. "What's the difference between that and buying you a pretty piece of jewelry because you're my girl? If I do that, Jules . . . you going to throw that back at me too?"

I open my mouth to tell him yes, that's exactly what I'll do, but then overwhelming shame hits me. Here Max is trying to do something nice for me—and let's face it, he's doing it for the kids too—and I'm being a bitch about it.

With a sigh, I mutter, "I'm sorry I'm being this way. It's just . . . hard for me to—"

"Whoever taught you that it's wrong to accept help, baby?" he murmurs. "Would you not help another person if you had the means to do so? I mean, haven't you done that in the past?"

"Yes," I whisper.

"You pay it forward, Jules," he says, and that causes a jolt of awareness to pulse through me. "I was taught to give and help, not only by my parents but when I've had others help me out when I needed it."

Of course you pay it forward. I know this. It's a great philosophy in life. But I hate that it makes me feel awful to have Max do this for me, because I never want to be viewed as a charity case.

I feel his hand slide over my shoulder then up my neck, where his fingers curl gently around the other side. He gives me a slight squeeze and says, "I'm not going to lie, Jules. From the start, your plight touched me like it would any human with an ounce of compassion, but what you have to realize is it's more than that with me. I've got a vested interest in making you happy because that makes me happy, so you got to know . . . I do this as much for myself as I do it for you. It makes me feel like your man when I can do things for you, and while I've sat back and let you figure things out on your own and stubbornly work your fingers to the bone, we're at the point in our relationship that I should be able to do nice things for you and not have you freak out."

"Max—" I say as I turn my head to face him.

"Jules," he cuts me off softly. "Give this to me, okay?"

God . . . this man.

This utterly beautiful man with a heart made of pure gold and a soul guaranteed to ascend to Heaven the minute his time is up on this earth.

This man who is mine and who cares for me like no man ever has before.

I reach my arm up, wrap it around his wrist and pull his hand away from my neck. I bring it to my mouth, where I turn it and press a kiss to his palm.

"I'll give you anything you want, Max," I tell him quietly. "Anything at all."

And I mean that.

# CHAPTER 19

# MAX

I walk into the training room and see Hawke on one of the tread-mills, running at a breakneck speed. He's drenched with sweat and his face is beet red as he pounds the rubber belt that whizzes under his feet. I'm due to train with Vale in about ten minutes, but I always arrive a little early to get in a short, easy run for warm-up.

I hop up on the treadmill next to Hawke and look over at his screen. He's going into his tenth mile and I blink in surprise. He's not a long-distance runner.

"Dude," I say as I start my treadmill up, set it to a moderate pace and begin a jog. "You're killing it."

He responds with nothing but a grunt. I take this to mean he's too winded to talk so I leave him alone and focus on my own run. Well, not really focusing on the run, but rather enjoying memories of last night with Jules. I ended up taking her to her apartment and going home myself because she was right . . . I needed a good night's sleep and her couch would not have given that to me.

But rather than pull right up to the staircase that led almost directly to her apartment door, I pulled into the back of the lot, right under a large streetlamp that was burned out. In the dark, I leaned across the console and I made out with Jules. We went at it for several minutes, necking in a dark car and fogging up the windows.

We didn't do anything but make out, although I did jack off when I got home, thinking about making out with Jules because she is so fucking fantastic, just memories of kissing her is part of my spank bank.

After fifteen minutes I look at my watch and note that Vale's late.

She's never late, and the first thing I do is worry that something may have happened to her father, although if that were the case, surely Hawke would have said something to me the minute I walked in, right?

I turn my treadmill off and as it slows to a walk I turn to Hawke, who has slowed down his pace quite a bit, and ask, "Where's Vale? We're supposed to train."

He's silent a moment and then his hand reaches out and he stabs the Stop button while he mutters, "She's gone."

"Gone?" I ask in confusion. "Gone where?"

"Back to Sydney," he says, and turns to hop off the treadmill, grabbing a towel he had draped over one of the arm rails and rubbing his face. He doesn't look at me but starts to head out the door and toward the showers.

I grab my own towel along with my iPhone, which I'd put on the treadmill tray, and scramble after him.

"She went back to Sydney?" I press, hot on his heels. "Sydney, Nova Scotia?"

"Yup," is all he says, but there's no mistaking the underlying hint of anger in his voice.

I reach out, grab his arm and turn him toward me. He pulls violently and wrenches away from my grasp but pins his eyes on me, and they are blazing with fury.

"What the fuck, dude? Why did she leave?"

Hawke actually gnashes his teeth together and practically spits out, "Because apparently I can't tell her I love her and so she's punishing me for that."

"What?" I ask, completely dumbfounded.

Hawke takes a step toward me and lowers his voice. "Last week she told me she loved me. I couldn't say it back to her. Thus, she decided she can't be around me anymore and just chose to leave."

"I can't believe it," I mutter, my eyes dropping down in contemplation.

"Well, believe it. She jetted out of here last night."

"No," I say as I raise my gaze back to his. "I can believe Vale left. I can't believe you didn't say it back to her."

Hawke actually rears backward, his face awash with stunned surprise. "Are you serious?"

"Yeah," I tell him honestly. "I am. Life's too short to be hung up on past bitterness. Let it go, man, and wise the fuck up."

He narrows his eyes at me. "I can't make myself feel something that's not there."

"Bullshit," I tell him smoothly. "It's there, you're just too fucking chickenshit to acknowledge it."

He opens his mouth to say something back to me, but then snaps it shut just as quickly. He stares at me a long moment, and I cringe a little when I see disappointment in his eyes that I'd take Vale's side.

I should tell him though that I'm not taking her side. I'm taking love's side, and if Vale were here right now, I'd tell her to get her head out of her ass too and work with Hawke to figure this shit out.

Some of the anger fizzles from Hawke's eyes and his lips press together in a grimace. He gives me a little nod of acknowledgment for my position, but I can tell he doesn't agree with a thing I just said. He turns away and walks into the showers, and I turn in the opposite direction, deciding on a longer run for my workout today, since clearly my session with Vale is not going to happen.

After I get done with my run, I hit the weight room and work on lats and shoulders, finishing up with some core work. I then head into the hallway that winds around the arena and do some reflex work. It's one of my pregame rituals but I also do it when I need to think about something in my personal life.

I take a small ball, bounce it hard from the floor to the wall and then catch it as it comes back my way. But I do it fast, zipping the ball with lightning speed at the floor so it hits the wall and flies back at me in a nanosecond, only to sling it away just as quickly. Someone once told me I looked like Forrest Gump playing Ping-Pong and that I was moving so fast you couldn't even track the ball with your eyes.

I liked doing this though while I let my mind wander, so that my inherent reflexes would get sharpened and my brain wouldn't think too much about where the ball was. I did it so my body just trusted itself to snatch the ball from midair, and while my mind drifted from my actions of catching and throwing, I could ponder other things.

I set up a quick pace, ball going from concrete floor to painted cinder-block wall then back to my hand. I walk down the length of the hallway as I do it.

*Throw, bounce, grab, throw again.*

"Max," I hear from my left, and my rhythm is broken. My

fingers miss the ball by a millimeter and it zings by me to hit the back cinder-block wall before bouncing off the back of my head.

I turn to see Garrett walking toward me.

"What's up?" I ask as I bend over and pick up the ball, which is rolling away from me.

He comes to a stop before me and says, "I take it you haven't seen it yet."

"Seen what?" I ask as I snap the ball to the ground again. I get ten more repetitions in while I see from my peripheral vision Garrett pulling something up on his phone.

"It's a SportsGab article," he says, and I snatch the ball from flight as I turn to him.

"What the fuck's a SportsGab article?" I ask.

"It's like this online blogging community that has articles on all different types of sports stars, focusing in on their personal lives rather than the actual sports they play. Stevie apparently saw this a little bit ago, showed Olivia, and she called me.

I step to Garrett's side and my gaze drops to the screen of his iPhone and I see a headline in big bold print that says, "Cinderella or Gold Digger?"

My eyebrows knit inward in confusion and I look up to Garrett. He nods back down to the phone, which he hands to me and says, "Just read."

I take his phone and with my finger start to scroll the article as I read along silently.

### Cinderella or Gold Digger?

By Camille Parks
SportsGab Contributor
While the hardcore hockey fans probably don't give two iotas about this, you ladies that were holding out hope of

finding your very own Max Fournier to come sweep you off your feet . . . hate to tell you, but "too late." It appears hockey hottie Max Fournier, star goalie of the defending Stanley Cup champion Cold Fury team and current top ten candidate for *Sports World* magazine's Hottest Sports Bachelor, looks to be officially off the market.

I had the pleasure of sitting down for a candid gabfest with Fournier's sweetie, Julianne, and boy did she talk my ear off. I was also able to snap some photos of the two lovebirds while they attended a photo shoot for *Sports World*.

I look at a photograph that scrolls up next and it's a picture from last night of me kissing Jules just before I went over to the wardrobe rack.

I scroll past it to the lines underneath.

They look like a genuine couple, right?

Well, on its face, it would seem so. Julianne has a sweet personality when you first talk to her, and she's not shy at all about telling you how her romance with Max started. But the more of the story you hear, the more skeptical you get.

According to Julianne, Max saved her from possible attack by two very suspicious and aggressive men when she was working at a convenience store.

That's right, ladies!

She works at a convenience store.

Julianne went on and on, and then on and on some more, in nauseating detail about how Max was her hero and saved her from destitution. She apparently is raising some kids from a family member or something, but one has to wonder if this is a true Cinderella story or, in the words of Kanye West, is she a Gold Digger?

I can't tell, but to me, in this photo, I can see a hint of opportunism in her eyes, right?

Or is it just me?

I scroll to the photograph that comes up next. It's with Jules smiling up at me, her hands on my chest, and she does not look like a fucking opportunist. She looks like she adores me.

Below that photograph are just a few more lines.

So pardon me if I'm being a little skeptical here, but I'm sorry . . . no one's story is really that good. There are no real Cinderellas, and let's admit it . . . we see a hot woman who is essentially a nobody on a celebrity's arm, we all pretty much know what she is.

Right?

My blood pressure, which had been consistently rising as I read through the article, peaks out as I digest those last lines and my hand holding the phone starts shaking. I raise my eyes up to Garrett and he stares at me with sympathy.

"This is going to hurt her so bad if she sees it," I rasp out, my head already spinning with how I can tell Jules about it.

"Whoever that chick is, she's a fucking bitch," Garrett growls. "Stevie already left a comment on that post, trying to set the record straight, but man . . . I'd advise you not to read any more. Most of the comments aren't nice."

"Son of a fucking bitch," I snarl as I thrust Garrett's phone back toward him. "Tell me again what this SportsGab thing is? I've never heard of it before, so I'm assuming it's not well known."

Garrett winces. "It's pretty fucking big, dude. Like millions of readers."

"Christ," I mutter as I scrub a frustrated hand through my hair.

I've got to go see Jules.

Now.


I wait in the lobby of Sweetbrier no more than fifteen minutes before Jules comes walking toward me, her step bouncy and her smile warm. I'd had her paged when I first got here but it took a while for her to be able to break away.

"What are you doing here?" she asks in a voice filled with happiness to see me.

I stand from the couch and she halts in mid-stride, the smile sliding off her face.

"Okay," she says slowly. "That's twice in less than a week you've had that look on your face. What's wrong?"

I nod toward the door and reach my hand out to her. "Let's go outside to talk."

She takes my hand, no balking, but I can feel the tension in her grip. I lead her over to what I've come to think of as *our* bench, and we're completely alone as there's a slight nip in the air today, which would ward off the residents from hanging in the courtyard.

When she sits down, I turn to her and lay it out as bluntly as I can. "That girl you talked to last night during the photo shoot . . ."

"Camille," she says hesitantly.

I nod. "She wrote a SportsGab article about me and you and it's not flattering."

"What?" Jules gasps, and my skin crawls with disgust that I have to share this with her.

I hold my phone out to her, the article already queued up. She takes it from me as I murmur, "I'm sorry, baby."

I watch Jules' face as her eyes move back and forth along the lines. Jules has always shown pure grace when she's had to deal with some of the pitfalls that come with my celebrity, but I know she won't laugh her way out of this one.

Her lips pinch tight, her skin goes pale and her eyebrows knit together in confusion and then dismay as she reads further. When she gets to the end, her head slowly rises and she looks at me. "Why would she do something that's so horribly mean?"

I shake my head, rage and sorrow and frustration coursing through me. I take the phone back from her and set it on the bench between us so I can take her hands in mine. "I don't know, Jules, but anyone that knows you knows that's a pack of lies."

"And the millions of others that don't know me?" she whispers, her face awash with humiliation.

"I don't know what to say, Jules," I tell her truthfully. "I never wanted my fame to hurt you, and I know it's done exactly that. I just realized . . . I can't protect you from it. The only thing I can do is tell you to do what others do in this situation and that's ignore it. Come tomorrow, it will be someone else's name in the news."

"And when the kids come home and ask me to explain what a gold digger is, what exactly should I say to that?" she asks, and her voice is now shaking with anger. Before I can answer, she asks with near hysteria, "Or what about my boss here when he sees this? Or my coworkers? What do I say to the people on the streets who will now recognize me? Should I ignore them too if they say bad things?"

My hands go to Jules' shoulders. "Baby . . . trust me that it will blow over—"

"No," she growls at me, and shrugs to dislodge my hands. She stands up from the bench and looks down at me, and my heart nearly crumples in on itself when I see the sheen of tears in her eyes. "This is why I don't want you buying me TVs and shit. I am not a gold digger."

I stand up, now angry at her leap from this article to even remotely hinting I view her that way. "That is not fair, Jules."

She throws her arms out in frustration. "I know it's not. But I'm operating on an overload of emotion right now. Give me some latitude."

My mind immediately eases a little, as Jules—God, dear beautiful but reasonable Jules—is actually seeing this for what it is. Just a really crappy slap at her that's laced with jealousy and vindictiveness, but that doesn't touch who she is.

Not between me and her. She knows I know she's nothing but perfection in my mind.

"Tell me what you want me to do to fix this and I will," I tell her softly. "I'll do anything you want."

"Quit hockey?" she asks, her head tilted to the side.

"Yup," I say without thought, and realize I'm actually okay with that answer.

She rolls her eyes at me. "You are not quitting fucking hockey because I got picked on by the neighborhood bully."

And I'm okay with that answer too.

"Want me to track this bitch down and we go slash her tires?" I ask.

"Maybe," she says, her lips just starting to twitch upward.

"Want me to break into her place and switch out her shampoo for hair removal solution?"

"Now you're talking," Jules says as her smile curves even more.

I step in to her, slip my arms around her waist and look right into her eyes. "I'm sorry someone hurt you. It hurts me that you're hurt."

She nods in understanding. "I'm sorry I took my bitch-moment out on you."

"I think I can handle it," I tell her.

She sighs and rests her forehead against my chest. "I don't understand. I hardly told her anything last night. Just that we met at the convenience store, and eventually I told her about the kids, but it was small talk . . . you know?"

I kiss her on the head and then rest my chin there. "Babe . . . sometimes you have to put a wall around you when you're in the public view. You almost have to treat people with a healthy degree of suspicion. I hate to tell you to do that because one of the things I respect most about you is your openness. Your genuine human nature. But I will tell you . . . if you stick with me, you're going to get photographed and recognized. It's the nature of the beast."

She's silent a moment and then she murmurs, "You kept me so well guarded against this up until now. I was in this protective little bubble and now it's been burst."

"I know," I tell her softly. "And again . . . I'm sorry."

"Don't," she admonishes as she lifts her face to look at me. "That article isn't on you. It's on that bitch who wrote it. I'm just going to have to grow a thicker skin and take my lumps if I want to be with you."

"And you do still want to be with me, right?" I ask . . . you know . . . just to make sure.

She smiles at me, lifts to her tiptoes and gives me a soft kiss. "More than anything."

CHAPTER 20

# JULES

The bus pulls up to the front of the Four Seasons Hotel, and Sutton and I patiently wait for the people in front of us—all friends and family members who traveled to Boston—to disembark. The mood is jubilant and the group is boisterous, and that's because the Cold Fury just whipped Boston's ass 5–2. Max, of course, played brilliantly, and I'm proudly sporting his jersey, which he gave me the other night.

Actually, he gave me and each of the kids a Fournier jersey and I can't wait for all four of us to watch a home game wearing them.

I have to say, this trip to Boston has been awesome so far, and the Cold Fury organization is very thoughtful. Apparently, for every away game, they reserve a block of tickets for traveling family and friends so we can all sit together, and if there's enough coming to a game, they arrange transportation to and from the arena for us as well.

That's not the only thoughtful measure that was taken.

Max found out that Alex Crossman's wife, Sutton, was coming to today's game, although she's not staying over for tomorrow's. Still, he worked with her to arrange it so we would take the same flight, and she picked me up at my apartment first thing this morning to take me to the airport. A friendly gate agent quickly maneuvered us around and got us seats together, and when the tickets were printed, I was stunned to see us sitting in first class.

"We're in first class," I whispered to Sutton.

"Yeah," she said. "Is that a problem?"

Well, shit.

Is it a problem?

Max insisted on buying my plane ticket. I tried to argue with him and I lost. He pulled that whole "I'm your man and I want to do nice things for you" card on me again, and while I can't fault him for that, I'm still feeling overly sensitive about that SportsGab article a few days ago.

I totally tortured myself by reading it over and over again that night, along with the multitude of comments, most of which were hurtful and nasty. I did have to smile when I saw Stevie commented and called Camille a "skanky wannabe reporter with no writing skills and clearly a heroin problem," but I was absolutely floored when I saw that Max had commented.

It was short and simple and fucking awesome.

It simply said: *Camille, this is Max Fournier. I met you the other night at your father's studio. I really like your father; he's a totally stand-up kind of guy. I also have to think that he has to be utterly ashamed at the depths you've sunk to humiliate a woman that is kinder, stronger, smarter, and all around just a better human being than you could ever hope to be. Seriously . . . shame on you.*

I, of course, called Max that night after I read it and I blubbered on the phone to him about how he was my hero.

So when Sutton asked me if flying first class was a problem, I had to admit to myself that deep down it was, because of my sensitivity to that gold digger article. But I also had to give latitude to Max so I could let him be himself with me, which included unparalleled generosity.

I smiled at Sutton and said, "Of course not. That was incredibly sweet of Max to do."

Finally the seats in front of us on the bus empty out and Sutton and I make our way off. I had a blast sitting with her at the game, finding her to be just as open and personable as Stevie and Olivia were with me. Vale, for that matter, too, although Max is a little upset about her leaving the team suddenly. He filled me in on what was going on with her and Hawke and it makes me so sad for them both.

I follow Sutton into the Four Seasons lobby and we sort of follow the rest of the group to a private room the organization booked for a family and friends meal. Because this was an afternoon game, it ended at the perfect time for those who traveled to support the players to come together to celebrate with a dinner. Again, a very nice touch from the organization.

"It will probably be another half hour before the team bus arrives," Sutton says as we enter the private ballroom, which is set up very nicely. Large round tables covered in crisp white linen and studded with china and crystal, each seating ten people. A large bar setup on one end with three bartenders manning it, and at the other end long buffet tables with silver warmers, holding God knows what, but it smells divine. "Come on . . . let's go get a drink and I'll introduce you around."

Sutton was able to introduce me to a few people at the game, but that was just those sitting to the sides, front, and back of us. There were probably forty or so people altogether so I had not met most of them. I suppose as the team captain's wife, Sutton knows everyone.

We make our way to the bar and she and I each order a glass of red wine. We walk around for a bit, talking to a few people, and I impatiently check my watch every five minutes, excited about seeing Max. To tell him what a great game he played. And to make sure he knows how much I adore him.

Sutton's phone rings and she fishes in her purse, bringing it up to her ear. "Hey, kiddo. What's going on?"

I watch as an amused smile plays on her mouth and she shakes her head as she says, "Hold on just a sec," and then looks to me with her hand coming up to cover the speaker. "My little brother . . . with girl issues apparently. I'll just be a minute."

I laugh and wave her off. "I'll be fine."

Sutton walks away and I smile at her retreating back. A happy and a sad smile. Happy for her that she's so close to her brother, and sad for me as a reminder I don't have that special sibling to talk to anymore.

"Well, we want to know if it's true," I hear from behind me, and when I spin around, my guard immediately goes up strong and fast. Cassie and her sister, Allie, are standing there with full resting bitch faces leveled at me.

"Know if what's true?" I ask smoothly, although I'm quite sure I know where they're headed.

"If you're a gold digger or a Cinderella," Cassie says as she looks at me haughtily. "That article was quite interesting."

Allie snickers and then eyes me up and down, taking in the jeans that I got on sale at the Gap and worn New Balance tennis shoes I've had for probably five years. I know she can't find fault with the jersey, since it's brand new, but I know what that look means.

"I'm thinking Cinderella," Allie says to her sister, and I notice her words are slurred. "Just look at those rags she's wearing."

Great . . . I'm dealing with two drunk mean girls who are decked out in high fashion with plenty of sparkling jewelry on display.

I give them both a tight smile. "Well, it's been a pleasure talking with you, but I'm just going to—"

"Oh, boo," Allie says with the fakest smile I've ever seen. She lightly taps my shoulder. "We're just playing around with you. It's part of the ritual . . . a little ribbing from the veteran wives."

"Cassie's not a wife," I can't help but say as I slide my gaze to her.

"No, but I'm with Mikkel," she snaps. "He invited me here this weekend."

"Well, good for you," I say with a sweet smile. "I'm just going to go get another glass of wine."

*After I chug the hell out of this one,* I think to myself.

I start to turn away from the women and a blur of movement catches my attention.

Sutton Crossman stalking across the ballroom floor, furious eyes flicking back and forth between Cassie and Allie. She doesn't cause an actual scene but there is no doubt she is a woman on a mission. I see both women tense up and Allie goes a little pale.

Sutton walks right up to them and in a very low voice that's laced with fury says, "I'm going to advise you two women to turn around and march your nasty, petty asses away from Jules, and I'd advise you to do it quickly."

Allie immediately starts backing up, a mixture of fear and respect on her face as she stares at Sutton. Cassie, however, doesn't take the hint and puffs her chest out like a peacock. "You don't scare me, Sutton. I'm not afraid of you just because you're married to the captain of this team."

"Of course you're not scared," Sutton scoffs. "You're merely jealous I married the captain, and I find it really pathetic."

I take a sip of my wine, hating this confrontation and needing the fortitude.

"Oh, I think you're the jealous one," Cassie hisses, and leans in closer to Sutton. "After all, I had Alex first."

I nearly choke on my wine and feel a little start to come out of my nose, which I hastily wipe at as my eyes turn wildly to Sutton.

Sutton throws her head back and laughs, and it is a genuine, amused laugh. "Oh God, Cassie. Do you know how bad you were in bed? Alex said you would scream like a cat in heat and there was nothing attractive about that at all. Also, he said your blow jobs were awful and he always had to close his eyes and think of some porn he'd watched just to get off."

Cassie's mouth falls open in shock and then sort of opens and closes like a gasping fish. Allie simply turns and walks away, I think embarrassed for her sister's beat-down by the captain's wife and hoping to stay out of the crosshairs.

Finally, Cassie mutters, "That's not true."

"Yeah, well neither is the shit that was written about Jules," Sutton snaps at her with narrowed eyes. "My point being, don't do anything to spread nasty rumors, okay? I won't take kindly to it."

The threat is clear.

Cassie takes the threat to heart and I can see her mind whirling, wondering if she really is that bad in bed, and I can even see her wondering if this will have negative repercussions on her standing with Mikkel. I mean, I'm sure he's already dived into that but she sure as hell wouldn't want him hearing this stuff.

Spinning on her heel, Cassie totters away with her metaphorical tail hanging between her legs. I stare after her just a moment, my mind blown over that exchange, and then I turn to look at Sutton in wonder.

"I thought Max was my hero, but damn, Sutton . . . you're

giving him a run for his money," I murmur as I hold my wineglass up. She clinks hers to mine. "Cheers."

"What was all that about?" I hear from behind me at the exact moment strong arms wrap around my waist. I crane my neck to see Max smiling down at me.

"Cassie and Allie being bitches," Sutton says matter-of-factly. "I ran them off."

I nod in agreement. "Sutton's my hero too."

Max's eyes darken and he growls so deeply I feel it rumble down my own spine. "What the fuck did they say?"

"Nothing," I assure him quickly as I turn around to face him fully. "They're drunk, I think. Just let it go."

Max's eyes travel from mine across the ballroom floor. I turn and see he's locked them on Cassie and Allie.

"Max," I murmur, sliding one hand around his neck. "Let it go, okay?"

He doesn't look at me but keeps his narrowed eyes on the two women.

So I repeat to him, "Max . . . baby . . . it's fine. Right, Sutton?"

I turn to Sutton and . . . she's gone?

I look around and see her standing on the opposite side of the room, on her tiptoes to give Alex a kiss.

"Babe," Max mutters, and I turn to look back at him. "Are you sure you don't want me to say something? I told you those girls are trouble and you should ignore them, but I'm not going to have them treating you badly. The organization won't allow that to happen."

I slide my hand back down and pat Max on the chest. "Honey . . . while you are strong and manly in many ways, and while I get a little horny when you come riding to my rescue, I think in this instance it's best not to stir the hornet's nest, okay?"

And it works. He gets completely distracted.

"Horny?" he asks with a cocked eyebrow.

"Mmmm-hmmm," I answer with a sultry purse of my lips. "I'll show you when we get back to the room."

"Let's go now," he suggests.

"Let's eat dinner first," I counter.

He grins before leaning toward me and kissing my forehead. "Dinner first. But just so you know, I have a special surprise planned when we get back to the room."

"You do?" I ask in delight. "What is it?"

"You do understand the meaning of *surprise*, right?"

I give him a tiny punch—love tap really—in his stomach and grin up at him. "Well, I might have a surprise for you."

"Well, shit," he says sourly. "I obviously want to know what it is."

"Sucks, doesn't it?" I quip.

"Okay, I'll tell you if you tell me. Let's just out our surprises," he suggests.

"Fine. You first."

"Without giving away all details, let's just say I had the hotel do a little romantic setup for us in the room. It might involve candles, roses, and champagne."

My jaw drops open and I give him a harder punch to his stomach and he winces. "I can't believe you just told me that. The surprise is ruined."

"You told me to tell you," he says with a grimace, rubbing his stomach.

I huff and give him a look of mock annoyance. "Well, it's not a surprise anymore."

"Which is what happens when you tell me to tell you the surprise," he points out with a laugh. I can't help it . . . the smile comes.

"So what's my surprise?" he asks as he leans in closer to me. With his lips against my ear he asks, "Am I going to like it?"

I nod and turn my mouth so it's now near his ear and I whisper, "I'm going to give you the best blow job you've ever had. I'm going to suck you until you blow harder than you've ever blown before. Right. Down. My. Throat."

Max shudders and he growls, "Jesus fucking Christ, Jules. You cannot say that to me and not think I'm not going to drag you out of here . . . possibly by your hair like a caveman."

I giggle and step back from him, my hand dropping to his waist, where I give him a little squeeze. "Patience, baby. The wait will make it better."

"I need a drink," he mutters and grabs my hand to lead me toward the bar. "Come on."

I start to follow but he abruptly stops and turns to me. I look up at him and see a soft, tender look on his face.

"And Jules," he says quietly.

"Yes?"

"Thanks for coming this weekend. It means a lot to me."

My heart starts tripping madly over the sincerity in his voice and I have the sudden, maddening urge to fling myself into his arms and kiss him crazily in front of all these people. Then I want to scream out to this entire room that he's mine, mine, mine, and I'm never letting him go.

But I don't do any of those things for fear of being labeled a fool and a gold digger. So I just smile up at him. "*You* mean a lot to me, Max."

He beams a smile at me that lights up the freaking room, and I think I could stare at him like this for hours on end and not ever get tired of it.

Never.

# CHAPTER 21

# MAX

I'll have to admit. This is a weird fucking feeling I've got going on as I step off the team bus and head into the hotel.

We got our asses handed to us tonight. I guess it's payback from the Eagles for us whipping their asses yesterday. One of the main reasons we lost tonight is because I played shitty. I was just a little off, and it was nothing major I could put my finger on, but two goals I'd allowed were definitely my fault.

That is the nature of the beast in professional sports. You play at an elite level because your talent is better and your training is harder than the others. You have more drive and determination. Stronger mental fortitude. Your spirit of competition is unrivaled.

But that doesn't mean you don't have bad games. I learned long ago we're all human and there are going to be some games where I am just off.

Tonight was one of those nights. I accept it and my team accepts it, but it still doesn't mean it's not a pisser. Normally when

I lose a game I'll be in a bad attitude for a solid twenty-four hours. I'll replay in my head every goal I allowed in and what I could have done differently. I'll sulk. I'll be a douche to any team-mate that tries to talk to me, which is okay, because they're all in the same mindset as me. No one is happy after a loss.

The interesting thing is, I haven't had the opportunity to see Jules after a loss. There haven't been many since the regular sea-son started and each one that occurred happened either on the road or on a night when I did not go to see Jules after the game, mainly because I didn't want to disturb her painting with my sour attitude.

But right now, as I walk through the lobby to the elevator doors, along with my entire sulking, grumbling team, I've just got a weird fucking feeling going on. I'm pissed at myself for the loss and I'm in generally bad spirits. That's normal. But I've also got this underlying hum of excitement that Jules is upstairs wait-ing in my room for me, probably prepared to give me emotional support.

I know Jules is in the room because I texted her while I was still in the locker room. We'd made tentative plans to go out for some drinks together.

Alone.

Just me and her.

But my text to her was simple. *Not feeling like going out. See you in the room.*

She wrote back. *Totally understand. See you soon.*

She totally understands.

Because she's Jules.

I cram into the elevator with about ten other guys and we ride up silently, the car stopping on two floors before reaching mine. I get off with two other teammates, none of us saying a word as we walk to our rooms.

Yeah . . . we're all in shitty moods but tomorrow we'll get our heads back on straight and look to the next game.

I slide the plastic key in the slot on the room door, and before I push it all the way in, I consider what is waiting on the other side for me.

Not a team loss.

Not a shitty performance by yours truly.

Not a bitter night of moping.

No second thoughts, recriminations, or self-loathing.

Certainly no fear that I'm losing my touch.

On the other side of this door is a woman who brings so much fulfillment and joy into my world, who believes in me so thoroughly—a woman who utterly fucking brightens even my most miserable fucking situation—there can only be one way that this evening is going to end.

I push the keycard all the way in and when the little light turns green I push down on the lever and open the door.

And there she stands, face all pinched with worry for me and in her hand an icy cold Molson beer that's extended toward me in offering. She took off her Fournier jersey and only has on a pair of jeans and a black turtleneck sweater, her feet covered in fluffy socks.

Stepping in, I shut the door behind me and lock it. I shed my winter coat as my eyes go to the beer. "That for me?"

"Figured you could use it," she says hesitantly and I now see that the worry in her eyes is not only for how I'm feeling after such a loss, but how I'm going to react. "They didn't have any Molson in the minifridge so I went down to the bar in the lobby and got a few for you."

I stare at the beer a minute, then slide my eyes to hers.

"Um . . . I can get more if you want some," she adds quietly.

I hate that uncertainty in her voice. I hate the way she's unsure of how I'll be tonight after a loss. Or how I'll treat her because I might be in a bad mood.

It's just not something we've had to deal with yet in our relationship.

I walk farther into the room, straight to her. I take the Molson and turn to set it on the dresser that holds a large flatscreen TV.

When I turn back to Jules, she looks up at me with sympathetic eyes tinged with quandary. I step closer, bring my hand to her face to lay my palm against her cheek before I slide it around her neck. My fingers go up into her long hair and I feel the cool silkiness slither over my skin. I sift my fingers through briefly before bringing my hand to the back of her neck. My thumb idly grazes her skin while I look down at her.

Noting those eyes that I've come to realize are my favorite part of Jules, because they're so expressive and she can communicate with their power alone. They speak to me when her lips don't.

"Max?" she murmurs. "You okay?"

I nod at her with a smile, let my eyes roam her face for a moment before coming back to lock with hers. "I love you, Jules."

A tiny gasp flutters past her lips and her eyes seem to burst with light, causing them to bloom into golden orbs, which then immediately start to shimmer with a translucent veil of tears. My hand moves from the back of her neck to her cheeks, where I rest my thumb, ready to catch any tears that fall.

"I was going to tell you last night," I say softly. "Had it all planned . . . candlelight, roses, champagne. But honestly, it didn't seem the right time because while last night was magical and romantic, it wasn't really us, you know? I mean, not that I can't be romantic, because I can, but it's not the real us."

She nods at me, and I think she's getting what I'm saying, though just to be sure, I continue on.

"But tonight . . . walking in here and seeing you after I just had a really shitty game, and ordinarily would sulk and bitch and moan about my performance, I took one look at you standing there holding my favorite beer and I realized . . . this is us. Me coming to you after I've had a shit day, and you standing there waiting to take it on. Jules, this was the right time to tell you that I love you. In fact, this was the perfect time."

I watch as she swallows hard and blinks her eyes to chase away the moisture. "I, um . . ." she says in a voice cracking with emotion, and then coughs a little to clear it. "I never thought I'd love someone with the depth that I loved Melody. But then those kids came along, and I realized I was given a gift. And I never thought I'd have room in my life after them to love someone else that deeply, and then you came along, and I knew I'd been given a miracle. Max, I simply can't help but to love you too. You've made it impossible for me to have anything less than love. I don't know what I did to deserve it but I'll be damned if I'm going to ever waste it or take it for granted. I just want to make you as happy as you make me."

In my entire life, there has never been a moment I've experienced like this one. Her words fill me up with such replete gratification . . . such tranquillity . . . absolute realization that I just became a complete man.

I bring my other hand to her face, frame it, and rub my thumbs along her jaw. "Big night for us, huh?"

She winces. "Well, except for the loss."

"What loss?" I ask her with a grin, but she knows I haven't forgotten it.

Merely that I'm choosing to ignore it because this is more important.

"I'm still not quite sure how this happened," Jules says softly. "I mean . . . the chances on how we first met, or that you saw me for a second time at Sweetbrier. It had to be, right?"

"I think so," I agree. "I think someone was telling us we're meant for each other."

She gives a small shake of her head . . . a bit of a skeptical move. "There are times I just don't understand why you're with me. My life has been a shit storm lately. And I come with three kids. What sane man wants that?"

Leaning down, I brush my lips against hers. "Babe, there's no doubt, your life is a bit warty. But it's because of those warts and the way you handle them that causes me to have such deep respect for you. That's part of why I love you, not a reason for me not to."

"Not sure it's really hitting me . . . the enormity of what we just said to each other," she murmurs.

"Or the implied commitment that brings," I add on. "You're stuck with me now, babe. Not going anywhere."

She grins. "Don't want you to."

"On second thought," I say mischievously, "I wouldn't mind moving this to the bed."

Her head turns slightly to look at the bed and then back to me with an impish smile. "Is this the part where you make love to me since we've now professed our deep feelings?"

I look to the bed and then back to her. "No," I drawl out. "I'm still going to fuck you. But I'm going to do it while being deeply in love with you."

Jules laughs, because that's just Jules and her internal sense of humor is so closely matched with my own. Our teasing and lame jokes lobbed at each other are simply a part of the way we communicate. It's part of what makes us both happy to be with each other. I love that despite the fact that Jules' life is complicated, messy, and downright stressful, she still has the easy ability to laugh at any given time.

In fact, that's sexy as fuck to me.

I bring my mouth down to hers and she meets me halfway by pushing up on her toes. Solid, warm . . . so Jules. The minute our lips touch, a ripple of sexual heat moves through my body and my desire for her is magnified by the fact that I know she loves me.

My hands only stay on her face a brief moment, but once that kiss is fully engaged, they're on the move. Dropping to shoulders, skimming down arms, turning inward to grab the hem of her sweater. It's up and over her head, causing a brief disruption in our kiss, but the minute it's free, our mouths are back on each other. Her hands don't stay idle. I push my jacket from my shoulders and then get to work on the buttons of my shirt. I make quick work of her bra, and only because I took the time to use both hands to work the clasp in the back.

I manage to toe my shoes off but no way I'm breaking the kiss to get those socks. I'll worry about them later.

One more brief disruption as Jules tries to frantically get my shirt off but is hampered by the fact that I'm wearing a white cotton tee under it. I take a moment . . . help her out and rip both pieces over my head.

She stares at my chest for a long moment, simply just taking me in before her hands shoot out and start to work at my belt. That spurs me into action, and by the time she's pulling my cock out, I've got my hand shoved down the front of her pants and into sleek wet pussy, which is all mine.

"Oh, wow," Jules mutters against my mouth as I circle her clit with the pad of my finger.

I'd say the same but my breath is nearly robbed when her hand tightens around my dick. An overwhelming sense of urgency grabs hold and I wrench away from her, my chest heaving.

"Get your pants off, baby. No more of this playing around."

She hops to it, shimmying them down her long and perfect legs then sitting her ass on the bed to get them off. Jules gives me a brief glance. "You got to get naked too."

Fuck yeah I do. I start pushing my pants down and then almost bust a rib laughing when Jules adds, "And take your socks off too. There is nothing sexy about fucking a woman while wearing only black dress socks."

She grins at me as the last of her clothes peel free, and I'm just four seconds behind her. I practically lunge at her, grab her around the waist and haul both of our bodies onto the bed, where we come to rest on our sides facing each other.

Her eyes so mesmerizing . . . still golden . . . the color of a lion's mane really, but now with dilated pupils because she's turned on. They stare at me intently and she whispers, "Love you."

I smile, wrap an arm around her waist and tell her, "Love you too."

"Okay, let's get to the fucking part," she exclaims and I'm all over that.

I roll her to her back, settle in between her legs and kiss her again. Long, slow, and wet . . . my tongue works against hers. Her hands slide around me, drag down to my lower back and press in. She rotates her hips, trying to maneuver her body, which puts my cock more in line with the sweetest pussy to grace this earth.

I dig my elbows into the mattress, haul myself up her a few inches and, without taking my mouth from hers, flex my hips. My cock knows exactly where to go and presses against her opening.

Jules gasps into my mouth when I breach her, my leaking tip sliding in easily against her own wetness.

Fuck that feels good. So much better than it ever has before, and I'm man enough to admit that it has to be love. It must change things, because that's the only difference between how it felt fucking Jules last night and tonight.

And last night was awesome, but this . . . sinking into her slowly and knowing that I haven't just conquered her body, but fucking own her heart right now . . .

That's the difference.

When I bottom out in Jules, I lift my mouth from hers and peer down at her. Her eyes are glazed, her lips wet from my kisses, and there's a faint blush running down her neck and across her chest.

Christ, she's so sexy.

I push my torso up, going from elbows to palms on the mattress. I give a test move . . . pulling back and sinking in once again, and Jules' moan in response hits me right in the balls.

I'm afraid I'm not going to last long, but that's okay. This won't be the last time we do this tonight.

I grab one of Jules' hands and drag it between our bodies. I push it right against her pelvis, my hand ultimately wrapping around her index and middle finger. I look down, move her hand slightly down and make her touch her clit.

"Max," she groans and gyrates her hips.

"Touch yourself, baby," I urge her. "I'm pretty sure you'd get off on just what I'm getting ready to do to you, but I don't want to take any chances, okay?"

"Okay," she says with a breathy sigh, and I feel her hand start to move. I watch as she rubs herself for a moment then I push up even farther. I take one of her legs, stretch it out then up and place the back of it running up my chest, her calf coming to rest just below my collarbone.

I slide my palm to her other thigh and lift it to my waist, then rub my hand over her knee, down her shin and to her ankle, where I pull at her leg so it curves around my waist. I feel her press her heel into my ass and I know she's locked in for the ride.

I look down at her again and she stares up at me with foggy lust, but I see a hint of challenge in her eyes. She knows I love her but she also knows I'm going to fuck her.

Leaning over her, I bring my hands back to the mattress. Her leg straight up my chest gives me leverage, causing her to fold slightly at the waist but spreading that pussy a little wider for me. I suck in a breath and then I start to fuck her.

Long, measured strokes . . . making sure I pull almost every inch of my cock out before I thrust it back into her deeply. Each time I power in, she huffs out a breathy moan. I can feel the tips of her fingers as she rubs her clit, sometimes tapping against the base of my dick. I look down in between us and it's hot as fuck watching my cock piston into her . . . see how wet she is because she's so turned on by me.

"Max?" Jules pants at me.

My head snaps up, my hips still powering hard.

"I want it harder," she huffs out, the words sounding staccato because of the pounding I'm giving her.

Fuck . . . harder?

Um . . . yeah, can totally do that.

"I got you," I assure her and kick up the pace. Turn up the speed. Punch my dick deeper into my sweet Jules like she asked me to, and the headboard starts a rhythmic beating up against the wall. I send out a mental apology to whoever's on the other side right now.

"Yes, yes, yes," she starts to chant and that right there adds fuel to my already blazing fire.

I start driving into Jules with an abandon I've never felt. I lurch into her body, possibly wanting to crawl all the way in and brand myself inside of her. Fuse us together.

Make what we have infinite.

I'm caught off guard when Jules' pussy clamps down tight on me and her back bows clear off the bed. Her eyes squeeze tight and her teeth dig into her lower lip and she orgasms so fucking beautifully that I'm completely enthralled.

And when her back relaxes and sinks down to the mattress, she opens those eyes that are now brighter than ever . . . looking like the sun, and she whispers, "I love you," I feel those words all the way through to my balls and straight through to the end of my dick, which slams into her one more time before my entire body seizes up.

Extreme pleasure grabs ahold of me, and the most exquisite and explosive orgasm I've ever felt ricochets through me. A massive shudder quakes up my spine, ripples back down, and when Jules' pussy contracts again on me, a second wave of pleasure hits me so hard, I pull my cock back involuntarily and slam it in again.

I feel myself shoot off again inside of her.

"Oh, fuck," I groan as I pull her leg from my chest so I can drop down onto her, grinding the last of my orgasm out.

Causing her hand that's caught in between us to press back against her clit, and she gives a cry as I feel her body shudder again. I lay there, still in her, completely on her, and wait for our bodies to quiet.

"Motherfucker," I gasp as I move my forehead to rest against hers. "That was . . . that was fucking unbelievable."

"I can't even . . ." she says and then doesn't say anything else because apparently she can't even.

It takes every bit of strength I have to lift my head so I can look down at her. She smiles back up at me, her eyes now glowing softly with complete satisfaction.

"You know the bad part to what just happened, right?" I ask her.

She shakes her head.

"You and I just set the bar incredibly high for ourselves," I point out.

"I am quite sure we can outdo that," she returns confidently.

I grin at her. "I look forward to trying."

"Me too," she agrees.

# CHAPTER 22

# JULES

"Any idea if Max has a pie pan?" Marilyn Fournier asks me from across the island counter of Max's kitchen.

I look up from the green bean casserole I'm putting together, the last item on the list of dishes I'm making for Thanksgiving. I nod toward the stacked set of cabinets beside his refrigerator. "Try in there."

She turns and walks two steps to the cabinets, opens up the top set and hits pay dirt. "Hot damn," she says as she reaches inside. "He actually has a pie dish."

I laugh and return to my task, sprinkling french-fried onions on the top of my casserole.

Max's mother is nothing like I thought she'd be. When he told me she was a public speaking coach, I just assumed that meant she would be professionally sedate. Instead, she's an absolute firecracker, and while I haven't met his father because he's at a medical conference, I totally see he gets his humor from his mom.

Marilyn's just a tad shorter than I am, with golden blond hair that's worn a few inches above her shoulders in big barrel curls. Her face is so youthful, I can't believe she has a twenty-seven-year-old son, and about the only thing that gives her away as a mom is that she does wear mom jeans that sit high on her slim waist.

I only met her yesterday but that was not the first time we'd talked. Max had put me on the phone with her the night he called to invite his parents for Thanksgiving, and I was at an utter loss as to what to say. Turns out, Marilyn was chatty enough for the both of us and she was very excited for the opportunity to come see her son. Since that first talk, she's continued to text me, including several times this week so we could iron out the Thanksgiving meal.

Marilyn is American so she's all on board with the traditional turkey and side dishes, but she's also making some classic French-Canadian dishes for Max and his brother Lucas, who should be arriving very soon from the airport. Max left to go pick him up about half an hour ago and he's beyond excited. He's super close to Lucas, and given that he's just a short plane ride from New Jersey, Lucas also jumped on the chance to come to Raleigh to see his mom and brother.

I am beyond excited as well, to get to know his family better. I'm not quite sure the extent of what Max has told them about me but they'll figure it out soon enough.

Glancing into the den that bleeds right into the open-air kitchen, I see the kids are still firmly rooted to the couches, watching *The Incredibles*. They've been angels today and I can't decide if it's because they're in Max's house for the first time or if they have sensed something's changed between me and Max or even that they're a little shy because of Marilyn being here, although she's been quite engaging with them. Still, she's an older authority figure and maybe that's it.

"I'm going to make a *tourtière* for Max and Lucas," Marilyn says. "It's one of their favorite dishes."

"What is it?" I ask companionably as I pull a piece of Saran Wrap off and cover the casserole. It won't go into the oven for a few hours yet, once the turkey's done.

"It's a meat pie with ground beef and pork, sage, thyme, garlic, cloves. I'll give you the recipe if you want and you can make it for Max."

She smiles at me as she starts pulling items from the refrigerator. Marilyn arrived last night, and first thing she did this morning was hit the grocery store so she could make her dishes, which include obviously the *tourtière,* but also *sucre à la crème,* a sweet, creamy treat the consistency of fudge, and *pouding chômeur,* which is a vanilla cake with maple syrup sauce.

Because it was me and Marilyn doing the cooking and because I had to work yesterday, I went with store-bought pie, even though that brings me a little shame. Still, her homemade desserts will more than make up for it, and we'll just have to suffer with Mrs. Smith's pumpkin pie.

"So how's the painting going?" Marilyn says as she moves to Max's spice cabinet. I wet a washcloth and start to wipe down the counters. "Your work is just stunning."

One of the first things that happened after Max introduced me to his mother was that she raved over the painting Max had bought and shipped to her. She went on for over thirty minutes, which completely embarrassed me. Max got a total kick out of it though.

"It's going well," I say, not willing to admit it's going so much better than I'd expected. I'm still having a hard time accepting that my talent is really worth money. "I'm hoping maybe I can cut back my hours at the nursing home since the money from my art is so much more than I expected. Certainly better than what I made at the gas station."

Marilyn chuckles and shakes her head. "I still can't get over that story about how you met. You know Max called me after he saw you the second time at Sweetbrier and told me how he got your job back for you at the convenience store?"

"He did?" I ask with surprise.

She nods and gives me a sage look. "That boy knew from the start you were the one, Jules."

My heart swells, contracts, and then swells larger with this knowledge, remaining full and light with happiness. "Took me a bit longer to give in to it," I admit candidly. "Your son is so . . . overwhelmingly confident. I'm still convinced he's crazy to be attaching himself to me."

"Why would you say such a thing?" she asks, her head tilted to the side and a jar of cloves in her hand.

My eyes flick to the kids and then back to her. "I'm not an easy person to be with."

"Max isn't easy either," his mom says, and I blink at her in surprise. "He has a grueling work schedule and is gone fifty percent of the time. That has to suck in a relationship."

"But it doesn't," I tell her quickly. "I mean . . . I accept that about him. We work with it."

She nods wisely. "Just as he accepts those kids come with you. And all the trials and tribulations that come with that."

Huh.

Is it that simple?

Do we just accept all those things about our lives, be thankful that there's more good than bad, and work with what we've got?

I think that's what she's saying.

"I love your son," I tell her, my eyes once again sliding over to the kids, who are still engrossed in the TV.

She smiles, her eyes warm and soft. "I know. And let me tell you something about Max. He's the type that loves deeply. He'll not only give you every bit of his heart, but he'll give you his soul."

Oh, wow.

Marilyn pauses, and while the smile remains as warm as ever, I see a bluntness filter into her eyes. "He deserves to have that back."

A lump forms in my throat and I nod in agreement. Max absolutely deserves that in return from me, and with all my heart, that's my intention. I just hope I'm good enough for a man such as him. I hope that as strong as Max thinks I am, I can prove to be exactly what he thinks.

Before I can offer reassurances or at the least a wan smile of agreement, I hear the front door open and a man's voice yell out, "Marilyn Fournier, your favorite son has arrived!"

That is not Max's voice, although there's the same understated accent that Max has. I'm going out on a limb and say it's his brother Lucas.

My guess is proven correct when Max walks into the kitchen, and a man that could pass as his twin walks in behind. Lucas Fournier is almost the exact spitting image of Max, except he wears his wavy hair much longer. But past that, their facial features are almost identical, as well as their body size and height.

Unreal.

Lucas locks eyes on his mother, who puts the spices on the counter and rounds it to greet him. He opens his arms and scoops her up from the waist and spins her around until she cries out, "Stop it, Lucas. I'll get sick."

Max comes to stand beside me, his hands going to my shoulders and his lips to the back of my head briefly.

When Lucas sets his mother down, he turns immediately to me and grins. "And this must be the angel that is rocking my brother's world?"

"Hi, Lucas," I say as I step around the counter and start to reach my hand out for him to shake.

But he's having none of that, also grabbing me around the waist and spinning me like he did his mother. My hands grab on to his shoulders and I hang on for dear life until he puts me down and gives me a smack of a kiss on my cheek. "And you can call me Luc. Only my mom really calls me Lucas, but I will answer to both."

He steps back, runs his eyes up and down me—not lewdly but more in an analytical way—and then he turns to Max. "I approve, bro. Totally approve."

"I'm so glad," Max says dryly and then points into the den. I look over and notice the kids are not watching TV but are instead turned around, all three staring at Luc with their mouths hanging open.

"That's Annabelle, Levy, and Rocco, in order," Max says to introduce my brood to his brother.

Luc takes one look at them, then the TV screen, and says, "Dudes . . . *The Incredibles*. I love that movie."

He walks into the living room and plants himself on the couch right in between Levy and Annabelle. The kids only take a moment to accept his presence then they turn and resume watching TV again.

All but Annabelle. Her gaze slides back to Luc and she says, "You look just like Max."

Lucas winks at Annabelle. "Not true, princess. I'm way better looking than he is."

"I don't think so," she says solemnly.

Luc grins at her and then says, "I'm way more fun though."

Annabelle glances at Max, then back to Luc, trying to ascertain if this is true. She can certainly tell from a glance that Max is absolutely better looking than Luc.

Hands down, in my opinion.

She's not so sold on the fun aspect yet.

"What can I do to help?" Max asks me and his mom.

"I think we're all good," I say as I push past him, giving him a tiny pat on his stomach as I do. I open the oven door and peel back the foil on the turkey to check it out.

When I stand back up, Max is leaning his hip against the counter and his arms are crossed over his chest, and he's blatantly staring at me.

I close the oven door and ask him in an affronted voice, "Were you just staring at my butt?"

"Yup," he says with no remorse.

His mother snickers.

"And it's a damn fine butt too," he adds.

I roll my eyes at him and point to the fridge. "Get a beer for yourself and your brother and go away. You're only in our way."

Max grins at me, but rather than do as I command he merely pulls out the barstool next to him and plops down. He crosses his forearms on the counter and leers at me. "I'd rather watch you."

"Pervert," I mutter under my breath.

"Is your friend Hawke still coming?" Marilyn asks Max.

He glances at his watch and says, "I think so. He told me when I talked to him last night that he'd probably make it."

"How's he doing?" I ask as I pull a pot out from a cabinet beside the oven before setting it on the stove burner and filling it with water from the totally awesome pot filler Max has built into the wall. It's time to get the potatoes going.

"He tries to act like everything's okay but I know it's not," Max says, and I can hear the worry in his voice for his friend.

"What happened?" Marilyn asks, curious.

"His girlfriend broke up with him last week," Max supplies, but doesn't elaborate. While I got full details, I think that's only because I'm Max's girlfriend, and I believe there's some rule that you share shit like that or something. But moms probably don't need the minute details.

"Oh, that's so sad," Marilyn says. "Holidays are a tough time to be alone."

Wiser words.

I wonder what my dad's doing. He totally backed out of Thanksgiving dinner, telling me by phone a few nights ago that the load he'd expected to be driving east from the West Coast got delayed and he wouldn't be able to make it. But he's going to try to come in sometime before Christmas.

I wish I could say I was angry he's not coming but I'm not. We've never been close, and because he was away so much of my time growing up, we just sort of have this very casual relationship. If I see him, great. If I don't, that's fine too. He checks in with me a few times a month, lately a little more frequently since Melody died. He took it really hard, I think perhaps out of regret for not having a better relationship with his daughters and then his grand-children. But as Melody told me once when he would miss yet another holiday or birthday with us, "You can't really miss what you never had."

So true.

Now, Max, on the other hand?

I've only had him for just about two months. I've known my father infinitely longer than Max, and yet I think if Max walked out of my life, I'd never get over that loss. That's how deep my feelings are where he's concerned.

So sit on that little barstool, Max, and stare at me all you want.

You can even think you're being cute and annoying me in that adorable boyfriend kind of way.

Only I know the full truth, that I like having you close by because that's when I'm happiest, so sit on that stool all day long, Max.

I like it.

# CHAPTER 23

# MAX

I look across the room at Hawke, and while he's facing the TV in a slouched, casual position, looking on the verge of a post-turkey coma, I can tell he's not into the football game at all. In fact, he's radiated nothing but tension since he got here. His outgoing personality is completely dampened and it was painful watching him try to interact with all of us when you could tell his mind was hundreds of miles away.

In Sydney, Nova Scotia, with Vale.

I've texted her a few times since she left, and she's responded quickly. All surface stuff, and I don't quite have the guts to ask her point-blank how she's doing, because our friendship has not extended that far. But Hawke's different and I don't have any such qualms.

My gaze slides over to the couch where Luc is conked out, snoring deeply in complete submission to the meal we just had. My mom and Jules took the kids up to the small park in my neighborhood that has an elaborate jungle gym set as well as swings, slides, and other fun things for the kids to climb on. This was my mom's suggestion and I know she did it only so she could spend more time getting to know Jules. My mom and I stayed up pretty late last night talking about her, and I didn't hold anything back.

I'm not a mama's boy by any means, but I am very close to her and I very much respect her opinion. I respect her opinion because she and my father have an incredibly close relationship that has maybe become a little comfortable over the years, but it has never dulled. They're the type of couple that displays affection and shamelessly flirt with each other, even after almost thirty years of marriage. They still joke and laugh together. They still talk. Deep, long discussions.

That's what I want for my future, and I think Jules is the woman I could have that with. It's why I want my mom to really get to know her as best she can while she's here, so I can have her perspective too.

My eyes slide back to Hawke and I say quietly, so as not to wake Luc, although that would be sort of like waking the dead the way he's snoring, "Dude?"

Hawke's head turns my way, eyes completely flat, but one eyebrow raised.

"Want to go play some pool?" I ask.

He doesn't look enthused but he nods and pushes himself up out of the deep cushioned chair he occupies. I push myself up out of the same type of chair, which sits opposite him, and head into the kitchen, grabbing us two beers to take with us. I pop the tops and hand one to Hawke, then he follows me down the back staircase to the basement.

When I reach the bottom landing I turn right into my billiards room. To the left is another sitting area with massive leather furniture and another big-screen TV. On the other side of that room is my home gym, but I rarely use it during hockey season as I do all my training at the arena. It's mostly for me to keep in shape during the summer.

Hawke walks over to the rack on the wall that holds the cue sticks and pulls one down. He then plops down onto one of the high-backed barstools I've got scattered around. I didn't give much thought into furnishing this room other than the red-felt-covered table and vintage Molson beer light hanging over it, so I just purchased the same type of stools that are in the kitchen and threw them down here.

"Before you even ask," Hawke says as I head to the end of the table to rack the balls, "I'm doing fine."

"Don't think you are," I return with a grin to lighten the mood. "It's the eyes, dude. Windows to the soul."

Hawke snickers and takes a sip of his beer. "She's been gone a week and a half. I've moved on."

"You are so fucking full of shit," I tell him as I place the last ball in the rack, roll it, then tighten it before I pull it free.

I step off to the side as Hawke sets his beer on a high round table and walks up to the opposite side of the pool table to break. He bends over, lines up and pulls the stick back, launching it forward quickly. The cue ball hits the tip of the first ball with such force, it hops off the table and hits the wall, where it leaves a dimple in the Sheetrock. I notice that a solid drops into a side pocket, and Hawke doesn't spare my poor wall another glance.

Neither do I because that's not the first time one of my teammates broke the rack in such a way and pelted my wall. There were four other dimples there, and it's why I moved off to the side before he stepped up to the table. Last thing I need is for one of those to catch me in my nuts.

Hawke grabs the cue ball and tosses it to me. I catch it, grab a stick off the wall rack and head back to the table.

"Solids," I call out, since it's my choice, and I place the cue ball back on the table, lining up for an easy shot. But before I bend over I tell him, "Neither one of you are going to be able to move on, Hawke. You have too much history. Fate brought you back together. That shit shouldn't be ignored."

"What the fuck do you know about fate?" he asks with his eyebrow cocked at me.

"Hey, you're looking at a man who is now a true believer in it," I tell him as I line up my shot. "It's what's steering my life right now."

I give a tap to the cue ball and cleanly make my shot.

Hawke snickers at me. "I'm dying to hear this one."

I move around the pool table, trying to figure out my next shot. I stall by picking up the blue chalk and rubbing some on the end of my cue stick. I do this to collect my thoughts because what I'm getting ready to say is as important to me as it is to Hawke.

I clasp my hands at the top of the cue stick and rest my weight against it as I look at my friend. "To boil it down in its simplest form, shit happens for a reason."

"Shit happens for a reason?"

"Pretty much," I say with a grin. "Simplest form and all that."

"Well, the only thing I agree with that you've said is you've equated fate with shit," Hawke says dryly.

I don't respond but go ahead and work on my next shot. I sink it just as easily and start walking around the pool table again. "Listen, all kidding aside, I really don't think you should just write off what you and Vale have together. Your history is deep and you can't take it for granted. Just imagine the odds of her coming back into your life and give some credence to that."

Hawke sighs and his shoulders slump marginally. "You couldn't possibly understand, dude. Things are going so utterly fantastic between you and Jules that you just don't get it."

"Then explain it to me."

His eyes are tortured and filled with pain when they look at me. "Relationships are a two-way street. There is give-and-take on both sides. If you're lucky, it all balances out. But if you ever get out of whack, if just one thing becomes unbalanced, it can cause incredible self-doubt on one or both sides. And it only takes a tiny sliver of that doubt to poison everything."

I give a slow shake of my head. "I can't accept that. If what you have is strong, a tiny shred of doubt shouldn't destroy everything."

"Maybe what we had just wasn't that strong," he offers softly, and I have to say, if Hawke isn't willing to try to work this out with Vale, then he may have a point.

I hear footsteps coming down the wooden staircase and I turn to see Luc trotting down, a small plate with pumpkin pie on it. When he hits the bottom step he says, "Appreciate all this racket down here. You're interfering with my holiday nap."

"You're Canadian," I point out. "This isn't really your holiday."

"Bite me," he says, and then to punctuate his position, he takes a huge mouthful of pie.

Hawke snickers and I turn to the table, line up my next shot, and then miss by almost a mile.

"I see you still suck at pool," Luc says with his mouth half full as he stands there and watches.

"When I finish whooping Hawke's ass here," I tell him with a good-natured smile, "I'll gladly whoop yours too."

"Pipe dream," he mutters and goes back to his pie.

Hawke and I continue trading shots, and we all make small talk. It turns from the serious talk about fate and love I just had going with Hawke to, weirdly enough, an argument over the best technique to get rid of fire ants in the yard.

Ultimately I win, so Luc grabs the rack and starts to load it up with the balls. As he bends over the end of the table he says casually, "Your girl seems nice."

"She's more than," I return.

"Kids are cool too," he adds on.

"Totally," I agree.

"Deep conversation," Hawke mutters as he watches from his barstool, sipping on his beer.

After Luc tightens the rack and removes the triangle, he looks at me across the table. "So how serious are things with you two?"

I chalk my stick up but take a moment to look over at my little brother. "Very serious."

His eyebrows raise up slightly but he nods. "Figured . . . what with you having us come in to meet her and all."

I lean over, position the cue ball, and let it fly at the racked balls. There's a resounding crack and then balls scatter in all directions, but none drop in.

Lucas reaches his hand out for my stick and I give it up. He walks around the table, and as he does, I casually drop, "I'm thinking about asking Jules to move in with me."

My brother's eyebrows shoot halfway up his forehead and he stops his pacing around the pool table to face me. "The kids too?"

I roll my eyes at him. "No, Luc, I thought I'd just leave them where they're at. I'm sure they can take care of themselves."

He's now the one to roll his eyes at me. "I'm just saying, that's a lot. It's one thing to ask a girl to move in but another to ask a girl plus three kids."

"Where Jules goes so too do the kids," I say with a shrug. "It's not a big deal."

"You don't think that's moving a little too fast?" Hawke asks hesitantly, breaching the conversation. I can tell by his tone of voice he's worried about offending me with his skepticism.

But I get it. I think most people would think it's too soon. I intend on talking about this with my mother tonight and I'm quite sure she will have the same concerns.

But I'm not most people. I'm Max Fournier, who is crazy, head over heels in love with Jules Bradley. I don't see that ever changing. And I don't consider her having three children to be a burden. That's part of what makes Jules, well . . . Jules. It's part of why I love her, and fuck if I haven't started to love those rug rats too.

"Is it too fast?" I ask them rhetorically. "Time's subjective, right?"

Yeah, I feel good about this. Still going to talk to my mom about it, and I'm also still going to give it some consideration. While I might be ready to take this next step, I'm anticipating Jules will balk. The key is in making her understand that this is good for the both of us, not something I'm doing to give her a handout, but to further our relationship as a whole.

It sucks that I still must have those considerations in dealing with Jules, but she's still very sensitive about how she's been perceived by others regarding this relationship. This renews my anger against that bitch Camille for writing that article, which did nothing but inflame Jules' own self-doubt.

Luc takes a step toward me, seems to hesitate and then squares his shoulders. "Listen, bro . . . I like Jules. I really do. And those kids are really great. But this is fast. You've only known each other . . . what, a month?"

"Two," I correct him, but even that sounds incredibly short.

"All I'm saying is, how well can you really know someone in that time frame?" he says softly, and I know he's trying to gentle his tone so I don't take offense. "You're rich and famous, and well . . . that attracts—"

"Don't even go there," I growl at him. "Jules isn't like that."

"No, I'm not." I hear her voice from the doorway and all three of us turn around to see Jules standing there, staring at Luc.

I immediately want to punch by brother in the face and then perhaps hit him a second time for good measure, because he's responsible for that closed-off look on Jules' face right now. Just one more person looking at her and assuming she's in this for all the wrong reasons.

"Christ, Jules," Luc says as he takes a step toward her. "I'm sorry . . . I didn't mean it like that. I just—"

Jules holds her hand up, palm facing him in a clear indication to stop. He snaps his mouth shut.

She gives him a hesitant smile and says, "It's okay. I get it."

She then turns to me. "Listen, I'm going to get the kids packed up and head back to my apartment. I just wanted to say goodbye to everyone."

Just . . . fuck. Jules had planned to stay much longer when we made plans for today, but clearly that's her saying she wants out of here.

And now.

I brush past Luc, who looks at me with truly miserable eyes, and I can't really be mad at him. He's being a protective family member. He's known Jules all of a few hours.

I get it.

But he's not my worry right now.

I reach Jules and take her by the elbow, steering her through the TV area and out the back French doors that open up onto a patio. When I close the door behind us, I say, "I'm sorry, babe. He's just being a protective brother."

Her voice is understanding but I know she's still peeved. "No worries. I understand."

And I know she does.

I know she gets it.

But does she truly get that I don't give a fuck about what others think? And that I wish she didn't give a fuck either?

"How much did you hear?" I ask her.

"Not much," she admits. "The part about us not knowing each other long, and then the clearly obvious . . . that you're rich and famous, and the implied statement that I'm not and that obviously is the reason I'm interested in you."

I wince but try to ignore that. "The part you didn't hear . . . the part that spurred that conversation, is I was telling them both that I was going to ask you to move in with me."

She blinks at me in surprise. "With the kids?"

I force my eyes to hold her and not roll around with frustrated annoyance. "Yes, Jules. You and the kids . . . come live with me. They'd each have their own bedroom and you and I could have more time together. And I know how you are, so you can pay me rent or whatever . . . we'll work out the details."

"It's not good timing," she says quietly.

"Why not?" I ask a little forcefully. "Why isn't this good timing?"

"Because I'm clearly a little sensitive to this whole disparity of income thing," she snaps at me, and then immediately looks apologetic. She takes in a deep breath and lets it out. "Look, I'm sorry. I totally understand that's not where you're coming from. I just need to be able to reconcile some things. Your offer is lovely, and I'd be a fool not to consider it. So why not let me think on it a bit. We can talk about this some more, okay?"

"Okay," I say with a forced smile before I pull her into me for a hug. Because I know it will do no good to press her on this. I know Jules needs to arrive at an answer her own way. "But don't go yet. I want to spend some time lounging on the couch together. It's a holiday tradition, I hear."

"You're Canadian," she points out. "What could you possibly know?"

"I'm half Canadian," I tell her with a grin. "My mom is American and I have it on good authority that's what you do after eating volumes of turkey. This isn't my first Thanksgiving rodeo, you know."

Thankfully, she laughs and relaxes in my arms, her prior pique forgotten at least for now. I let out a small smile of relief that I haven't fucked things up too terribly with my girl.

# CHAPTER 24

# JULES

I step out of the dressing room, careful to pick up the long skirt so I don't trip on it. It's about two inches too long but I figure with high heels, it will be the perfect length.

I think.

Not really sure.

Last time I wore a formal gown was for my senior prom. It wasn't the magical, romantic evening most senior high school girls dream of spending with their honeys. I went with a good friend of mine, Johnny Davidson. Neither of us were dating anyone at the time so it seemed like a good idea. There was nothing memorable about that night to me and the memories are dull because of that. I do remember Johnny lighting a joint as we sat in the backseat of his best friend's car, and he was driving, with his date riding shotgun. When he passed it to me, I shook my head to decline, and before he could pull it back across the seat, a single ember broke free and dropped down onto my gold lamé dress, which promptly melted a hole in it the size of a dime.

Good times.

I exit the dressing room, looking for Sutton. I had asked her to come shopping with me because I had no clue what one wore to a celebrity charity gala, for I had never been to a gala, much less a charity one, much much less one that would be swarming with celebrities.

I look down at the strapless silvery-blue dress. The top is done in satin with a shimmery tulle overlay, and the skirt is nothing but several layers of the same shimmery tulle extending full length to the ground so it puffs out just a bit. When I turn back and forth, it swishes prettily and I feel totally fucking awkward in it.

"Oh my God, Jules," I hear Sutton say as she walks back into the dressing area, another gown draped over her arm, this one done in a cranberry red. She looks me up and down, her eyes wide with appreciation. "That's the one."

"Really?" I ask with a healthy dose of skepticism. I haven't had a single "aha" moment with the dresses I've tried on so far, but the choices haven't been that great. I'm working on a very limited budget so I only picked from the sales rack.

"Trust me," she says with a firm nod. "That is totally the one. I'm not even going to let you try this one on."

I look down at the dress and reluctantly admit it's probably my favorite. The color looks really good on me, I suppose. And it's definitely affordable.

Looking back up at Sutton, I say, "All right. This is the one."

"Perfect." She beams at me and then pushes past to the dressing stall I was in and grabs the five dresses I'd already tried on. "I'll just hang these up and then I'll start scoping the perfect pair of heels to go with that. Come meet me in the shoe section when you're done."

"Okay," I say halfheartedly, because honestly, I hate shopping. It's never been something I'd been keen on, probably because

I've always kind of known what I wanted, so browsing racks of clothes never did anything for me but waste time. I was more of an online shopper for the convenience, but I couldn't do that for a formal gown. It was important to nail the fit as time was ticking down. I was a week and a half away from the gala that Max had invited me to weeks ago.

Back then I'd promptly agreed because things were new and exciting.

Since then I've not been as eager, and I think I put off shopping for a dress because the excitement had all but dried up.

That, of course, had mostly to do with the article written about me, which I see still continues to circulate around social media, particularly after Max has a game. I know I shouldn't torture myself by reading that stuff but I can't help it. I'm like the proverbial kid who will put her hand to a hot stove even though her mom told her it would burn and hurt.

After I get the dress off and back on the hanger, and I'm dressed in my own clothes again, I step out of the dressing room. My head is down as I take one more look at the sales price tag to make sure it really is in my price range, and run into another person.

"I'm sorry," I say as I stumble, correct myself and look up. "I wasn't watching where I was going."

A young woman stands there—maybe my age—her arms crossed over her chest and looking at me with absolute disgust on her face. Another woman—about the same age—stands just behind her, not quite as much disgust on her face but her nose is slightly wrinkled.

"Sorry," I mumble again.

"You're totally not good enough for Max," the first woman says prissily.

I blink at her, stunned beyond words. All I can say is, "Excuse me?"

She repeats it slowly, her words sharper. "You're. Not. Good. Enough. For. Max."

My mind swims, trying to figure out who this woman is. A former girlfriend who wants him back?

"I'm sorry," I say as I tilt my chin up at her. "But who are you and how do you know Max?"

She rolls her eyes at me and says, "I don't know him personally. But I am a Cold Fury fan and he's my favorite player. I read that article about you, and he doesn't need someone in his life trying to take advantage of him. It will totally mess up his game and his fans don't want his heart broken when your true nature comes out."

I drop my face, looking down to the gown in my hand and mumble to myself under my breath, "You've got to be fucking kidding me."

Taking a deep breath, I lift my gaze back up to her and paint on the brightest smile I can muster. It's completely fake and my cheeks immediately strain trying to hold it. "Well, I respect your opinion on that but have to disagree. Now, if you'll excuse me, I have to be going."

As I push past her and the other woman, she gets her last dig in by muttering "Gold digger" as I walk away.

I exit the dressing area and turn to the rack just outside that holds an array of shirts and blouses. Not caring that the dress doesn't belong there, I shove it in until the hooked end of the hanger catches on the bar and then walk away.

A slight sting in my nose alerts me to impending tears, so I take in a few harsh breaths and try to conjure up images of puppies and babies, two things guaranteed to brighten any day. It doesn't work on my current mood but it at least averts a full-fledged crying jag.

I quickly locate the shoe section and Sutton sees me coming. She holds up a pair of silver high-heeled sandals and beams at me. "These will be perfect with that dress."

Conjuring back up that fake smile, I tell her, "I'm not sold on it. I want to think about it a bit more and maybe try some other stores."

"Okay, let's go," she says as she puts the shoes back down. "Let's do this."

"Maybe some other time," I tell her softly as we walk through the department store. "I'm really tired and want to call it a night."

Tina's watching the kids for me as Max is at an away game. There's nothing I want more right now than to go home and cuddle with them for a bit. Levy and Rocco probably won't be hip to that but Annabelle is always good for some snuggles.

Sutton looks at me doubtfully but she doesn't say anything.

Which is good.

I don't feel like talking about all of the crappy feelings overwhelming me right now.


I sit before my easel, staring at the blank canvas. The apartment is silent, the kids having gone to bed a few hours ago. I do my painting in the kitchen, as it affords the most room to lay out my materials, and my easel is a tabletop model so it's really the only place to paint.

I've been sitting here for as long as the kids have been down, trying to get some inspiration, but nothing's coming.

My gaze drags over to the envelope sitting beside my easel.

Blocky, messy handwriting with my name and address.

Postmarked from Atlanta.

The return address is one I don't recognize, but the name above it I do.

Dwayne Collins, my brother-in-law.

I've been trying to ignore it, knowing that the minute I open it and read what's inside, my world is going to be turned upside down. I know this because it's a statistical impossibility that the contents of that envelope contain an apology or back-due child support. This is Dwayne we're talking about. He's an opportunist, and so that means whatever is in the envelope is geared toward benefiting him and hurting his kids.

No doubt whatsoever.

I turn back to the canvas and stare at it. I haven't even bothered picking up my brush. Haven't bothered to mix colors or fill my palette with my choices. I just stare at the blank canvas because right now my brain doesn't seem to be able to handle anything more than the soothing white of it staring back at me. It's simple and uncomplicated.

Something I desperately need right now.

Simple.

Uncomplicated.

Easy.

My eyes go back to the envelope, and with a sigh I pick it up because I can't ignore it forever. I break the seal, run my finger along the inside to rip an opening down the length, and pull out a pack of papers that once I unfold them look to be no more than four to five pages.

The top is a handwritten note from Dwayne, which I don't read right away but pull off to see what's underneath. My blood goes icy within my veins when I take in the fact that it's clearly a legal document and it's entitled "Petition to Terminate Guardianship."

I try to suck in air but precious little gets in, and when it comes back out, it's in a painful wheeze. I drop the document and look back to the handwritten note by Dwayne, feeling that same sting in my nose that I felt earlier today at the department store when I was reminded that I'm considered by most to be a gold digger.

My eyes fly over the page.

> *Julianne,*
>
> *I've been to see an attorney to discuss my rights as a father to Rocco, Levy, and Annabelle. I'm told that I have a good shot at getting them back from you. The attorney drafted this up and all I have to do is file it with the court.*
>
> *I'm still considering what's best for all involved. Call me and maybe we can work things out.*
>
> *Dwayne*

He's bluffing.

He has to be. Dwayne doesn't want those kids. He's never wanted those kids. He's only wanted freedom to do what makes Dwayne feel best, and he wants the money to do it.

I look back at the petition and it appears legit. I'm thinking maybe he invested a little bit of cash into an attorney to draft this, hoping the payout would be bigger.

At least that's what I hope is going on. To consider that he's actually serious about this is something my already overtaxed and emotional head can't handle right now. Let's not even discuss what this is doing to my heart.

I consider calling Dwayne right now but I know deep down it's not a good idea. I take stock of my emotions, and in addition to helplessness and frustration, I'm feeling a great deal of anger toward him.

Toward that woman in the dressing room.

Toward Luc.

Toward Camille.

Toward everything and everyone that has caused me so much anxiety and self-doubt lately.

I turn to my box of paints and pick a few colors. Blue, black, purple.

Dark colors.

They match my mood.

Because inspiration has hit me like a freight train, I decide to go with it and leave Dwayne until tomorrow, when I'll have a clearer head. I decide to focus these feelings onto the canvas and perhaps create something that will not only help to purge me of this nastiness, but will be evocative enough to entice someone to buy it.

I paint, getting lost in the feeling and letting my talent transform my emotion into a story on canvas. I paint solidly for over an hour, never once taking a break or second-guessing where I'm going with this piece of art.

I paint, and I paint, and I paint, sinking deeper and deeper into it.

My phone rings, and at first it barely penetrates. My psyche seems to want to shut everything out.

But it continues to ring and I finally drag my gaze away from the canvas and look down at it.

Max is calling.

I note the time and realize he's been playing an away game the last few hours against the Chicago Bobcats. I've gotten used to watching all of his games on the big flat-screen TV he'd bought for me and I reluctantly accepted.

*Not a gold digger. Not a gold digger.*

But tonight I completely forgot about it, so completely immersed in my problems. A flash of guilt sweeps through me and I feel terrible because in addition to all of my other perceived failings, tonight I've forgotten to be a good girlfriend.

I set my paintbrush down, the loaded bristles resting on the edge of my palette, and reach slowly for the phone.

But then I stop.

Today has gone down as one of the shittiest I've had in my life since Melody died, and I know if I pick up that phone, I'm going to have to tell Max all about it. I have no idea if my man won or lost his game, only that I have nothing good to offer him tonight. I absolutely do not want to burden him with my oversensitivity to what others think of me or the messy problems that Dwayne has created.

I don't want to tell him any of these things because I'm scared that one day soon he's going to really wake up and notice what he's getting with me, and I'm terrified that it will become clear to him that I'm not the catch he thinks I am.

So I pick my brush back up and I keep painting.

# CHAPTER 25

# MAX

"Can I get your autograph, Mr. Fournier?" I hear from behind me. I only give a quick glance over my shoulder, keeping my hands firmly gripped to Annabelle's waist as she navigates a horizontal rope bridge that sits a few feet off the ground. "Sure thing. Give me just a second."

I walk with Annabelle along the entire length of the bridge, the kid asking for an autograph following along with me. As Annabelle hops down, I glance over at Jules, who's pushing Levy on a tire swing. Beyond her, Kate and Zack are standing atop a wide slide built into a little hill, watching as Ben and Rocco take turns sliding down it and running back up the hill again.

"I want to do it again," Annabelle says as she tugs on the hem of my shirt.

"Anything for you, cutie," I say as I ruffle her hair. "Give me just a second."

I turn to the kid. A boy, maybe about ten. His parents are hovering close by, looking worried they may be imposing. And they sort of are, but it's what you do when you're in my position. You never take for granted any child who might be looking up to you as a role model. If I were to be an ass to this kid, tell him I'm too busy, what does that teach him?

To be an asshole.

I take a moment, sign the autograph, and then pose for a few pictures, all while Annabelle watches me carefully. When I'm done, I take her by the hand and lead her back to the beginning of the rope bridge. It's a moderately chilly day for North Carolina, which means mid-fifties for December, hence there aren't a ton of people out here today.

"Why did you write on that piece of paper?" she asks me as I lift her back up. She places her feet carefully, one in front of the other, her hands holding on to the ropes at her side. My hands go back to her waist as she starts walking it.

"You know I play hockey, right?" I ask her. "As my job."

"Uh-huh."

"Well, I have fans . . . and they like to collect my signature or take pictures with me," I explain to her.

"What's a fan?" she asks, not taking her eyes off her feet, but truly invested in the conversation.

I laugh and try to give the simplest explanation. "A fan is someone that really, really likes me."

"Then I'm your fan too," she says, and fuck . . . if that doesn't cause my heart to melt.

Seems it's been doing that a lot around these kids, the more I spend time with them. Jules has done just a remarkable job of keeping them centered and grounded. They're good kids—not without some faults, but for the most part my day is always better anytime I can spend with them.

A glance back over at Jules and I see her watching us, a light smile on her face. I wink at her. Her smile doesn't lessen but it doesn't get any brighter either as she turns back to give another push to Levy.

Something's wrong with her.

I have no clue what it is, because when I ask her she insists nothing is wrong.

But I know differently. She's been a little distant since I got back from Chicago yesterday. Hell, the distance actually started when I was in Chicago, because for the first time ever, she didn't answer the phone when I called her. It has become our ritual when I'm at an away game: I call her as soon as I make it back to the hotel and we talk about the game: She'd taken to watching my games with fervor, chattering away at me excitedly if we won, or with softly empathetic tones if we lost. But she didn't pick up the phone the other night and it made me wonder.

If I'd had my way about things, I would have preferred to spend today alone with her. We'd talked about it earlier this week, because Kate and Zack were going to use his day off today to take Ben to the Durham Life and Science museum. They'd invited Annabelle, Levy, and Rocco to go along and thus it was the perfect opportunity for me and Jules to have a day to ourselves. I figured maybe we'd go out to lunch, and then perhaps back to my house, where we'd spend the rest of the day in bed.

Good plan, except Jules didn't want to do that. Instead she wanted to go with the kids, and I wasn't about to tell her no. Spending time with them was just as important to me, and I figured that one day Jules would be mine in all ways. That might mean moving in together or it might mean marriage, but for now I had to take what I could get from her and it didn't bother me in the slightest. As long as we could be together, it didn't matter if it was when I was balls deep in her or hanging out with her and the kids.

Any Jules time was perfect time.

Except when she's like this.

Distant.

Closed off.

Unapproachable.

I have no fucking clue what's going on, but figure I'll try again tonight after the kids go to bed. I'm staying the night whether she likes it or not, and I'm willing to battle a sore back from her couch.

Annabelle jumps down at the end of the ladder and yells, "Again."

"Of course, again," I tell her.

I glance again at Jules as she pushes Levy on the tire swing, and hesitate when I see him grab the ropes and pull himself up to a standing position.

"Levy," Jules snaps at him. "Sit back down."

He doesn't obey and instead uses leverage on the peak of the back swing to propel the swing higher.

"Watch, Aunt Jules," he exclaims when at the peak of the front swing he launches himself off the tire. He doesn't get much air but I'll admit my heart jumps into my throat as I watch him hurtle toward the ground, where thankfully he lands with grace on his two feet.

I start to lift Annabelle up the ladder, but Jules is stalking toward Levy, her face a mask of fury that stops me. She reaches him, grabs him by the arm and leans over to get in his face, where she yells, "Damn it, Levy. When I tell you to do something, you better damn well do it."

To perhaps any other parent, this wouldn't seem like an over-the-top reaction for a child who doesn't listen and willingly does something stupid where they could be hurt. But not once since we've been together have I ever heard Jules yell at one of the kids. And it's not just that she yelled, but that she did it while holding on to his arm and with anger vibrating from every pore on her body. She yelled loud, and it garnered the attention of everyone in the vicinity.

"I'm sorry, Aunt Jules," Levy says, the tears immediately welling up in his eyes.

I start walking their way and then pick up the pace when she tells him furiously, "I'm so tired of you not listening to me. Just sick and tired of it."

She says this last part as she releases his arm and practically snarls at him, "Come on. We're going home. If you can't behave, you don't deserve to play out here."

"Whoa," I say softly as I reach her, my hand going to her lower back. I note Zack and Kate watching with worried eyes, and they start to come down the hill now that they've heard Jules proclaim we're leaving. I drop my voice lower and lean in toward Jules' ear. "Babe . . . let's just calm down."

She spins on me, Levy forgotten. "Don't tell me to calm down, Max. I don't need your patronization."

"Hey," I say softly, my hand coming to her cheek. "I'm not patronizing you. I'm sorry. If you want to go, we'll go."

Jules doesn't meet my gaze but her eyes take in Levy crying, Zack and Kate hovering nearby, and a few other parents in the area watching carefully.

Finally, her eyes lift to mine and it's a gut punch when I see the self-loathing in them burning through the layer of tears that are welling up. She whispers to me with a husky voice on the verge of a meltdown. A small voice. "Can you take me home?"

I nod and turn to Kate. "Mind taking the kids for the rest of the day? I'll come pick them up a little later."

Kate nods, holds her arms out silently, telling the kids to gather near her. "Come on, kiddos . . . why don't we go get some hot chocolate."

They all walk toward Kate as Jules stares blankly at my chest. I reach down to take her hand, but she suddenly spins from me, rushes over to Levy and drops down before him on her knees. She wraps her arms around him and pulls him into a hug, squeezing him hard and whispering fiercely, "I'm sorry I yelled at you. You just scared me and it made me angry but I shouldn't have done that."

When she pulls back, Levy smiles at her and then throws his arms around her neck for another hug. "It's okay. I shouldn't have jumped."

She nods her understanding and releases him. She then gives Rocco and Annabelle hugs too, and a murmur of thanks to Kate and Zack before turning back to me.

"Come on." I hold my hand out to her. "Let me take you to lunch. We'll relax, maybe have a few beers and talk."

She takes my hand but she shakes her head. "I don't want to go out. Just to my place."

Her voice is still so small but it's also firm.

While I'd rather not have her go to the apartment to sulk, I'm not going to argue with her either. I have a sinking feeling that things are definitely off between us, so I need to give her the room to air those things as she sees fit.


The ride back to Jules' apartment was silent and tense. I had no clue how to go about effectuating conversation. Had no clue if she was receptive to it.

Ultimately, I decided to hold my tongue until we got to her place, because I suspected that my attention should be on her fully and not on the road while I was driving.

When we walk in, she immediately goes to the refrigerator. "Want something to drink?"

"I'm good," I tell her and watch as she opens the door, stares for a few moments at the inside, and then closes it with a sigh, not taking anything out.

When she turns to me, her face is worried. "I was awful to Levy."

"You were a mother to Levy," I correct as I walk to the couch and sit down. I pat the cushion beside me and she trudges my way, shoulders slumped.

When she sits down, I note it's not right beside me but rather she leaves about a foot between us. I let it go and turn to face her. "What's going on, Jules? And don't give me that 'nothing's wrong' shit you've been handing me since I got back from Chicago."

She stares down at her lap a moment, and I think she may indeed tell me nothing's wrong, but then she murmurs, "I don't want to go to that charity gala next weekend."

"What?" I ask, completely taken aback. Of all the things I thought might be bothering her, this wasn't at the top of my imaginative list.

Jules angles her head and brings her eyes to mine. "I don't want to go to the gala," she repeats.

"Okay," I respond slowly, sensing that this is just a front for what's really going on. "Want to tell me why?"

"It's just . . . overwhelming to me."

"I'll be by your side the entire time," I provide, hoping to not necessarily coax her into going, but rather trying to get to the root of the true issue.

"I know," she says with a frustrated huff. "I just . . . I don't like being on display like that."

"On display?" I ask, confused. No clue what she's talking about. "You wouldn't be."

Her eyes harden somewhat and she says, "Let me be clearer

then. I don't like people looking at me with you and second-guessing my motives to be there by your side."

And understanding hits me. "Is this because of what Luc said at Thanksgiving? Because I thought we were past that."

It's true. We haven't talked about that since, just as we've had no further conversation about her moving in with me, despite the fact I've brought it up twice and only got an "I'm still thinking about it" from her.

"It's not that," she mutters, her gaze dropping again.

My hand goes to her jaw and I make her look up at me. I lean in closer and urge her, "Then tell me what it is."

I'm stunned when Jules jerks her face away from me and shoots up off the couch, only to spin back around and face me with her arms outstretched in a plea for understanding.

"It's everything, Max," she says desperately. "You're rich and I'm poor. Women slipping you their phone numbers and bikini models at fancy photo shoots for hot bachelor competitions. It's people judging me . . . writing terrible things about me that I can't defend. It's your teammates' wives and girlfriends who don't even have the grace to whisper behind my back that I can't afford designer clothes, but instead snidely tell it to my face. It's about being out in fucking public and having your fans accost me, telling me I'm not good enough for you and calling me a fucking gold digger to my face."

"What?" I snarl as I come off the couch. "When did that happen?"

Jules seems to deflate in front of me, her anger expended by her rant. She lets out a pained breath and drops her eyes to the floor, "It doesn't matter."

"It does matter," I insist as my hands come to her shoulders. She raises her face, and my stomach pitches when I see a flatness there I've never seen before. "It doesn't matter because nothing can be done about it. It's something I have to accept, and Max . . . I'm sorry, but it's just not easy to be with you sometimes."

"Jules," I say softly as I pull her into me. I wrap my arms carefully around her, cocooning her in safety.

She turns her head and rests her cheek against my chest. I'm partially relieved when her arms come around my waist and gather me tight.

"Did you ever have something really good happen to you?" Jules murmurs as we hold each other. "Something so fucking fantastic that you start to worry about when that bubble will burst, and then you start worrying about the pain it will cause you. And you don't want pain. You're tired of it so you want to avoid it at all costs. So you end up not enjoying that really great thing because all you can think about is the inevitability of its loss and what that will do to you."

"You're not going to lose me," I assure her.

"Maybe not," she agrees. "But I can't help but worry about it constantly. I can't help being sensitive to what others are saying, and fuck, Max . . . I don't even want to go out in public with you. It's just not easy, and I really need easy in my life right now."

I don't even know what to fucking say to any of this. I have no clue how to alleviate her worries. But apparently I haven't heard it all, because she pulls away from me slightly and releases her hold. I do the same, sensing she needs a bit of space.

Jules steps back, puts her hands in her pockets and says, "Dwayne wrote me. He's contacted an attorney and he says he's going to petition the court to terminate my guardianship."

"That will never fucking happen," I growl, suddenly forgetting everything else that Jules told me, and I know that this wave of protectiveness that just burst forth is not only for Jules but for those kids.

She gives me a sad smile. "It's just another thing in my life that I have to deal with, and I will deal with it. But . . . I need to make my life easier so I can keep my head clear. If I have to battle for those kids—"

"Are you saying you want to break up?" I cut in, needing to know exactly where the fuck she's going with this.

My knees almost buckle when she shakes her head and says, "No. That's not what I'm saying. But I do think things have moved fast, and I have so many other things going on, that I'm not really sure what I want. I guess if I had to pinpoint what would be the best thing, it would be for us to maybe slow down a bit."

"Slow down?" I ask, my tongue thick and my head spinning as to what this means.

"I need some space," she says sadly. "I need to prioritize and those kids have to come first. So I don't want to have to be worrying about buying ball gowns or going out to lunch with you, constantly worried that someone's going to come up and say terrible things to me. I just need a little bit of peace in my life right now so I can focus on the important things."

Those important things not including me, I think bitterly.

"That sounds an awful lot like we're breaking up," I say harshly.

"No, Max," she says, and I have to admit, her voice sounds strong and steady. "I just want things to slow down. I don't want to go to that gala . . . it's simply too stressful for me. And I don't want to discuss moving in together. And I don't want to go to Houlihan's with you after a game, and I don't even want to show my face at the arena to watch you in a game, because it stresses me out constantly worrying what people think. It stresses me out to be on guard all the time, waiting for someone to attack me, and let's not even get into the fact I'm now worried that the kids will somehow get dragged into the spotlight and that is something I cannot ever let happen."

I finally reach my breaking point in this crazy conversation. "For fuck's sake, Jules. At some point you can't lead your life worried about what others think."

"You're right," she says softly. "And maybe if my life were normal, I'd have a bit more fortitude to push past this. But my life isn't normal. It's messy and stressful and tiring and I can't handle one more thing. So I have to cut out some of that mess."

"You need to cut me out," I throw out.

"No," she says again firmly.

"Oh, I get it," I say with a sarcastic smile. "You still want to see me, but you won't go out in public with me and you won't come to my games to support me. You only want it to be secretive, right? Maybe I come over here for dinner, or you come to my house once a week and we'll fuck. Is that it?"

"God no," she exclaims, taking a step toward me. "It's not like that."

"Let me see if I can get this straight," I say, trying to force my voice to be calm. "You don't want to go to any events with me, right?"

She gives a small nod.

"Or out to lunch or dinner? Anywhere in public basically."

Another nod, her mouth drawing into a frown.

"Don't want to come to my games?"

"Just until things settle down," she says softly.

"And when might that be, Jules?" I murmur. "Because your life is messy, yes, but it could be that way for a very long time. Fuck . . . it might be messy until those kids come of age and leave home. Want me to wait that long? Keep you hidden in my room and bring you out to fuck you periodically, but otherwise keep you a secret?"

"That's not how it would be," she maintains, her voice sounding a bit panic-stricken. "I'm not saying it right."

"No, Jules, you're saying it right. I understand. You don't have it within you to put aside some of this petty bullshit a handful of people have lobbed your way. You don't have it within you to focus on what matters."

"That's what I'm doing!" she cries out in frustration.

"But I'm not included in that small circle of things you're focusing on," I point out.

She almost growls in annoyance at me. "Max . . . I feel like someone's tied lead weights to my feet and then went and dumped me in the ocean. I'm getting pulled down and I can't fight my way back up because the weight is too fucking heavy."

I huff out a breath of frustration, jam my hands down into my pockets. "I've tried to help you cut that rope repeatedly, Jules, but you won't let me. I'm strong enough to pull you back up but you won't let me."

"I know. I get that—" she says, but I cut her off.

"More importantly, your little analogy about the weight and the rope . . . well, you pretty much are saying I'm dragging you down. Clearly I can't help take the weight off if I'm the one adding to it."

She opens her mouth to argue against that but then just as quickly shuts it. Her eyes drop to the floor and her shoulders slump farther. She gives me no further argument and that's fine.

I don't have it in me to keep going around in circles with her.

"I'm going to head out," I say softly, turning toward the door. When I reach it, I hesitate just a moment. I don't look back at her, but I leave the ball in her court. "If you change your mind and figure there's room for me in your life, let me know."

"Max, there is room," she says desperately.

"Not enough," I say as I open the door and step through it, pulling it shut quietly behind me.

# CHAPTER 26

# JULES

I push open the door to Fleurish with my hip, struggling with the three canvases under one arm and two under the other. A merry chime of bells greets me and I hear Stevie yell from somewhere in the back of the store, "Be right out."

Stepping in, I squat to release my hold on the paintings before they fall and then carefully restack them to lean against an open armoire standing up against the near wall. It's filled with a variety of knickknacks that appear to be for sale.

"Jules?" I hear Stevie's surprised voice and turn around to face him. "What are you doing here? You weren't supposed to come until Monday."

I shrug. "I got more paintings done than I figured I would, so I thought I'd go ahead and bring them by."

Yup. Got twice as many paintings done this past week because my time has been freed up yet again by the fact I haven't seen Max since our—um, argument?—a week ago to the day. Turns out, although we may have not seen each other every day before said argument, due to his travel schedule, he was still very much a daily presence in my life, with long telephone calls, FaceTime, or text chats. Without those taking up my time, and thus feeling the keen loss of his presence, I channeled my resulting miseries into my art.

It made me quite productive.

That's not to say it's been pure radio silence between me and Max. He's been gone most of this week with away games in Ottawa and Montreal but we have shared a few texts. Well, I texted him after each game—one win and one loss—and he texted back.

The texts were short.

They were impersonal.

It fucking hurt that he wouldn't engage with me.

"Well, let me see them," Stevie says, and I blink away my dark thoughts before they make me cry. I watch as he turns to where I'd displayed the paintings and he walks down the line of them, hand to his chin as he evaluates them with a critical eye.

"These are really different than your other stuff," he says casually.

"I know," I say with a low murmur. They're all moody, bordering on depressing, which is exactly how I've felt this week while I let my feelings out onto the canvases.

"But I like them," he adds, and turns to face me with a smile. "I'm going to keep two here for the shop and I think it's time we up the price on them a little. I'll send the others out to some of the local retailers."

"Awesome," I say, feeling somewhat heartened by the fact he thinks my work can get an even better price. I'm making a steady income now from my art, and even have a nice savings account started. I look past Stevie to the back. "Olivia working today?"

"Nope," he says and then looks at his watch. "She's getting

ready for the gala tonight, and speaking of which . . . why aren't you doing the same? It starts in a few hours."

My body goes stiff at the mention of the gala, even as my stomach pitches at the thought of Max going there without me. It's a fundraiser hosted by the Cold Fury organization, with the proceeds going to the funding of after-school activities for the underprivileged who can't afford such things. It's a great cause, and one that is and should be very personal to me, as I understand all about not being able to afford things for my niece and nephews.

"I'm not going," I say in a whisper of a voice.

"Why not?" Stevie exclaims. "These parties are always so much fun and who doesn't love getting all glammed up?"

"Me," I admit, although that's somewhat of a lie. I'm a girl. I like those things. I just don't have the ability to carry off the deception that I'm nothing but a poor girl being dragged into the celebrity lifestyle, and it's so painfully obvious I don't belong there. "I told Max I wasn't going because I just don't like the spotlight on me. I also told him I wanted to slow things down. Things have been a little strained between us."

"I straight up call bullshit on you," Stevie says dramatically with a wave of his hand. "Now, what's really going on?"

Stevie stares at me critically, almost as if he's looking for a nuance in my expression or voice to get to the truth. His look scares me because it tells me his bullshit meter is turned on and is finely tuned in. Ordinarily, I might still lie to him or even put him off with some excuse as to why I have to leave, but honestly, I want to tell him. I want someone to hear my side of the story and tell me if I'm crazy to be acting this way.

I suspect I am, but I won't admit it to myself, so I decide to just go ahead and lay it all out there.

"I'm scared of Max's world," I tell him by way of simple explanation.

"Go on," he prods me with a nod.

With a pained sigh, I tell him, "My life is a complete mess at times. Being a single mom trying to navigate the stressors of raising kids has taken a toll. And then Max comes into my life, and he's amazing and has done so much to help me—like recognizing my artistic talent and helping me turn that into something—that I should be over the moon about having a relationship with him, right?"

"Right," Stevie agrees.

"Except I keep focusing in on the negative stuff and it drags me down," I admit to him, almost shamefully.

Yes, shamefully because I know it's sort of a cowardly thing to do.

"Like what?" Stevie inquires.

"Max is famous. People are drawn to him. Women are drawn to him. He has fans so devout that some of them hate me just because I have his attention. Hell, I had a woman lay into me last week while I was out shopping. She told me I didn't deserve him. And I've been called a gold digger, and hell, even Max's brother questioned my motives. It's just too much for me to handle with trying to raise kids and deal with their father, who's now threatening to try to get them back. It's just . . . it's too much."

I look at Stevie expectantly, because I'm sure he'll agree . . . this is a lot of burden on a young woman's shoulders.

"So what?" Stevie says dismissively.

"What?" I ask incredulously.

"So. What," he repeats slowly. "It's really simple. If you love someone—and I know you love Max—then you take the bad with the good. The good totally outweighs the bad in this situation, so you ignore the bad. Figure out a way to suck it up, buttercup, because that's Max's life. If you want him, you take him as is."

"But—"

"He took you as is. You say your life is messy? Well, guess what? Max saw that from the beginning and he said, 'So what?' He took your bad and he reveled in your good. He wanted the good so much, he was willing to put the work into dealing with the bad. And sweetie pie, I'm here to tell you . . . all the negativity and second-guessing of you is going to go away. It's not here to stay. People may question your motives now, but why do you care? There will be a day when that won't happen, and even more important . . . who gives a fuck right now? Max doesn't question you, and really, he's the only person that matters."

A complete and massive wave of shame hits me as I take in Stevie's observation. Max took me with my messy life and he said, "So what?"

He never questioned my motives.

I mean . . . I knew this. This isn't a revelation. I've known from the beginning that Max took me warts and all, and I know this because I've often questioned why he would do such a thing.

Most of that shameful wave of guilt has to do with the fact that he takes all of it because he loves me.

It's as simple as that.

He loves me so he works with the bad.

He loves me despite the bad that comes with me.

And here I am, proclaiming to love this man—which I do— and I'm not willing to give the same to him in return.

It's really just that simple.

I didn't give Max back what he gave to me.

More guilt.

More shame.

Fuck. I'm such a goddamned idiot.

I let out a pained moan. "Ugh."

"You just had a proverbial slap to your face, didn't you?" Stevie asks with a grin.

I nod fiercely. "I think I knew deep down the truth of what you're saying, but I guess I couldn't see past my own frustrations to really understand the simplicity of it."

"Looks like my work as a fairy godmother is done then," Stevie says, and then looks at his watch again. "And you have plenty of time to get ready for the gala now. I'm sure Max will be thrilled. But I wouldn't tell him. Just show up and surprise the crap out of him."

My stomach pitches, first in a joyful way, to think that I can get things back on track with Max. There's no doubt he'll forgive my momentary lapse of sanity, because I know Max. I know him down to his soul and he loves me. But then it pitches like a bad drop from a roller coaster as I realize the gala isn't going to happen.

"I don't have a dress," I tell Stevie sadly. "I don't have a damn thing to wear to the gala."

He looks down to his watch, seems to think about something for just a moment, then says, "I'll be right back."

I watch as he turns and sprints to the workroom. I hear something bang and then he's sprinting back to me with keys in hand. He jingles them in front of my face when he meets me, then grabs my hand, dragging me to the front door.

I follow along, my head spinning. When we get out onto the sidewalk, he lets me go so he can pull the door shut and lock the flower shop behind him.

Then he turns to me and says, "Good thing you have a fairy godmother then. Let's go find you a dress and get you ready."

I'm all for that, but then I come to a screeching halt, exclaiming, "Wait. I can't. My friend Tina's watching the kids right now but she has plans tonight, so I don't have a sitter."

Stevie turns around after making a dismissive wave at me and starts pulling me along. "Auntie Stevie will be babysitting tonight. And when I say tonight, I mean all night, so that means you won't turn back into a pauper at midnight. That also means Max will take you to his house and, well . . . let's just say I expect a very big smile on your face in the morning when you come home."

Yes, I'm sure that's exactly what will happen!

The next two and a half hours are a whirlwind of activity. Stevie marches me three shops down to a designer consignment shop owned by a tall, statuesque woman with silver hair in a sleek chignon. After air kisses and introductions—her name is Stella—they lead me over to a rack of gowns. Without consulting me, only each other, they pull forth a gorgeous deep coral dress and usher me into a dressing room.

While Stella helps me try on the dress, Stevie gets on his phone and I hear him say, "I have a hair and makeup emergency."

Slight pause, then, "Not for me but for a dear friend."

Another slight pause. "We'll be there in twenty minutes."

By the time I get the dress on—which is beyond phenomenal, with a cut-out halter top with thin straps that crisscross over my upper back but leave the rest bare until you get down to my hips, where the material drapes almost indecently low while still looking elegant—Stevie's thrusting a pair of bronze-colored strappy high-heeled sandals to try on.

Another twenty minutes go by and my dress and shoes are paid for—which I got for a steal since they were on consignment—and I'm sitting in a hair salon that is located right next door to Stella's shop.

More air kisses, after which Stevie consults with the stylist—a plump woman named Moe—and it's decided I need an updo with lots of wavy curls.

More air kisses with the makeup artist—a man named Antonio, with a mass of dark curly hair in disarray all around his face—

and it's decided I need dark smoky eyes but coral blush and lip stain.

After I'm primped, powdered, and otherwise glammed from my shoulders up, Stevie instructs me to take my car home and follows me in his delivery van, which is painted bright purple to match the front door of his flower shop.

From there it's straight into my dress and strappy shoes, after which all three of the kids watch as Stevie does some last minute evaluation of my look, adjusts a curl that came loose in my hair, and shoves lip gloss at me to put a final layer on.

When I was done, he had me twirl around for a final look-see, at which all three of the kids clapped and cheered their approval. Tina graciously agreed to stay for another hour so Stevie could spare me a cab ride and take me to the gala, which was in downtown Raleigh at the Convention Center.

He pulled right up to the curb, and because the gala had started more than half an hour ago, there was no one outside. No long line of limos waiting to expel celebrities and no paparazzi and their flashing cameras.

Just me—Jules turned Cinderella—stepping out of Stevie's purple van with my heart racing and my palms sweating. I turn and lean back on the passenger door briefly as Stevie grins at me.

"Thank you," I tell him sincerely. "For not only helping me put my head on straight, but for making me feel like a princess tonight."

Stevie shakes his head. "I just helped get you dressed. Max is the one who will make you feel like a princess."

I take a deep breath, let it out.

"God, I hope so," I tell him as I shut the door and turn to walk into the Convention Center.

# CHAPTER 27

# MAX

"These things are such a drag," Hawke says as he tugs on his bow tie, looking incredibly uncomfortable.

"Bet you wouldn't be saying that if Vale was your date instead of me," I say with a chuckle.

"That is absolutely true," Hawke agrees with a laugh.

And I'm pleased to hear my friend has an easy, spirited laugh again.

That's because while we were in between the Ottawa and Montreal games this week, Hawke paid a surprise visit to Sydney, Nova Scotia. It was under the appearance of visiting his billet family—that is, the family that housed Hawke while he was playing major junior hockey in Sydney.

That truly may have been his intended mission, but I know damn well it was so he could check up on Vale. And the checkup proved fruitful, because they're back together again.

Except not in the literal sense, as she's supposed to be starting a new job at The Ohio State University in a few weeks.

"This long-distance relationship stuff sucks," Hawke grumbles, as if he were reading my mind. I'd almost agree with him, except he at least now has a solid relationship back on track, whereas I have no fucking clue what's going on with me and Jules.

"It's only temporary," I remind him. Apparently, Vale is going to try to find a job back in the Raleigh area as soon as she can. "So suck it up."

"Just like you're doing?" Hawke asks with a sly grin.

"Just like me," I agree as I survey the crowd. It's a hodge-podge of sports celebrities, state level politicians, and generally rich donors who will part ways with lots of money tonight.

Because Jules asked for space and I'm giving it to her. She texted me a few times this week, and while I responded, I kept my feelings dialed way the fuck in. So yeah . . . I'm sucking it up and giving her what she says she needs, with nothing but the hope that when she finally works things out in her head, she'll realize she needs me in her life.

"You should just go see her tonight," Hawke says, and my head snaps his way.

"Just go see her?" I ask with an arched eyebrow.

"Yeah, why not?" Hawke asks, and before I can give him a million reasons to answer his question, he adds on, "She did say she just wanted to slow things down, right? I take that to mean she still wants to see you."

Well, yeah . . . she did say that, but I'm not exactly sure it's what she meant. She insisted it wasn't a breakup and she just wanted to slow things a bit. But fuck that. I'm a guy who doesn't slow down. When I know something is good for me and I want it, I go forward with guns blazing until I get what I want.

It's fucking killing me to not just barrel my way into Jules' apartment and physically kidnap her and the kids so I can move them into my house.

Shaking my head, I look back around the ballroom as I mutter, "I don't think Jules would appreciate me just dropping by."

"I think she would," Hawke counters.

I snort. "That's just because you got your girl back and you've got all these silly ideals in your head."

"Maybe so," Hawke says affably. "But I still think you should push a little."

I'm shaking my head before he even gets the words all the way out. I turn to face him, shoving my hands in my pockets. "Jules isn't the type of woman you push. She likes to find her own way. She's independent and stubborn, but she's also smart and reasonable. I've got to let her figure this out on her own. It's the only way really."

"I get that line of reasoning," Hawke continues to pester me. "But if you stay away, she might forget all about you. Absence doesn't always make the heart grow fonder."

My stomach flips at the thought. Would she fucking forget about me now that I'm making myself scarce? Would she just move on with her life and figure that she can do things on her own, why in the hell would she ever need me?

A panicky feeling starts to claw at my insides. "Maybe I'll go see her tomorrow."

Hawke's eyes brighten and he nods effusively at me. "That's the spirit. So what's the first thing you'll tell her when you see her tomorrow?"

Fuck . . . I'd have a million things to say, all of them important, but there is one that stands out.

With a casual shrug I tell him, "Only thing that really matters . . . and that's to just simply tell her I'm madly, crazy, head over heels in love with her and I'm ready for her when she makes that same commitment."

Hawke gets this shit-eating grin on his face and then gives a subtle nod at something over my right shoulder. "Well, now's your chance, brother."

"What?" I ask as I turn around, and even though the ballroom is crowded, I immediately spot Jules walking in through the main double doors.

My jaw drops as I take her in, first because I'm utterly blown away that she came, and second because she's a fucking knockout in that dress. It hugs her body and exposes her graceful shoulders, and when she walks there's a slit in the front that gives me a peek of her leg up to right above her knee.

She doesn't see me but she's looking around, clearly on the hunt.

Hawke claps a hand on my shoulder, but I hardly pay him notice when he gives me a tiny shove her way and says, "Go get her, tiger."

My legs start moving, weaving my way in and out of the guests, some wanting to shake my hand and others wanting to pose for pictures. That's why we're here . . . to make it worthwhile for people to open their wallets for charity.

But I brush people off with a firm but polite, "I'll be back. There's something I need to do."

When I'm halfway to Jules, I see her gaze focuses in on something to my left and I turn to see Allie and Cassie standing there talking. The way their heads are tilted toward each other and by the looks on their faces I can tell they're engaged in some catty gossip.

Then I'm absolutely stunned as Jules squares her shoulders and starts to walk their way.

Whoa, fuck!

I turn that way too, hoping to cut her off because no way in hell am I going to let those two get into Jules' head any further.

Unfortunately, she beats me there by just a few strides and I watch as Allie and Cassie turn their heads to Jules as she walks right up to them. Both have their lips practically curled into sneers and I feel my hands start to clench into frustrated fists of aggression.

But just as I get to within five feet of Jules, I hear her say, "Allie . . . Cassie . . . you both look very lovely tonight."

Both women sort of jerk in place, their eyebrows shooting upward and their mouths hanging slightly open.

Jules then gives a little twirl in place and waves one hand down the length of her body to direct their attention to her stunning dress and comes out of her spin facing them. "And don't I look lovely tonight too? I actually feel just like Cinderella."

They say nothing.

"Now, if you'll excuse me, ladies, I'm off to go find my prince. Have a great night," she says and gives them a regal incline of her head.

Princess?

How about a queen?

Jules turns my way and barrels straight into me, which is completely fine. She gives a gasp of surprise as my hands come to her upper arms to steady her and her eyes travel slowly up until they lock on mine.

"There you are," she breathes out softly.

"Your prince?" I ask.

"The one and only," she murmurs back.

And yeah . . . so I go ahead and kiss her, because what else should be said?

Except when I pull my mouth from hers and take in her sweet sigh of contentment, I tell her what should have been my first words. "I love you, Jules. Madly. Head over heels. Crazy, crazy love."

Her eyes seem to glow with that shade of light amber that I

love, which tells me she really, really likes what I just said to her. "I love you too, Max. So much."

She opens her mouth to say something else but then abruptly looks to her left. I do the same and see Allie and Cassie still standing there, mouths agape as they watch us. Jules turns, dislodges my hand from her arm and then tucks her arm in the crook of mine. She starts walking through the ballroom and I follow along, loving the way she feels beside me.

Relishing the looks of appreciation she gets from some of the men.

Secretly even loving some of the jealous looks of other women.

When we reach the opposite side of the ballroom and find a space not occupied by people mingling and chatting, she turns to me, taking both my hands in hers. Her face tilts up and her eyes are apologetic. "I'm sorry, Max."

I try to cut her off with a shake of my head but her hands squeeze mine, a silent indication she wants me to listen and that, more importantly, I need to listen.

So I listen.

"I'm sorry," she begins again. "I love you so much and I've acted like such a fool."

"You're a cute fool though," I say, only to lighten things up because she looks so seriously disappointed in herself.

I'm rewarded with a little bit of a smile as she continues on. "Here you were . . . an amazing man that came into my life and swept me off my feet. You were always bucking me up and telling me how strong I was, and I believed you. I believed every bit of faith you placed in me and that changed my life. And then . . . I got all up inside my head and ended up doing the exact opposite of what you believed about me."

"You had a moment of doubt," I say softly.

"No," she says with an almost violent shake of her head, but then gives me a sheepish smile. "Okay, yes . . . a little doubt. In myself, and whether or not I deserved someone like you. But never doubt in you. Not really even in us as a whole. I guess I prefer to think that I just had a moment of stupidity."

I can't help it. I bust out laughing, and because she's so fucking adorable, I tug her into me so I can wrap my arms around her. She reciprocates, but tilts her head back so she can keep looking up at me.

"Seriously, Max. Just plain stupidity," she insists.

"Okay. I believe you," I tell her, only so she'll let that part go. My girl is far from stupid. Maybe silly and a little susceptible to her emotions, but never stupid.

"I'm strong, Max," she murmurs as she looks up at me. "I'm strong and I'm not going to let anyone get me down or get in my way of being with you."

"I hear you, baby," I tell her.

"I am never going to be put off by what people think about me," she asserts more definitively, as if she's desperate for me to understand that she's all in. "And I'm never going to not be by your side. I'll be at every damn game that I can and I'll proudly be by your side for every charity event, or whatever else you famous people do."

Chuckling, I give her a squeeze. "That's nice, Jules. All of what you said. Just really nice. But you're leaving out the most important thing."

She rolls her eyes at me and leans back farther to level me with a bit of a stern look. "I was getting to the good part if you'd just have a little patience."

I incline my head in apology. "My bad."

She huffs out a breath of annoyance but her eyes show anything but. They're warm and vibrant and full of emotion. "I love you, Max," she says softly. "Just like you . . . it's madly. It's crazy,

crazy. It's head over heels, tumbling further and further into it with you, but I am ready for every bit of dizziness that comes with it. I want it all, Max, but mostly I just want you."

Yeah . . . that right there.

That punch of elation hitting me square in the chest, taking hold of my heart, squeezing it almost painfully for just a moment before it starts to fill up with this feeling of joy and completeness.

That's a feeling I can get used to.

It's a feeling I don't ever want to do without, and now I'm hearing it straight from Jules . . . she doesn't want to do without it again either.

"Sounds like we're finally on the same page, baby," I murmur as I release my hold and move my hands to her face. Her own hands come up to lock around my wrists, holding me firm as she looks at me with shimmering eyes.

"We are so on the same page," she affirms softly, and then adds, "And Stevie's watching the kids tonight so I'm all yours until tomorrow morning."

I shake my head with an amused smile. "Uh-uh. You're mine forever."

She smiles at me . . . bright and brilliant and full of love. "My bad. I am absolutely yours forever."

# JULES

**One week later. Christmas Eve . . .**

"We should have gone tonight," I tell Max as I burrow into his side on the couch. All the lights are off and there's nothing but the glow of the Christmas tree by which we can see. His left arm wraps around me and gives me a squeeze.

"No way in hell we should have gone," he says. His voice is low and mellow and oh so very happy. "This is how I want to spend Christmas Eve."

We skipped the traditional Christmas party at Brian Brannon's house, owner of the Cold Fury. It's not a mandatory party, from what Max says, and it sounds super fun, also from what Max says, but when it came right down to it . . . he wanted a more traditional evening.

That included bringing me and the kids to his house, where we found the space under the Christmas tree—which we'd put up just two days ago—filled with brightly wrapped presents. The evening included a meal I'd cooked, including a ham, sweet potatoes, a corn soufflé, and a *tourtière* I made just for Max, using his mother's recipe. After, we watched *A Christmas Story* with the kids, and before they went to bed, we let them each open one gift.

After that, Max and I waited a sufficient amount of time for the kids to settle down, and with a quick peek inside each of their rooms, where we'd put them to bed, we both went a little nuts laying out the gifts from "Santa."

We overbought, no doubt. It had everything to do with the fact it was their first Christmas without Melody. Max bought a ton of stuff and I didn't even argue with him at all about it. I also bought a ton of stuff, depleting my savings account, but . . . oh well. I was happy and in love and I had amazing kids. This Christmas was going to rock!

Now as we're settled onto his couch and looking at the obscene number of toys under the tree, I'm just really glad we didn't go to Brian Brannon's party tonight, but rather celebrated privately our first Christmas together.

"Want to make out?" Max asks seriously, his hand sliding from my arm down to my hip.

"Of course I want to make out," I tell him as if that was the most stupid question in the world, because when don't I want to make out with Max?

With a low chuckle he hauls me onto his lap, positions me sideways, and then his mouth is on mine.

God, that just gets better and better.

This kiss is deep and passionate, and later we'll let it turn into a bit more before we go to sleep. But for now it's brief and I'm satisfied even as he pulls away and rests his cheek against mine so we can both look at the tree a little bit more.

"I can't wait for tomorrow," I murmur as I stare at the glowing lights.

Max gives me a squeeze. "They're going to flip out when they see the presents."

Yeah, they are.

I can't wait.

**Three weeks later . . .**

"This is the last one," Hawke says as he waddles in with a monstrous box housing all of my art supplies. "Where do you want it?"

"Sunroom," I say as I turn to point to the large glassed-in room just off the den area. My intent was to just set my stuff up in the basement somewhere but Max wouldn't hear of it. He said something about an artist needs natural light.

I started to argue with him because I didn't want to take over the sunroom. It was a beautiful place and didn't need my paints and brushes all around. But Max wouldn't engage with my argument and sort of put his foot down.

I kinda, sorta gave in very quickly, and let's just say . . . I'm learning when to be stubborn and when to let Max get a little alpha on me.

Which is kind of hot.

Hawke walks to the sunroom and unloads his burden, then immediately heads to the kitchen to pull a beer out of the fridge. He mutters, "Not sure how I got unloading duty."

I see Vale just behind him give him an eye roll, then a quick kiss, before she turns to open the oven and check on the lasagna she'd brought over as a housewarming present.

Yes, it's kind of my housewarming, because this is the day that the kids and I moved into Max's house.

It didn't take long for Max to convince me. In fact, he started working on me the evening of the charity gala a month ago, and when I say he worked on me, that means he kept trying to get me to agree to it while he was fucking me, but doing it so slowly I couldn't quite grab ahold of the orgasm that was fluttering just beyond my reach.

When I agreed, he slammed home and tipped me over the edge. I became very, very happy and Max got what he wanted as well.

The reason it's taken me a month to move in is because of the holidays, then Max insisted that each kid get to decorate their own room and pick out what furniture they wanted. I was slightly uneasy over this, but then Max did what he does best . . . he just simply reminded me that his commitment to me was a commitment to us as a family. That naturally included the kids, and his desire wasn't just to have me but to have them as well.

The thought still makes my eyes mist up.

Turns out, Vale got her old job back with the Cold Fury, so despite Hawke's grumblings, I know he's a very happy man. I note that Hawke is now kissing Vale in Max's kitchen—no, wait, it's my kitchen too now—and I use that as a good opportunity to sneak my way upstairs. I can hear Max's voice right away and I head to the room at the end of the hall. This brings me past Levy's room, which he chose to have decorated in a dinosaur motif, then past Rocco's room, which reflected his love of science. There was border wallpaper of all the planets and he had us put glow-in-the-dark stars on the ceiling.

Neither of the boys were in their rooms but rather outside playing in the backyard, even though it was a seriously chilly day.

When I hit Annabelle's room—which is my favorite by far, with its pink princess decor—I find Max sitting on the floor with her as she dresses her doll. He's not actively playing with her but merely sitting down cross-legged and engaging in quiet conversation while she dresses the doll.

"Think Levy and Rocco will like their new school?" she asks

him. Her back is to me so she doesn't see me lean against the doorjamb, my arms crossed over my chest as I listen in. Max does see me though and I know this only because his eyes come to mine briefly, where they smile at me, before turning his attention back to Annabelle.

"I'm sure they're going to love it," he tells her, and she nods in silent agreement. "Ben goes there, and so do Ruby and Violet."

"And do you think I'll like my new school?" she asks, her fingers working the buttons on the doll's dress. I can hear a little bit of tension in her voice and my heart squeezes for her.

We decided to enroll Annabelle in private daycare—well, they call them educational learning centers—to get her some more social interaction. She'll enter into prekindergarten there and then start public school in the fall.

This was a source of some contention between Max and me because I absolutely cannot afford that school on what I'm making. Well, I could if I didn't have any other expenses, but because I feel like I should be paying something to Max for my share of the house, that means I do have other expenses. While my share would be paltry in comparison to what it costs to run this monstrosity of a house, he knows it's something I feel strongly about at this point.

But once again we both proved we could talk things out, and I could let go a little bit of my stubbornness and pride. We eventually decided that my income would go toward groceries, utilities, and Annabelle's school. Max would cover everything else.

I capitulated and I didn't dwell on it. I decided I couldn't waste any more time in worries over how people would view me with Max. The only thing that mattered was what he thought.

"You will absolutely love your new school," Max tells her with exuberance, then my heart melts again when he takes his big hand and palms the top of her head in a reassuring manner.

It melts further when Annabelle finally raises her eyes to his and I see them filled with trust and acceptance of what he says.

**Four days later . . .**

My phone rings and my stomach cramps a bit when I see it's Dwayne calling. I'd not heard a peep out of him after his letter to me back in November. Max and I discussed how we should respond, and ultimately Max talked me into talking to an attorney so I could get some solid advice on how we should handle Dwayne. The attorney gave us great information, including until Dwayne got his child support caught up, he essentially had no rights nor any other leverage over us. Thus, we decided it was best if I didn't respond to him. Call him on his bluff and let's just see if Dwayne will be Dwayne and sort of disappear the way he's known for doing.

Looks like my reprieve from having to deal with him though is over.

I put my paintbrush down, take a deep breath, and pick up my phone. "Hello, Dwayne."

"Where are you?" he asks in a bewildered voice. "I'm at your apartment and someone else is living here."

I consider lying to him for all of about two seconds, but I know I can't do that. If I'm going to handle Dwayne, I have to do it with everything laid out on the table. "The kids and I moved in with Max."

"Oh," is all he says, and he neither sounds put out by this information or happy about it. "Well, I need to see you. We need to talk."

I agree. We need to talk, but it's going to be done on my

terms, and that essentially means that I want Max by my side when I do this. He's my rock solid support and I need his strength. Unfortunately, he's in New York and won't be home until tomorrow evening.

"I can do it day after tomorrow," I tell Dwayne.

"It has to be today," he says, again . . . not overly put out but more just in a rush or something.

"Well, it can't be done today," I tell him. "Day after tomorrow. I'll have to text you the time as I'm not sure what Max's schedule will be that day."

I brace for an argument, but instead he says, "Okay . . . fine. Just text me when and where."

**Two days later . . .**

The doorbell rings and Max gets up off the couch we'd been sitting on to answer it. I go ahead and stand up, wiping my sweaty hands on my jeans.

Max decided to have Dwayne come here, and I had to agree with his logic. His reasoning was that Dwayne was still the kids' father, and while he didn't have guardianship, he did have some visitation rights. Granted, those rights were suspended by the court because his child support was past due, but Max wanted to try to show him we could all get along.

So Max opens the door and Dwayne is standing there, looking in awe of Max's house.

Correction . . . our house. *Still having a hard time getting used to that.*

Max steps back and says to Dwayne, "Come on in."

Dwayne does so, and looks around at the bronzed tiled entryway before looking up at the massive iron light that hangs from the second-story ceiling, with the staircase winding around it.

When his gaze drops, it locks on mine. "Hey, Jules."

*Jules? That's interesting.*

It's also interesting that his voice sounds almost humble.

I don't trust it for a minute.

"Come on into the kitchen," I tell Dwayne, and turn my back on him. I can hear him and Max following as I walk through the formal sitting area, past the wet bar area with the staircase that leads down to the basement, and into the kitchen. "Want some coffee?"

"That would be great," he says.

It's a tense silence as I throw a K-Cup in the Keurig and wait for his coffee to brew. I know he takes it black, so after the last drop falls, I turn and hand the cup to him. I nod toward one of the kitchen island stools and he takes a seat. I walk to the opposite side of the counter and stand before him, Max coming to stand beside me.

I don't say anything. I watch as Dwayne takes a tiny sip of his coffee, then he sets the cup down and looks at me. "I'm not here to fight about the kids."

My eyebrows raise in surprise but I don't say anything.

His gaze drops to his cup and he says, "I, um . . . I'm going to head back to Oklahoma. My girl and I broke up, and well . . . you know I can't afford to have an attorney fight about those kids right now. Maybe once I'm settled and get into a job . . . I can work to catch up the child support."

I don't believe a word he says, but I do say, "That would be a good idea."

Dwayne is silent for a moment before he looks at me. "I could use some money to get set up back in Oklahoma. You know . . . to rent a place and give me some cushion until I find a job."

I stare at him.

He continues, "And I was thinking . . . you know, since I'm not going to fight you for the kids, you could front me some money to get back home."

My mouth opens to tell him he's got some nerve, but Max says quietly, "Jules . . . will you give me and Dwayne a minute? I'd like to talk to him privately."

At first I feel a rush of anger that Max would think to exclude me, but when he turns his gaze on me, the anger fizzles because before me I see a man who wants to be my champion and he's simply asking me to let him do it.

"Sure," I say quietly, and I walk out of the kitchen.

Now, I am in no way not going to listen in on what's being said, so I make a production of climbing the stairs with some mild stomping so Dwayne thinks I'm out of earshot, but I stop right at the top landing and lean my forearms on the banister. Looking down over the open foyer with the front door just beyond, I know the sound from the kitchen will travel well enough for me to hear what's going on.

"Just a little bit of money," Dwayne says, his supplication now aimed at Max. "I know you got plenty, man, and I swear, you won't ever see me again."

I'm surprised when Max says, "And what about Annabelle, Levy, and Rocco . . . will they see you again? You just going to jet out of their life for good?"

"Man . . . you know I'm not a good daddy," Dwayne says with an actual measure of genuine self-disgust aimed at himself. "Wasn't a good husband either."

"Doesn't mean those kids don't need to know their father," Max says, and this again surprises me. I sort of thought when he asked for privacy, he was going to lay into Dwayne.

"I'm no good for them," he says, and that sounds like self-pity now, and I never could tolerate that attitude, so my nose involuntarily wrinkles. "So maybe just give me some money and I'll be out of here for good."

There's silence, and I can almost envision Max staring Dwayne down. I can also envision Dwayne doesn't have the bravery to hold Max's critical gaze.

Finally, I hear Max's voice, and it's empathetic but uncompromising. "We're not going to give you a dime, Dwayne. You've managed to take care of yourself this long in life, I'm sure you'll find some way to survive. But I will tell you what I'll do. First, if you ever think to threaten Jules again about taking those kids away from her—when you've never once showed an ounce of interest in their well-being or in their mother as she died—then I want you to know I will use every penny of my vast and incredible fortune to fight you. I will bankrupt and bury you before I ever let that happen."

There's a small pause, and Dwayne doesn't say a word.

Max continues, his voice a little softer now. "But, what I will do is talk to Jules about perhaps rescinding the order for child support. Take that monkey off your back, since you clearly have no desire to pay it. In return, I want you to relinquish all of your paternal rights so Jules can officially adopt those kids. She's their mom now. She's been more of a parent to them in these months than you've been in their entire lives."

More silence, and I can no longer even envision what Dwayne's or Max's face looks like at this point, because this is so not where I thought their conversation would go.

"However," Max says, this time as if he were talking to a child who needed some type of encouragement. "I know Jules would still want you to be a part of their lives. You don't have the maturity to care for them and raise them the way a parent has to sacrifice to do so, but I do think you have the power to love them. So I would propose you still have some type of regular visitation.

Jules and I will bring them to you when our schedules permit, or I'll pay to fly you here to see them."

Immediately, my nose starts stinging, and I don't even try to quell the tears that start to form.

Oh, God . . . sweet, genuine, generous Max, doing right by not only me and those children, but also doing right by Dwayne. Still trying to include a wayward father into those kids' lives.

I don't bother listening anymore. I have no clue what Dwayne will decide to do, but I know Max would never make decisions without me and will call me down when I'm needed. Besides, it really doesn't matter what he decides. Nothing will change the fact that those kids belong to me and Max.

So I turn and head into Levy's room, and make myself busy picking up his toys and clothes he'd left lying around this morning before going to school. I'll do the same for Rocco and Annabelle when I'm done.

**Three weeks later . . .**

"It's finally here," I shout out as I barge into Fleurish, not caring if I scare the crap out of any of Stevie's customers.

Stevie calls back, "I'm in the back."

I hurry back there, vaguely noticing that the shop actually has a few customers, but they're currently being helped by one of Stevie's employees and don't give me a second glance.

I find Stevie at a large worktable, creating a floral arrangement of such beauty, it takes my breath away for a moment. "Oh, wow. That is stunning."

"Never underestimate the value of a gay man arranging flowers," he says dryly and then pushes the large container of what looks to be lilac and lavender sprigs mixed with baby white roses away from him. "Let's see it."

I round the worktable and come up to stand beside him, plopping the latest issue of *Sports World* on the wooden top.

Max's gorgeous face grins back at us with the title "Hottest Sports Bachelor" across the top.

I have to say, I love the photo they chose. It was one of him sitting on a chrome barstool, holding a goalie stick across his lap as he wound tape around the base. I remember the photographer telling him to look up and "smile," and when he did so, they captured the perfect picture, complete with shining eyes and panty-dropping dimples.

"Have you read it yet?" Stevie asks as we stare at the cover.

"Nope," I tell him. "Thought we could do it together and maybe giggle like girls when we do so."

"I can totally do that," he says, and starts flipping through the magazine until we get to the article, which starts with the preceding page filled with Max and the two bikini babes on either side of him.

Doesn't even bother me in the slightest.

"He's so hot," Stevie murmurs.

"Tell me about it," I say dreamily.

"Okay, let's read the article," he says, and starts to do so out loud. " 'Voting was contentious and close, but we're pleased to announce that Max Fournier, hot goalie for the Carolina Cold Fury, has been named as *Sports World*'s Hottest Bachelor.' "

Stevie continues to read aloud, the article actually giving a lovely recitation of Max's accomplishments, all the way back to when he played hockey as a little kid in Montreal. While he reads, I just stare at the hotness of Max, completely able to disregard the gorgeous women beside him.

When Stevie flips to the next page, I blink for a moment but then immediately my eyes are locked onto the next picture and

I'm stunned. It's not one from the formal photo shoot, but rather one of the candid photos Camille took of me and Max. The reporter must have reached out to her for them.

It's not one that was in her horrid article but appears to be the moment just before he'd kissed me. He's got one hand wrapped around the back of my neck and he's peering down at me with such utter love that my knees start to shake.

Did I recognize that in his eyes then?

I don't remember, but it's clear as day now.

Max is looking at me as if I matter more to him than the air he breathes. And my gaze back at him . . . it mirrors his perfectly. I'm staring back with the same look of almost awe and devotion.

"'. . . and Max was more than happy to talk to us about his love life,'" Stevie says, and my ears definitely perk back up at that.

I lean in closer to him and my eyes start scanning the article, trying to pinpoint exactly where he's reading from. But the magazine is snatched out from under my nose and Stevie steps back from me, holding it up to read further.

"Stevie," I say with a growl.

He just holds his hand up and says, "Cool it, sister. And just listen."

I give out a huff of frustration, but then Stevie's reading and I'm suddenly lost to Max's words. "'Let me tell you something about Jules. She is without a doubt the most amazing human being I've ever met. Not woman . . . I'm talking out of all the people I've ever encountered, she's the best of them. I could go on and on, but I know it would embarrass her if I did. That's because she's also one of the most humble people I've ever known. I know she's taken some flack from a few of my fans, but I have to believe that most of them aren't like that. That they're truly happy for me that I've found someone to share my life with.'"

Prickles in my nose again, and that's the sign a good cry is coming. It's my cry-o-meter.

Even Stevie gets a little choked up when he continues on, " 'And while I wasn't all that crazy about being named hottest bachelor and all that, because let's admit it—it's a little embarrassing—I'd at least like to accept this title as sort of my last hurrah. So Jules . . . I know you're reading this, babe . . . I'd like to officially take myself off all bachelor lists and ask you to marry me. You know it's not too soon, and you know it's right. So as soon as you finish this article, give me a call and tell me yes, okay?' "

"Holy shit," I wheeze as Stevie's eyes fly up from the magazine and lock with mine.

"Did he just?" Stevie whispers.

"Ask me to marry him?" I whisper back.

He nods at me, almost afraid to say it again. But then he lowers the magazine and, still whispering, asks, "What are you going to do?"

I don't even hesitate as my hand dives into my purse and I fish my phone out. My hands are shaking as I pull up Max's number and tap it. As it starts to ring, I look back to Stevie and grin. "I'm going to say yes, of course."

Read on for an excerpt from

*Roman*

A Cold Fury Hockey Novel

by Sawyer Bennett
Available from Loveswept

# CHAPTER 1

# ROMAN

I pull open the glass door that leads into the Cold Fury executive office suite. It's posh and sumptuous, with its thick cream carpet and sleek European furniture. It tells the story of exactly how much money is generated by this organization.

My eyes immediately land on a young woman sitting on a low-slung, gray leather couch set up against the far wall. She has one leg crossed over the other and her head is bent down over her phone, upon which she is texting. I can't see her face as her dark hair forms a curtain with her head bent down and is obstructing the view. She's dressed very casually in a pair of dark jeans, fuzzy-looking boots, and a heavy cream wool sweater. There's a navy wool coat sitting beside her on the couch.

"Can I help you?" I hear a smooth female voice say from the reception desk.

My gaze turns that way and I come under the cool appraisal of a stern-looking older woman with pale blond hair pulled back from her face in a tight bun. "Roman Sýkora. Got an appointment with Gray Brannon."

The woman actually sniffs at me and says, "You're fifteen minutes late, Mr. Sýkora."

"Yup," I tell her before turning away and walking to a chair that sits adjacent to the gray couch. Nothing else really needs to be said about that. I'm chronically late and will probably be that way until the day I die.

Just before I take a seat I hear the receptionist say from behind me, "Ms. Robertson . . . Mr. Brannon is just finishing up his ten o'clock appointment and should be with you shortly. I apologize he's running late."

The woman sitting on the couch lifts her face, looks right past me to the receptionist and gives a small smile with a nod. "That's quite all right. I don't mind waiting."

And damn . . . what a face. Creamy, flawless skin with silvery blue eyes that absolutely pop against the dark lashes surrounding them. She lifts her hand and tucks a lock of her hair behind her ear, and then I'm stunned when her gaze slides over to me. She gives a slight nod toward the reception desk, leans her body a little closer toward my chair and whispers, "Seems like a double standard to me."

"Double standard?" I ask with confusion, and more than a little fascinated by the husky, almost raspy tone of her voice.

She grins at me, which draws attention to her lips. Full, pink, and pulled back to reveal sparkling white teeth with a tiny gap right in the middle. Totally sexy.

"Well, yeah," she says as she lowers her voice in a more conspiratorial tone. "It's okay for management to be late to a meeting with me, but it's not okay for you to be a few minutes late with management?"

She's got a damn good point.

I, in turn, lean toward her as if we are sharing a great secret. I also drop my voice, not because I care if the receptionist hears me, because let's face it—I don't give a shit what anyone in this organization thinks about me—but because I'm merely enjoying my banter with this really pretty woman.

"I think you may have isolated the issue," I tell her, my Czech accent coming on a little bit thicker only because I've slowed my words down a bit. "You and I are not management, therefore we do not enjoy the privilege of being able to be late. We are too far down on the . . . what do you call it . . . totem pole?"

The woman nods in agreement and gives me a wink. "Definitely at the bottom of the totem pole."

I think about introducing myself to her, as I'm not sure she knows who I am. She's clearly sitting here in the lobby of the Cold Fury executive office suite, but that doesn't necessarily mean she knows hockey. For all I know, she could be here selling Girl Scout cookies.

But before I can even push my hand toward her, the receptionist behind me says, "Mr. Sýkora, Miss Brannon is ready to see you now."

With a sigh, I push myself up out of the chair, and the woman gives me another smile and says, "Good luck. I hope you're not in too much trouble."

I give her a grin, and a wink of my own. "Unfortunately, I have a feeling I am in quite a bit of trouble."

Her jaw drops open slightly and her eyes round in sympathy, but before she can even extend her sympathies, I lean over to her and whisper, "But it's nothing to worry about. I'm sort of a troublemaker."

Her eyes sparkle with mischief as she nods in grave understanding, "I can kind of tell that about you. But hey, you carry it really well."

"And don't you forget it," I say with a chuckle as I turn from her to face the receptionist. She laughs softly behind me, and with that raspy, grit from her vocal chords . . . yeah, it's totally sexy.

But the minute I face the receptionist and she points me down the hall toward the executive offices, I put the woman and all her sexy ways out of my mind. I stiffen my spine as I walk toward Gray Brannon's office because I know I'm getting ready to have my ass handed to me.

"She's the office at the end of the hall," the receptionist says smoothly.

I don't even acknowledge her because frankly her attitude is snotty and doesn't deserve an acknowledgment. I merely stride down the hall until I reach Gray's office door, which is open. With a slight tap of my knuckles against the wood, I announce myself and stick my head in.

Gray Brannon is the general manager for the Carolina Cold Fury hockey team. This is her second year in the position and she is proudly sporting a Stanley Cup Championship under her belt. This is also my second year with the team, as I was added on last year after Gray took over management. I owe a lot to her for her faith in me, believing I could be a great contribution to this team.

However, just because I'm grateful to her does not mean I'm going to take her shit or change my ways.

Gray lifts her head from some documents she's reviewing on her desk, and for a brief moment I'm captivated by the sheer beauty of this woman. I've never been a fan of redheads, but I have to say Gray Brannon wears the color well and her face is almost angelic. So yeah, our general manager is hot as hell, but she's also fucking brilliant at her job, and while I'm sure every man on this team has eyeballed her in a way a man will look at a gorgeous woman, she is more than respected for her abilities to do right by this organization.

As I step into her office, Gray stands from the desk and holds her hand out to me to shake. My eyes immediately draw down to the rounded bump of her belly before coming back up to lock with her own. Gray announced a few weeks ago at the team Christmas party that she and her husband, Ryker Evans, were expecting their first child together in May. Ryker was the starting goalie last year for the Cold Fury and was instrumental in us winning the Stanley Cup. He retired this past summer and is now one of the goalie coaches for the team.

I take Gray's hand and give it a quick shake before releasing it. She waves to the chairs behind me and I take one, settling in casually. While I am most assuredly going to get an ass-chewing during this meeting, I don't ever want her to have the impression that it bothers me.

Because it doesn't.

I pretty much do what I want and I take my lumps when I deserve them. And I probably deserve this ass-chewing.

Gray sits down in her chair, rests her elbows on the top of her desk and steeples her hands in front of her. "No sense in beating around the bush. You have to pick your battles better, and frankly, a little less frequently."

"Not sure I'm following," I say with utter honesty. I thought I was going to be given the affirmative command to cease and desist my wild ways completely, not telling me to dial it back a notch.

"Well, let's take a look at your history," she says blandly and with a touch of sarcasm. It causes me to give an involuntary smirk, which she chooses to ignore. "A year and a half ago you celebrated joining the Cold Fury by going out and getting extremely drunk at an away game in Toronto, and got into a shoving match with a fan from the other team."

"He started it," I say with a smile.

She ignores that too. "You got arrested for being drunk and disorderly."

"Those charges were dismissed," I point out.

"Then," she says, barreling right past my excuses, "you pulled the infamous 'possum' stunt."

I snort. That was a good one. I took a high stick to my shoulder, then dove to the ice. It hurt but not enough to put me down. The other players didn't know that though, and while a shoving match started right in front of me, my teammates clearly coming to my defense, I laid there on the ice playing dead. One of the trainers even came over to check on me. The scrums around me got broken up by the refs and about the time all the players started to slowly skate away I jumped up from the ice—scaring the shit out of our trainer, Goose—and attacked the fucker that gave me the high stick in the first place. Got a few solid hits on him before the refs jumped on me.

That earned me a game misconduct ejection.

Gray Brannon does not laugh, but continues to extol my "virtues" to this team.

"You've been suspended for eleven games over the past two years," she says distastefully. "Three for boarding, two for cross-checking, and six for abuse of an official," she recites.

"Well, the abuse of an official was for ten games, but it did get reduced to six, so that's good, right?" I ask without a hint of apology. "Besides, you and I both know that guy is a douche."

"You're late to practice most of the time," she throws at me.

"I need my beauty sleep," I say as I bat my eyelashes at her. "And it's not personal. I'm late to everything."

I can tell she wants to roll her eyes at me but she never breaks that direct, hard stare. "You've heckled and threatened fans, gotten into a public drunk spectacle on several occasions—the last just four days ago—with your girlfriend, which made the social media rounds—"

"I fucking hate Snapchat," I say glumly but very truthfully. "And that was an ex-girlfriend. We'd been broken up a while and had just run into each other at a bar, and she's the one that—"

"And then today," she cuts in on me, grabbing the newspaper off her desk and sliding it across to me. "You make the front page of the sports section."

My eyes drop down and I have to practically bite my tongue not to grin at the photograph taking up the entire top of the page. It's of me, sound asleep in bed. I'm lying on my back, covers pulled up to my hips, but it's clear I'm naked underneath. And next to me is a woman, also clearly naked but with the sheet pulled up over her breasts, taking a selfie photograph with me.

Unbeknownst to me.

Didn't find out about it until she sent me a text with the photo day before yesterday along with a short but clear demand for money, and said if I didn't pay it, she would go to the press with it.

My text back to her was simple: *Fuck off.*

Of course, that text exchange ended up in the paper too, along with a quote from yours truly. After all, the reporter called me for my side of the story and I told him I'd never be bribed by anyone, not to mention a two-bit model who would jump into bed with anyone just for the attention.

I actually think I handled the situation well.

Inclining my head toward the paper, I try for my most seriously affronted expression. "You can't honestly be mad at me for that. I had no clue she took that picture."

"She was previously engaged to one of your teammates," Gray grits out.

I hold my hands up in mock surrender. "I did not know that. Well, not until after the clothes came off, but still . . . she wasn't engaged at the time."

"Jesus Christ, Sýkora," Gray mutters as she runs her fingers through her hair in a sign of frustration. "You have a goddamned answer for everything. But surely you can see you're taking things a bit too far. For fuck's sake, you even had a rule instituted by the league named after you," she adds on. "They named a goddamn rule after you."

I give a lift of my chin in pride. Because that was epic. There was nothing in the rules preventing screening the goalies. It happened all the time. I just chose to do it more blatantly, actually getting right up in his face when the puck was in his end and waving my hands in front of his face. It was a guaranteed goal-getter, as my teammates had no problems slipping pucks past while the goalie was otherwise occupied with my hands in his face.

The league enacted a swift rule prohibiting it and it's known as the Sýkora rule.

"You got to admit, before the rule was enacted, I was pretty brilliant, right?" I say confidently, knowing that I'm starting to get on her nerves by the way a muscle at the corner of her mouth starts ticking.

"I'm not amused," Gray says stiffly.

"Not even a little?" I ask with innocent eyes.

"Cut the shit, Sýkora," Gray growls at me as she leans across the desk, eyes blazing. "You know the reasons why I brought you to this team, and I like that you've got a reputation about you. You're an amazing defenseman and I like the grit you bring to the game. But you're taking things too far, and regardless of what you think, this organization still has a reputation to uphold."

"I am who I am," I say with challenge.

"That may be," she retorts. "But if you want to be on this team, you need to heed what I'm saying."

"And what exactly are you saying?" I ask, leaning forward in my chair.

She sighs and sinks back into her own. She gives a tired rub to her eyes before looking at me. "I'm saying to cut the stunts out. Be tough out on the ice but quit being such an obvious jackass. Clean up your act. Lay off the booze. Quit making a spectacle of yourself. Play by the rules. Show up on fucking time. It's not rocket science."

"And if I don't?" I ask, even though I know the answer to this. I'm just being a dick.

"Then you ride pine," she says softly, but it doesn't lessen the punch. Especially when she says, "Or worse . . . I'll release you."

"This team needs me," I growl.

"Yes, we do," she says with a nod. "But we need more than just stellar play. This is a championship team, and your antics could go south very quickly and drag all of us down."

"They're not antics," I tell her firmly. "This was who I was before I came to the Cold Fury."

"And I'm telling you it's not meshing with our vision," she counters.

I lean back in my chair, cross my hands over my stomach and give her a lazy look. While I very much do not want to lose my job, and while I very much will probably take what she says to heart, I don't ever let on that I'll do such a thing. It's about maintaining some level of control in this situation, and call that an ego thing, fine, but I'm not one to back down.

"What exactly would you have me change?" I ask casually.

"For starters," she says with a hard stare, "show up for practice on time. Show up to your training sessions. Maybe even take an interest in the team off the ice. Quit doing stupid things. Grow up a little."

I suppress the snort. While, ironically, I do play a team sport, I'm not overly close to my mates, outside of partying with some of the single guys. But I don't really buy into this "family" sort of vibe that the Brannons have instituted.

Not saying it's bad.

Just not me.

"Anything else," I ask blandly.

"Maybe lay off the alcohol so you can control yourself," she returns harshly.

Before I can even retort, because I'm not a fucking alcoholic—I just like to party on occasion—she says, "And try to be a little more frugal in the game-suspending penalties. You don't do a damn thing to help us from the stands."

Okay, she may have a point there, but honest to fuck . . . it's not like I plan to go out there and get suspended. I just go out there and play my fucking heart out, and I know that's something she appreciates even if I'm not getting that vibe from her right now.

I've heard enough, and even though it borders on disrespect-ful, I stand up from the chair, effectively calling this meeting at an end. Looking down at her with clear eyes and a resolved attitude, I say, "I'll do my best to adhere to your wishes."

"I sure hope so," she says casually, but the threat is clear.

Shape up or ship out.

As much as I respect Gray Brannon for her hockey smarts and for putting together an amazing team, I'm not liking her very much right now. I simply nod and walk out of her office without a backward glance.

PHOTO: MARIE KILLEN

Since the release of her debut contemporary romance novel, SAWYER BENNETT has written more than thirty books and has been featured on both the *New York Times* and *USA Today* bestseller lists on multiple occasions. A reformed trial lawyer from North Carolina, Sawyer uses real life experience to create relatable, sexy stories that appeal to a wide array of readers. From new adult to contemporary romance, Sawyer writes something for just about everyone. Sawyer likes her Bloody Marys strong, her martinis dirty, and her heroes a combination of the two. When not bringing fictional romance to life, Sawyer is a chauffeur, stylist, chef, maid, and personal assistant to a very active toddler, as well as full-time servant to two adorably naughty dogs. She believes in the good of others, and that a bad day can be cured with a great workout, cake, or a combination of the two.

sawyerbennett.com
Facebook.com/bennettbooks
@BennettBooks

## ABOUT THE TYPE

This book was set in Galliard, a typeface designed in 1978 by Matthew Carter (b. 1937) for the Mergenthaler Linotype Company. Galliard is based on the sixteenth-century typefaces of Robert Granjon (1513–89).